The Jacq of Spades

"This was the first steampunk book that I've read that I actually really loved."

— GABBY'S HONEST BOOK REVIEWS

"A mystery, a damn good one … your characters are still living in my head."

— DAVID BRIDGER, author of A Flight of Thieves

"The Jacq of Spades hooked me immediately, almost against my will, and pushed me through a story that both captivated and puzzled me."

— LILYN G, blogger, SciFi and Scary
scifiandscary.wordpress.com/

"Mobsters, corrupt police and a novice private detective. This story was amazing."

— ALLIE SUMNER, blogger, Allie's Opinions
alliesopinions.wordpress.com/

"… a good read for anyone who likes mystery and suspense mixed with science fiction. I can't wait to read the second book!"

— IVORY MORTON, blogger, Beautyful Word
beautyfulword.com

For more reviews, visit JacqOfSpades.com

BOOKS BY PATRICIA LOOFBOURROW

FICTION

RED DOG CONSPIRACY

Part 1: *The Jacq of Spades*

Available in paperback, audiobook, and all ebook formats

NON-FICTION

Edible Landscaping on $1 A Day (Or Less!)

Available on Kindle

The Queen
Of Diamonds

Part 2 of the Red Dog Conspiracy

Patricia Loofbourrow

To De + Don
Best wishes
[signature]

To Andy, who gave me a chance.

The City of Bridges

(not to scale)

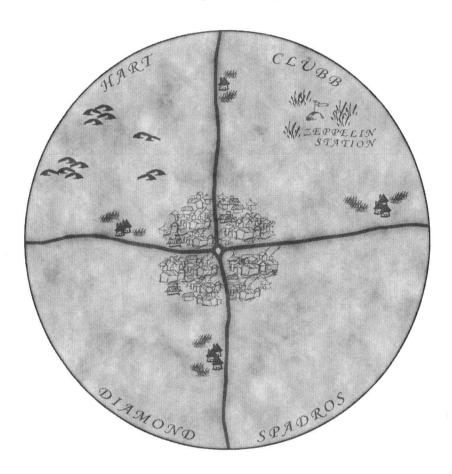

The Headline

A domed city split by four rivers, an island at its center. In the southeast quadrant, a white mansion stood on 192nd street in a heavy downpour. On the second story, a folded newspaper lay atop a tea-table.

I sat at the tea-table gazing at the curtain of water formed by the rain as it passed over the eaves. Thunder cracked, whip-like, as lightning flashed. Black clouds hung in the early morning sky.

Seven days ago, the gentleman investigator Blaze Rainbow and I rescued twelve-year-old David Bryce from his kidnappers. Could I ever forget the sound of blood dripping, the gore splattered on white walls, the screams and moans of dying men?

This past week in my sickbed, I had ample time to consider this matter. The men I killed had friends, families, people who loved them. Could I have found another way to escape that basement and avoid whatever horrors Frank Pagliacci and Jack Diamond planned for us?

A coughing fit struck, and when it passed, I drew my robe around me, exhausted. I had been ill ever since I was caught in the storm after delivering little David to his mother. Between sickness and my more womanly troubles of a monthly nature, the past week had been miserable. I lit a cigarette, gulped down honey-lemon tea, and unfolded the newspaper, hoping to find something more pleasant. Then I saw the headline:

Alcatraz Coup 100th Anniversary Celebration Planned

Clubbs Host Zeppelin Station Spectacular

Back home in the Pot, March 1st was a day of mourning. Here, they celebrated.

The Pot was once the most beautiful part of the city of Bridges. A hundred years ago, Xavier Alcatraz betrayed his king, Polansky Kerr. With the help of the first Acevedo Spadros, he slaughtered my people. Today the Pot lay in ruins, its inhabitants despised. The idea of celebrating their treachery almost made me throw the paper away.

But then I discovered this article:

'Miracle Gem' Health Benefits

A Breakthrough in Modern Medicine

The esteemed physician Dr. Overs Gocow of London presented a report at the Royal Academy of Science General Conference Tuesday with the results of his research into the spinel gemstone. According to his studies, this jewel provides benefit in various illnesses and a general health improvement to those without malady.

Dr. Gocow produced a document specifying illnesses treated with each gem color, with recipes for various tonics and elixirs. His document was received with acclaim from the physicians at the conference, who were interested in conducting their own research on the subject.

Spinel is a naturally appearing gem, dug from the earth near the tonic spring near Agree, at the outpost located in Old Montana. It is thought that the gem's proximity to the tonic spring may

2

contribute to its beneficial properties.

Being ill myself (and weary of it), I found this article fascinating. If I obtained a gem, perhaps I might avoid illness in the future. Where might I purchase one? I searched for more about these gems, and found this article in the financial section:

Gemstone Merchants Posting Record Sales

Trade in the so-called 'miracle' gemstone spinel has been brisk over the past two weeks, with the price of the gems going up weekly. The Bridges Daily editor, Mr. Acol Durak, interviewed the noted Market Center financier Tenace Mitchell:

AD: What are the future prospects for spinel sales?

TM: This is the best investment in decades.

AD: How did you come to this conclusion?

TM: Any time you have a new product combined with a scientific breakthrough, the opportunity for profit is good. In this case, where the product brings clear health benefits, the price can only go up.

We in Bridges are fortunate to have leading gemologist Dame Anastasia Louis with us. She obtained license to produce the tonics and elixirs according to Dr. Gocow's specifications to be shipped for sale to the rest of the country.

AD: So this discovery will bring jobs and commerce to Bridges as well.

Could this be true? I didn't recall the name Tenace Mitchell, but I had no knowledge of finance. I searched the paper further. In the classifieds, a large advertisement read:

Louis Gemstones And Fine Jewelry

Cut, Polished, And Set By

"The Queen of Diamonds"

Dame Anastasia Louis, Expert Gemologist

Featuring "The Miracle Gem"

15116 Snow, Spadros

This sounded terribly exciting. Dame Anastasia had been one of my informants for years. Not only that, she lived on our very street. Why had she not once told me of it?

My lady's maid Amelia Dewey came in. Amelia was short, middle-aged, and plump, with brown eyes and graying brown hair. "Ready for me to draw your bath, mum?"

Being a "grand lady" (as Amelia put it once) was mostly a matter of routine. Wake, tea, newspaper, toast, bath, hair, dress, prayers, breakfast, morning meeting, and so on. Running a home with several dozen servants and supporting my husband in the Business was close to a full time job. Today, though, my husband Tony made it clear my only duty was to make myself presentable for luncheon. Joseph and Josephine Kerr were invited, and their visit needed to go well.

The Kerrs and I had once been the closest of friends. And my relationship with Joe had become so much more. But time seemed to have put distance between us, at least for their part. At our last meeting I was drunk, and behaved rudely. This luncheon was our attempt to learn how much damage had been done, and if possible, to make amends before the Queen's Day dinner.

I stood. "Yes, I'm ready." I felt I had already survived the worst I might ever face. No matter what happened, I knew I could handle it.

I was a fool.

The Luncheon

I clung to Tony's arm, exhausted from my illness, eager to see Joe and Josie, yet afraid at the same time. I was so rude at our last meeting, yet they didn't dare refuse our invitation. Had I offended my friends past forgiveness?

But when our butler John Pearson opened the parlor door, I knew something was terribly wrong.

The parlor itself looked perfectly normal: white paneling, pale blue sofa, white coffee table.

Josephine Kerr sat, face in her hands, alone. She glanced up as Tony and I entered. Her skin was pink, her curly blond hair plastered around her face, her blue eyes red and full of tears.

Now, looking back, I'm ashamed to say that all I thought of was Joe. Where was her twin? My heart began pounding at the thought that something might have befallen him.

I glanced at Tony. He nodded, his blue eyes somber as he turned to go, but Josie said, "Please, Mr. Spadros, stay. I sorely need your counsel."

Josephine Kerr was a year older than I. As a young girl, she led the High-Low Split, the most notorious (and now only) street gang in the Spadros section of the Pot. The girl who taught me to fight with knives in the streets and alleyways of the worst section of Bridges. The woman groomed to run her grandfather's estate, chosen over her twin brother Joseph.

Josie never asked anyone for counsel. I'd known Josie since I was born, and I'd never seen her cry before.

I took Tony's hand to keep mine from shaking, and drew him to sit across from her. "Josie, what's wrong?"

Her gaze was both horrified and bereft. "Oh, Jacqui," she said, "Joe's been hurt."

I felt an enormous sense of relief. Hurt. I feared from her demeanor that he had died.

Tony ran a hand through black hair. "How? What happened?"

Josie wiped her face with a handkerchief. She took a deep breath, and let it out. Then she spoke, slowly and with hesitation:

"We were in the Hart countryside, a week ago. The day was … so … beautiful! Joe and six of his friends rode beside the carriage on horseback, while I and three of my friends rode inside.

"You know how Joe is, Jacqui, always sporting. We passed a field, and he told the carriage to stop. It was time for luncheon so I asked if he wanted to eat there. He did, so the ladies and I began taking out the blankets and baskets with the help of our driver.

"Joe was still a-horse, and challenged the men to race across the field to a thicket. It wasn't far, oh, maybe a hundred yards off. I told him not to, Jacqui, I did. He knew nothing of the field, or of its dangers, but his friends joined in, urging him on, and off they went. I screamed for him to stop, but they raced — full on. I felt terrified for his horse, and I was right: just before the thicket, his horse stepped in a hole and threw him … at speed."

I gasped, stomach churning, and Tony squeezed my hand.

Josie nodded. "He went into the thicket and flew over. But beyond that was an embankment, with a stone wall at its base, and then a terrible far drop."

I leaned forward. What happened?

"A stand of trees and bushes lay there. A large branch went through his leg, then he hit the wall at the bottom of the embankment so hard it cracked. The top part of the wall had blood all over it."

It seemed incomprehensible. He hit a wall?

Josie shook her head, face in her hands. "He hung … by his

6

leg ... over a cliff. I still can't believe it. That branch was the only thing which kept him from going into certain death."

Joe might have died? "A week ago?"

When Josie spoke, she sounded afraid and defensive. At the time, I felt ashamed: I imagined she thought I blamed her. "It was terrible, Jacqui. A friend spoke to me and I glanced away right as the horse threw him. Then the men began to cry out for help, screaming for a doctor. I felt terrified Joe might be dead. I told the driver to unhitch the horse and go for a doctor, then my friends and I ran across the field to him. He lay in the branches, unmoving, blood dripping from his wounds. The men shouted and wept, distraught at the thought he might be dead.

"It took us the rest of the day to bring him home. We were far in the countryside. It took two hours for a doctor to arrive. Thank the Floorman the other horses were unhurt, for we had to send for ropes so we could climb down to him. We had to saw the branch with our pocket knives to free him, to bring him safely away from the cliff. After the doctor came, we lowered him to Joe's side so the doctor could remove the branch from his leg. Oh," her voice broke, "I can still recall how Joe screamed as we did so." She wiped tears from her cheeks. "We got a stretcher down to him so we might hoist him up. It took ten men to do so. The horse Joe rode had to be put down, it screamed as much as he did. It was terrible. Its leg ...." She shuddered. "Thank the Dealer Joe's friend had a pistol to release the poor animal from its pain."

"Oh, Josie." I went to her, holding her as she sobbed in my arms. After she calmed herself, I asked, "How can we help?"

But Josie didn't seem to hear me. "I came myself, the next day, once the doctor said he would live. I knew you'd want to see him, but they said you weren't home. Didn't they send my card?"

"They did." I sighed. "I've been ill. I'm sorry. If I would've known it was so serious, I would have come straight-away."

Josie stared at me. "You're ill? I'm so sorry. I should never have come." She began to rise. "I —"

"Of course you should have come," Tony said. "You've done everything well. Sit, please. Mrs. Spadros is well now, and feels strong. We should have luncheon together, as we planned. Let's go to the veranda. The sight of the gardens will be relaxing." He paused. "When you feel able to, Miss Kerr, of course."

She sat staring at her hands. "How did you come to fall ill?"

Tony smiled. "She went boating with Helen Hart. Can you believe it? All these years the Harts have been estranged from her, then invited to luncheon twice now. They were caught in that rainstorm last week and she's been sick with coughing and fever ever since — until today, of course. What terrible luck."

Josie stared at me unmoving, and I felt a spike of panic. I hadn't been with Helen Hart that day. Did she know I lied? If so, what would she do?

But she nodded without expression. "The same day we were in the Hart countryside. The day Joe fell. I saw the storm far off over the city while we waited for help to arrive." She took a deep breath. "I'm ready."

I took her arm as we went out of the parlor, Tony following behind. Our butler met us in the entryway.

"Pearson," Tony said, "we'll take luncheon on the veranda."

"Yes, sir." A middle-aged man with thinning brown hair, John Pearson strode ahead of us. We ambled after him, past the white paneled doors to Tony's library, his study, my study, and the breakfast room.

Josie said nothing as we walked, which was just as well: my mind was in turmoil. Joe was terribly hurt, for a week now, and I hadn't been there for him.

Of course the staff gave me her card. But they wouldn't have known to tell me of the situation even if Josie shared it, which she wouldn't have. Josie was a most private woman; she must trust us very much to let her distress show, especially in front of Tony, who she barely knew.

The sun peeked through the clouds as we passed the breakfast room windows. The twigs in the garden glistened as we turned right, towards the dining hall. The veranda doors were at the left side of the large hall, halfway down the room. A maid opened the glass-paneled doors for us.

The air was warm for this February afternoon, and smelled of damp earth. My bird, white with blue-gray markings, chirped at us from its large white cage as we emerged. Amelia's son walked far out in the meadow with our bomb-sniffer dog, Rocket.

Josie seemed to notice none of this, going straight to the table. Tony pulled her chair out, then pulled out a chair for me to her left. The wide gray roof hadn't let a drop from that morning's storm reach the table, so the chairs were clean and dry.

Pearson emerged. Two of his sons brought out a side table. Maids followed with serving platters and tablecloths, and began setting the table. The maids set out large white service plates and tea cups, with a small bowl of rosemary sprigs in the center. The scent of rosemary wafted in the air. I rose to pour the tea, then returned to my seat. Josie continued to stare dully at the table.

Pearson's daughter Mary came to the table in her maid uniform, black with a spotless white apron, and curtsied. "Smoked ham, roasted new potatoes, baked beans with fat pork."

Josie nodded. I smiled up at Mary. "Thank you."

Mary curtsied and began placing filled white luncheon plates edged in black atop the larger ones.

Tony smiled at me. It was then I realized how nervous I was.

Josie let out a weary sigh, and sipped her tea.

We began eating. My bird chirped, another answered.

"You mentioned that you needed my counsel," Tony said. "How may I help?"

Josie nodded, not meeting our eyes. "The horse Joe rode was valuable, a beautiful sorrel. It belonged to my grandfather. Mr. Charles Hart gave the grand-sire to him when he first sponsored my grandfather into the Hart lands. My grandfather loved the horse's offspring dearly, as he does Mr. Hart himself." She took a deep breath, let it out. "My grandfather is distraught at the loss, almost as much as with Joe's injuries. But … we only had the two horses to begin with. We have no way to replace it in a timely manner, and Mr. Hart has done so much for us already …"

Tony nodded. "Would it help if I spoke with Mr. Hart —?"

A spike of fear. What if Tony learned I had never met with Helen Hart? That I lied to him all those times?

"Or would one of our horses help? Until you can get another."

Josie brightened. "Oh, Mr. Spadros, a horse would help so much. Just until we can replace it. We're fortunate that his sire still lives. He is our carriage-horse, old, yes, but reliable. We can get a foal from him in the spring, I'm sure."

Tony smiled. "You're welcome to choose any from the stables you like. Keep it as long as you need."

Josie's face filled with gratitude. "Thank you so much, sir. You have no idea how much it will help."

"It's no trouble at all," Tony said. "Lady Luck has blessed the Spadros Family. I'm happy to help you."

Josie's eyes lowered. She smiled, blushing. "May I speak on another matter?"

"Why, of course," I said.

"Joe would be most obliged if you visited him," Josie said to Tony. "He's been bound to his bed a week now, and is starved for company." Her shoulders drooped as she glanced aside. "Many of his friends no longer visit."

I turned to Tony. "Might we go tomorrow after luncheon?"

Tony shook his head. "I have a meeting tomorrow. But you can go, if you feel well enough."

Pearson told me Tony had a meeting tomorrow, which was why I suggested it. "I'll take the unmarked carriage." This plain brown carriage resembled a taxi, if you ignored the black horses and silver tackle of the Spadros Family. By using this carriage, we might visit other quadrants without attracting undue notice.

Tony nodded. "Good idea. It'll be safer that way."

Always his concern was for my safety. Tony meant well, but his idea of "safety" often felt like life in a cage.

Josie stirred at Tony's remark. "Have you had trouble?"

Tony put his fork down and leaned back in his chair. The room Crab and Duck died in was still being cleaned from the ordeal. "You might say that."

My best friend Air, murdered in front of me the night I was sold to the Spadros Family ten years ago, had two brothers. Frank Pagliacci kidnapped twelve-year-old David Bryce (Air's youngest brother) a month ago, framing the Red Dogs street gang for it. David's seventeen-year-old brother Herbert and a fifteen-year-old

Red Dogs member named Stephen Rivers tried to find David. The police found them strangled; I felt certain Pagliacci killed them.

Two of Tony's men were killed and two others kidnapped by Pagliacci's men. Then they attacked Tony in his own warehouse. Frank Pagliacci released the kidnapped men after blackmailing them into spying on us. Pagliacci claimed he did all this to capture me then lure the rest of the Spadros Family to their deaths. But I believed this was a ruse to cover up his real intent.

The two spies were dead: Duck, of infection after Tony shot him; the other, Crab, died at his own hand. David Bryce, now home safe, had so far refused to speak, his mind having reverted, it seemed, to that of a babe. I shot Frank Pagliacci, but I was no closer to bringing Frank's mad accomplice Jack Diamond to justice than I was a week ago.

I gazed at Tony. *They tried to destroy us. Yet we survived it.* Feeling a surge of fondness, I kissed Tony's hand and turned to Josie. "We have had some trials, yes, quite serious ones, but they've brought us closer together." And they had. For the first time, I felt as if Tony valued me as more than just a woman, but something closer to an equal.

Tony let out a breath, color rising in his cheeks, his gaze part incredulity and part hope.

Sadness washed over me. Somehow, he knew that I held my heart from him these three years of our marriage.

Josie gaped at us.

And I felt ashamed.

Her brother Joe and I promised ourselves to each other before I was kidnapped and brought here. Everything in his actions indicated he had lost interest in me. But what might her dreams have been?

I dropped Tony's hand. "I forget my manners sometimes."

Josie smiled. "I'm glad to see you happy."

I let out a breath. Yes. In spite of my worry for Joe, my grief over David's ruin, my fears for the future … yes, I was happy.

The Regrets

After luncheon, Tony and I went with Josie to select her horse. Josie didn't seem to care which one she took, but once she pointed at one of our black stallions, Tony hurried to have our stable-man Peter prepare it.

Once Tony was out of view, I said, "How's Marja?"

Marja was the Kerr's housekeeper, and the mother of our mutual friend Ottilie, who was now dead.

I brought our friends Ottilie, Treysa, and Poignee from the Pot to work here as kitchen maids. They said something to Tony after Inventor Call took me to see the Magma Steam Generator last month. I never learned what they said, but it offended Tony so much he had them killed.

Josie shrugged wearily. "As well as can be expected."

"I'm sorry you had to come here."

"I must do what I need to," Josie said. "I'm not above begging for anything that will help my family prosper. Even from him."

My vision blurred. *She's suffered so much. How can she bear it?* I hugged her, but she didn't hug me back.

After Josie and her driver left with the horse, I told Pearson cleaning could resume. He went to collect the staff.

I climbed the stairs to that room above the parlor where Crab and Duck died. Poor Josie, caring for her brother in addition to grieving our friends and managing her grandfather's business. No wonder the strain took its toll on her.

Josie's grandfather forbade her to marry so she might take care of his affairs. Yet he was, to all accounts, perfectly well. It seemed unfair to deny such a beautiful and talented woman as Josephine Kerr the chance at a home and a future. She sounded happy when we discussed the matter last month, but I wondered if she was beginning to regret agreeing to it.

A week had passed since Crab and Duck died. The rugs had been removed and the tiles pried up. The wall where Crab's blood lay after he shot himself had been scraped, scrubbed, and patched.

My day footman Skip Honor came in wearing work clothes; Peter Dewey, our stable-man, followed behind. I nodded at them. "You've done good work."

Peter ignored me. Honor said, "Thank you, mum."

Amelia's husband Peter hadn't so much as looked at me since my mistake with Thrace Pike last month. Roy Spadros tortured Amelia to learn what happened, and Peter never forgave me for it. I didn't know what to do to make things right.

Pearson came in. "Jane's ready for our meeting."

I followed him downstairs and through the house. We went through the dining room then down to the kitchens. A small table and three straight-backed chairs were set up for the meeting. A large pot bubbled on the stove; good smells filled the air.

A maid cried in Jane's arms, flinching when she saw me. The maid curtsied. "My apologies, mum," she said, then rushed away.

I hung back by the doorway. "I'm sorry to intrude."

Jane was a stout middle-aged woman whose straight blonde hair mixed with gray. She shook her head, frowning. "The girl mourns Duck's death." The way she said it ...

Ah. The poor girl fancied him.

Duck and his lover Crab betrayed the Family by spying on us for Frank Pagliacci, but ... "We all wish events passed differently."

Jane nodded. "Shall we sit, mum?"

Pearson held my chair, then his wife's, then sat between us.

Jane took a small notebook from her apron pocket. "We need another barrel of baking soda. We've used up almost all of the one we have in order to absorb the smell upstairs."

"See to it." I turned to Pearson. "How are the staff?"

"About Crab?" Pearson let out a breath. "We've never had such a thing happen here."

I felt much the same way, and I hardly knew the man. "What can we do to help?"

Pearson shrugged. "I'll ask. Time heals most wounds, as they say. But perhaps something for them?"

"That's a good idea. An outing, perhaps?"

Jane smiled. "That would be good, mum."

"I'll speak to Mr. Anthony about it." Then I came to what I wanted to say. "I'm sorry it's taken so long for me to speak of this. I must apologize for the burden I put on you by bringing Pot rags to your kitchens. It was unfair to expect you to train them, and I regret all that happened."

Jane became very still, staring at the table, face red. "It's kind of you, mum, but there's no need to apologize to the likes of me."

"There is need. I'd like for you to choose your replacement."

She shook her head slightly, head bowed, lashes moist, nose reddening. "Has my performance distressed you, mum?"

Oh, dear. "No! Not at all! I'm most pleased with your work. There's better work for you to do here. You perform the tasks of a housekeeper plus your own, and since we lack one …"

Jane's head jerked upright, her eyes wide. "Me? Upstairs, running the house?"

"I can't think of anyone better."

Jane looked to Pearson, joy in her face. "Oh, John, can you believe it?"

Pearson put his hand on hers then turned to me. "We're most grateful, mum."

"As am I." I smiled at the fond glance which passed between them, then rose. "You have until the outing to choose your replacement. Please inform me when you've decided."

They both rose hastily. "Yes, mum," Jane said, and curtsied. "Thank you, mum."

I took their hands. No one else was in the kitchen, but I spoke softly. "I'm also grateful to you. I've been here since I was twelve.

And you're near thrice my age. It feels strange for you to call **me** mum, especially ..." I felt at a loss for words, "me being a Pot rag and all."

"You must never say such things," Jane whispered fiercely. "Never. You're Mrs. Spadros now. Forget all else."

Something in her voice made me shudder: to this day I don't know why.

***

That evening after dinner, I took to my room and lay in bed. Even though my health had improved, I still tired easily. Tony leaned against the pale blue cushion at the head of the bed as we held hands in the golden lamplight.

I thought back to our luncheon with Josie, Tony's reaction to my comment, the things he had said and done.

Tony truly loved me.

A month earlier, I couldn't have said the same. But the way he stood up to his sadistic, brutal father swayed me. I felt proud of how he had grown as a person. Was this love? I had no idea.

I gazed past Tony to the pictures on the wall. Landscapes of places I had never been, portraits of strangers, all in pale grayish-white frames. My least favorite color for many reasons, not that anyone cared what I thought. But one picture looked familiar. "Who's that man?"

"What man?"

I pointed to the portrait of a pale, black-haired man with a sober face and blue eyes. He resembled Tony and Roy, so I assumed he was some relative.

"That's my grandfather, Acevedo Spadros II. My mother says he was the most loving, generous man in the world." He paused. "He died when I was two. I have no memory of him."

A week ago, our private surgeon Dr. Salmon told me of the affair Acevedo Spadros II had with Tony's mother Molly, and of Acevedo's murder by his own men.

Tony said, "Why do you ask?"

Then I remembered who the man reminded me of. "I saw the most beautiful child a few weeks ago. He looked very much like your grandfather. Well, if your grandfather had dark brown skin and curly hair."

"Oh?"

I rolled to face him, and raised myself on an elbow. The lamplight glared in my eyes, leaving Tony's face in shadow. "You should've seen him. He was exquisite: the sweetest black ringlet curls, dark eyes, and a lovely smile." I lay back on the bed, facing the ceiling. "He was about four. His little ball rolled past while I walked, and I fetched it for him. He said, 'thank you' with this tiny high voice ... he was the most adorable child I've ever seen."

Then I felt melancholy. *That could have been our son.*

Give him lighter skin, straighter hair ... but I could picture Tony and I having a child very much like him.

I secretly took a special "morning" tea to keep from bearing Tony a child. My monthly flow began the day Crab shot himself. After everything that happened in my life — kidnapped, forced to marry, unable to see my mother — I wanted some choice in when I would have a child. But now ... I began to regret it.

Tony took my hand. "We'll have children one day. The doctor says it can take time, especially with the first." He paused. "I read about new locking mechanisms for carriages. They lock from the outside, so children don't fall out. I told Pearson to have all the carriages fitted with them."

I stared at the ceiling, wanting to weep. Did Tony feel at fault for his lack of an heir?

I put his hand on my cheek and closed my eyes, feeling the warmth of his hand, willing back tears. *Tony would be a good father. Why am I denying him the chance to have a son?* It no longer made sense to me.

I would visit Joseph Kerr tomorrow. If he didn't speak of how he felt I would ask, as inappropriate as it might seem. I would know for certain one way or the other. If Joe no longer held feelings for me, I would stop taking my morning tea and let the cards be dealt as they were.

The Memories

Tony said, "Was the child alone? The little boy?"

I opened my eyes and sat up, turning towards him. "Oh, no, not at all. He had a young nanny with him, a girl of maybe eighteen. She said her name was … oh, yes, Octavia Diamond. She had skin a bit lighter than mine, and long blond curly hair! She looked nothing like a Diamond. I almost didn't believe her."

Tony gave a short laugh. "Probably a distant cousin, perhaps one 'under the table.' I have cousins that look more like Diamonds than some Diamonds do."

I thought of our Inventor, Maxim Call: wiry and brown, with those piercing blue Spadros eyes.

"She said they were from the country, so you're probably right. The boy, now he looked a Diamond, to be sure." I pictured his little face. "He looked very much like Jon and Jack, now that I think of it. His name was Roland."

Jonathan Diamond was my best friend. His decidedly unwell brother Jack, who threatened my life every time he got the chance, was Jon's identical twin. I peered at Tony, squinting at the lamplight's glare. "Jack's middle name is Roland, isn't it? Could the child be his son?"

Tony snorted. "Hardly. I don't think Jack Diamond has much regard for women, not in that way. And Roland is a very common name among the Diamonds."

"Yes, I suppose it must be. It's astonishing how much the boy resembles them, now that I think of it. But I suppose he could belong to one of their older brothers, or a cousin." I sat up next to him. "He must be an upper; the girl called him 'Master Roland.' I don't recall anyone using those terms to speak to a child until I came here." It was a puzzle, and I enjoyed such things. "Yes, Octavia must be a distant cousin; she and the boy didn't look much alike. She was pretty, though, and the boy seemed happy."

"Happy," Tony said. He sounded wistful, and I recalled his lonely childhood, forbidden all playmates but one after his older brother's assassination. "Was the boy well cared-for?"

"Oh, yes, the nanny seemed quite attentive. I loved the way he skipped after her as they went. They were going to see if a calf had been born yet, if I remember correctly."

Tony leaned back, closing his eyes with a deep sigh. I rested my head on his shoulder, remembering myself at that age, back home in the Pot. How happy I felt, playing in the ruins of old Bridges with my best friend Air and my Ma.

I would give anything to see them again.

Tony put his arm around me and held me until I fell asleep.

Blood dripped down the walls as I went up the stair, one step at a time. My friend Air, still looking as he did when he died ten years ago, his seventeen-year-old brother Herbert, and fifteen-year-old Stephen lay moaning and twitching on the steps, their wounds horrible to behold.

I held something in my arms that grew heavier with every step. I looked down: Joe gazed up at me.

The room was hot. When I glanced behind me, Jack Diamond, head shaved and dressed in white, crept up the stairs on all fours. Even though the stairwell was awash with blood, his clothes and hands were spotless. He drew closer behind me, and my terror grew as I tried to flee. I moved so slowly ...

Jack Diamond grabbed my ankle. "I have you now."

I shrieked and came awake, tangled in the covers.

"Jacqui?" Tony sat up, sounding more sleepy than alarmed.

Our night footman Blitz Spadros rushed in, candle in hand, his face glowing orange in the candlelight. "Are you well, mum?"

My heart pounded; I felt bathed in sweat. "A dream." Tears

of humiliation filled my eyes. "I'm sorry."

Tony flopped backwards onto the pillows. "I hoped maybe — maybe they were gone. You didn't have any for a whole week." He smoothed my hair, kissed my forehead. "I'm sorry."

Blitz gave us a small smile. "I'll leave you then." He closed the door behind him.

I clung to Tony and began to cough, to cry. "I thought maybe they were gone too." That one was bizarre, so unlike the others, which had up to now mostly been memories.

"You think the doctor has something to help you sleep?"

I shook my head in the darkness, discouraged. This had been my life for the past ten years. "I don't know."

I never returned to sleep after my nightmare. All I could think of was that I would see Joe again. Yet horrible visions of how his injuries might appear ran through my mind.

It felt like forever before I left home to visit the Kerrs.

The Kerrs lived in Hart quadrant, which was in the northwest part of the city. To get there, we drove past the slums and the Spadros section of the Pot (hidden safely from view by wrought iron and tall hedge) onto Market Center, an island in the center of Bridges. We then drove around the Plaza, over the bridge, and onto the close-laid red brick streets of Hart quadrant, where Joseph and Josephine Kerr lived with their grandfather.

The day was overcast and chill, and the air smelled of wood smoke. When my carriage arrived at the Kerr's home, my day footman Skip Honor helped me to the sidewalk. And I thanked him, as I always do. It was considered unseemly for uppers to acknowledge the servants in any way, but I didn't care. I treated them as people, even though ten years ago they despised me as much as anyone else for being a Pot rag.

No one met me out front, so I went up the brown stone steps and knocked on the wooden door. Marja, a middle-aged woman with brown hair, opened the door, tears rising in her eyes when she saw me. "My little J-Bird," she said, hugging me tightly.

The summer afternoon sun streamed orange onto the far wall of the

*cathedral while Ma and Marja cooked. Josie, Ottilie, Poignee, Treysa,
and Joe sat with me, playing dice on the floor.*

Grief swelled inside my chest. "I had nothing to do with
Ottilie's death."

"I know," Marja whispered. She let go and stood before me,
squeezing her eyes shut. "They was shot in the head and thrown
in the Pot like trash." She glanced up at me. "Did you know?"

I shook my head, horrified.

She stared into emptiness. "Leave the city. It's not safe."

"Why? What's going on?"

She glanced around. "Not here."

"Marja!" Josie's voice from the top of the stairs startled me.
"Jacqui is Mrs. Spadros now. She doesn't have time to speak with
servants. Mr. Kerr is going to have something to say about this."

Marja cringed. "Yes, mum. My apologies, mum."

I went up the brown wooden stairs. "Josie, don't blame her.
Her daughter just died. I was bringing condolences."

"You're too kind," Josie said, but she sounded annoyed.
"She's been reprimanded more than once about this."

I stared at Josie, appalled. "Marja has been like a mother to
you. Why are you treating her this way?"

Josie's beautiful face grew stern. "Do I tell you how to treat
your servants?"

"No, but —"

"Then don't tell me how to treat mine."

This wasn't like Josie at all.

"Jacqui," she said, as if explaining to a child, "we're Kerrs.
Not only that, we're Pot rags. Everyone here hates us. We have to
be like them if we're going to survive. Marja can't grasp that."

"No, you don't," I said. "We're better than this."

Josie shook her head, and her face turned pensive. "Our
situation's very different from yours." She patted my hand. "Be
grateful." Then Josie smiled. "Joe's waiting for you."

Something was terribly wrong here. Why would Josie treat
Marja so poorly? Surely she could help Marja understand without
being cruel to her. Had Josie's worry for Joe become too much for

her to bear? Heart pounding, I followed Josie, afraid of what I might see.

Josie took my hand. "I'm grateful you've come. He's spoken of nothing else since I told him you were to visit." She brought me down a hallway paneled in brown wood to a door.

Joseph Kerr had always been, to me, the most beautiful man in the world. Golden brown skin, green eyes, brown hair, he lay in bed wearing white flannel pajamas. He turned his head towards us and smiled.

Joe had the most glorious smile, the smile of a very small child. In it held pure unabashed happiness, the utter joy of life. Every time he smiled, I fell in love with him all over again.

"Oh, Jacqui," he said, "am I glad to see you."

Joe's right leg was in a cast, his left, strung up in a brass mechanism with many gears which held it aloft. Pulleys and weights attached to his left thigh, which lay bare. His left pajama leg was cut away, revealing the lower end of a well-muscled, badly bruised thigh. His right arm was in a burgundy and white sling. Many cuts and bruises adorned his face, along with a large bandage on his head. His left hand he held out to me. "My sweet Jacqui, you're finally here. You look just as beautiful as I remembered. Come to me."

I hurried to his side, sat on the chair beside his bed, and took his hand in both of mine. "Are you in pain?"

He lay back on his pillow, languid as a cat. "Some, but the doctor says it'll pass. Josie tells me I'm fortunate to be alive."

I nodded, mesmerized by his eyes.

"How are you, Jacqui? I've missed you so."

I took a deep breath. The room smelled of antiseptics and clean linens. "I'm well." I glanced at the contraption he was placed in. "Will you be well enough to come to dinner?"

"The doctor says in another week I can be free of this, if all goes well. Then I can be wheeled about like a babe in a pram." He chuckled, then his face turned solemn. "Josie told me not to race that field, Jacqui. You mustn't blame her." He gazed up at his sister, who stood beside me. "I understand now that she is much more intelligent than I." He turned to me. "I will follow her advice from here henceforth, to the letter. I promise."

I squeezed his hand. "I'm glad to hear you laugh. I feared you would be downcast."

"No," Joe said. "I feel good." He gave a contented sigh. "Especially now you're here." He paused. "Tell me more of the dinner. Who else will be there?"

"Let's see ..." my eyes lost focus as I went over the list. "Jonathan and Gardena Diamond, Lance Clubb and his sister Kitty, Dame Anastasia Louis —" His hand spasmed, as if he felt a sharp pain, but when I glanced at his face, he seemed well. "— and Major Blackwood. Tony and I, and both of you."

Josie said, "I look forward to it."

"Josie, would you fetch a blanket?" Joe said. "I feel a chill."

Josie left the room, closing the door behind her.

I had a sudden thought: Joe and I were alone, in his bedroom. He was partially clothed, and I held his hand.

I recalled Tony's outrage and terror for my reputation when I went to the Apprentice's area and the Magma Steam Generator "unescorted," even though our Inventor accompanied me, a man old enough to be my grandfather.

This scene was probably not what Tony had in mind when he allowed me to come here.

"I only have a little time," Joe said, "so I will be brief."

He sounded so serious that I felt afraid.

"I'm so deeply sorry for the time I've been away from you. Words can't describe how much I grieve over missing these years of your life. The torment you must've endured at the hands of the Spadros Family! And I wasn't there to comfort and protect you. The thought tears at my soul."

I felt astonishment, and hope.

"I think of you every day. I dream of you every night." He gripped my hand. "I — forgive me, but I feel this is my last chance. I must speak, though you never wish to see me again.

"The night you were taken, I was taken too. Taken here, beaten daily, told to do things I didn't understand. I still don't understand most of it. We're not like these people." He paused, glancing away for a long moment, then gazed into my eyes. "I long for you desperately. The only thing which kept me sane was thoughts of seeing you. But when I've been allowed near you, it was in the presence of others. I feared to speak or show any hint of my regard for you. I was in terror of what might happen. This," he held up our hands, clasped together, "is utter bliss. Yet I fear I've lost you."

I gaped at him, stunned. "I — I'm ... I'm —"

"Yes, I know. Married. Three years now." He lowered our clasped hands to the bed. "You're married. Bound to another for life." He closed his eyes for several moments. "What traps these quadrant-folk lay for each other." He paused, then turned to me. "Did you come to love him? Did you give yourself gladly? At least tell me that."

The coldness of the gun behind my neck as Roy and I stood outside the chapel ... the terrifying click of the hammer ...

I stared at my lap.

... the horror as Tony undressed me that first time ... Roy's words repeating in my mind: "Make us believe it, now and for all time, or you'll be dead."

Enduring that night had taken everything Ma taught me.

"... find a place to go inside, if you truly can't abide him," Ma said long before, when it became clear what was to happen to me.

So that night, I did ... and eventually, I found Joe.

I shook my head.

"Do you love him now?"

Tony's gentle touch, his loving words, his determination to stand against his father ...

My first impulse was to say yes.

But I couldn't say that with Joe here, his precious hand in

mine, saying he loved me. Tony never made me feel like Joe did.

No. I don't love him. Not like I love you.

"I don't know," I whispered.

Joe closed his eyes and pressed my hand to his lips. Then he opened his eyes. "I'm not going to tell you what to do, Jacqui. I don't know what you should do. All I know is — all you need to do is say the word and I'll be there."

My confusion must have shown, because he said, "Have you forgotten our last night together?"

... how we kissed, the way he smelled, the way he touched me ...

I smiled, the warmth of his love flowing through me. "How could I ever forget?"

"I meant what I said, Jacqui." His voice dropped to a whisper. "As soon as I'm well, I'll take you and we'll leave Bridges, lose ourselves in some other city. They'll never find us." He paused. "If you'll still have me."

If I would still have him? I had almost given up hope. "Dealer help me," I whispered. What was I to do?

"I have to get out of here," Joe said. "I can't live like this anymore. And I can't — I won't leave without you. My grandfather is a monster. The things he's done —" Joe shook his head. "He doesn't know you're here. We plan to tell him you came, then left when you heard I was unable to come down. He would kill me if he learned I told you these things."

I stared at him, horrified. "Why do you stay?"

"Why do **you** stay?" He turned his head away. "I know of Roy Spadros. I've heard of his brutality, his torture room, his disregard for life." He turned his head to look at me. "What keeps me from despair is that he threatened your home and family, and that you're a woman who values her kin. I have to believe this is why you stay in such a terrible place."

I nodded. "I tried to run once. Roy threatened to kill my Ma, burn the Cathedral with everyone inside, even the little children, should I step in the Spadros Pot again."

Joe stroked my fingers with his thumb, then he sighed. "My

grandfather threatened **you**, Jacqui. He vowed to kill you if we had any contact — this is why I never came to you, never wrote you. He vows to kill you every time I make a wrong step. The thought torments me." He gazed in my eyes, and I saw the fear there. "I live in terror of some harm coming to you because of me. He knows I would rather die."

I squeezed his hand in mine and kissed it, then held it to my cheek, my heart full.

My mother-in-law, Molly, had spoken of a threat directed at me. I couldn't fathom who would target me besides Jack Diamond and another of my enemies, Judith Hart. Now I had one more name for the list. I kissed Joe's hand, and gazed into his eyes. An electric feeling hit deep in my soul; our hearts touched, and became one.

Josie came in carrying a blue woolen blanket, and spread it over him. "Grampa will be back soon."

"Jacqui," Joe said, "you must go. He must not find you here."

I nodded, and rose, still holding his hand. "I'll visit when you tell me it's safe."

Josie grabbed my hand and led me to the door. I glanced back, and Joe mouthed, "I love you."

The Problem

Josie and I hurried down the stairs; my carriage and coachmen stood before us. The wind blew stronger, tiny sprinkles of rain falling here and there. But I barely noticed them.

Joe loved me.

No other carriages were on the street, and Josie let out a sigh of relief. "Grampa won't be angry at you being out here. But if he saw you were in the house, in Joe's bedroom —"

I nodded, picturing Tony's reaction. "I understand."

She lowered her voice. "Jacqui, there's something I must discuss with you."

"What is it?"

"Helen Hart was **not** out boating last week."

I stared at Josie, dismayed. That was my cover story the day Blaze Rainbow and I went to the Diamond Party Time factory to rescue David Bryce from his kidnappers.

"Helen ... Mrs. Hart ... is a dear friend. She's been ill for many weeks. She was with child, but the pregnancy went poorly. Very poorly. That day you were out, the day Joe and I were in the Hart countryside and he was hurt so badly, she lay bleeding. It was sudden and unexpected. She herself almost died, and the baby was born much too early, dead. Not many know of this; she has lost several babes in the past, and they didn't want the newspapers to get word. Her difficulty is why she wasn't at the Grand Ball with her husband Etienne, our Inventor."

I nodded. I had wondered about that.

"But Jacqui ... where **were** you? Why did you tell your husband you were with Helen Hart, of all people? I felt appalled when he said so. I didn't know what to say there at the luncheon. I felt you caused me to lie for you in front of all those people — your husband, the maids, your butler — to cover up whatever it was you were doing that day. Why would you lie about where you were? What were you doing?"

I had never seen her so upset in my life.

"Were you out with a man? Is there someone you love other than Joe?" She put her hand to her forehead. "I can't conceive you to be so false. It can't be true. It would break Joe's heart."

Of course I hadn't been with some other man; I had been saving a little boy's life. Could I trust her with that information, though? What had she gone through these six years? How had it changed her?

A carriage came down the street from far off. "You must go," Josie said. Honor stood beside my carriage door, waiting.

I stopped a stone's throw from my carriage, turned to her, and whispered, "Please don't speak of this to anyone. I beg you. There is an explanation, but I can't give it now, there's no time. Please. I ... I love Joe. I would die before harming him. Don't wound him further with these speculations. Please believe in me; await my story before making accusations."

"I will. But this 'explanation' had best be a good one." Her tone made her message clear: *I will not have my brother hurt by you.*

I felt stung, yet grateful of her willingness to hold judgment, at least for a while. "Thank you."

Honor stood by the opened door several feet off, a question in his eyes, but saying nothing. I took his hand and got into the carriage, and waved to Josie, who went into the house without waving back.

Honor glanced at me. "Is all well?"

I nodded. "Her brother is badly hurt and she's distressed. She'll be well; she has family and friends beside her."

Honor nodded. "Let us be off then. Spadros Manor?"

"Yes, thank you."

It was a long ride back to Spadros Manor, and I spent most of it in turmoil.

Why would Morton ... Master Blaze Rainbow ... why would he say Helen Hart invited me to luncheon? Why did I listen? Why did I go along with his plan?

I knew he was lying. I knew he was untrustworthy after he grabbed me in that alley. I would never have considered the idea of boating with Helen Hart if Blaze Rainbow had not brought it up. And I went along with it.

Now I was in a serious predicament.

Who thought I was with Helen Hart those two times? Would any of them be able to hear otherwise? Who besides Josie might learn of Helen Hart's illness and my 'luncheons' both?

I thought back. Pearson, the maids, Honor, the driver that day, Jonathan, Tony ...

The biggest problem was Tony. If he — or worse yet, his father Roy — happened to speak with one of the Harts ... for example, about the horse ...

Betraying the Family held the death penalty. My father-in-law Roy preferred torture to a clean bullet to the head. Probably one of the reasons Crab shot himself after Duck died, rather than wait to see which Tony intended for him.

I didn't want to die. Not when I finally had a chance at life.

Stop, I thought. I had to remain calm. As far as I knew, no one but Josie suspected me. Somehow I would reason this out. But I would never be able to do so while in a state of agitation.

Roy would never speak with Charles Hart; he hated Mr. Hart as thoroughly as a man could hate anyone. I couldn't imagine how Roy might learn of my visits with Helen Hart. He hadn't been to the house since he and Tony argued several weeks ago.

I sat watching the river as we crossed into Spadros quadrant, and I realized that all this thought and agitation was merely a way to distract myself from the real question: what was I going to do about Joe?

After dinner, Tony and I sat in his study in front of the fire as he held my hand. He said nothing about my somber mood, but I had learned to read him. Though he was a master at keeping his emotions from most people, he seemed to relax, even be vulnerable in my presence.

It made me feel sad.

When he finally spoke, I knew a moment before what he would say, and the sincerity with which he would say it. "How is Master Kerr?"

I shook my head. "Sorely hurt, but able to speak. I'm astonished he spoke with such clarity. He had a terrible large bandage on his head."

The realization hit me as a shock: would Joe remember our conversation? Could his words have come from being impaired in some way?

Did he really still love me?

What a fool I was not to see the import of the bandage before I sat with him. "He claimed the doctors would release him from bed in time for the dinner, but I'd be surprised if they attend."

Tony shook his head. "It's a pity; I hoped to spend the evening with them and have them meet others in our society. They need assistance in that regard: most doors are closed to them simply because of their name." He almost seemed to be speaking to himself, rather than to me. "It seems unfair." He paused for several seconds. "I understand being judged because of your ancestors — because of your father."

I patted Tony's hand. "Once Joe's well, we can have them over as often as you like."

He smiled and reached into his pocket. "I have something for you." He produced a small box. Inside was a silver chain with a single moonstone, which he placed around my neck. "One of the health gems," he said. "So you'll get well soon."

I gasped at his thoughtfulness, and threw my arms around his neck as I kissed his cheek. "Thank you so much."

Pearson's heavy tread approached the door, and he knocked. I extricated myself quickly and smoothed my hair.

"Come in," Tony said.

"A letter for you, sir, from your father. The messenger said it was most urgent." Pearson put the letter into Tony's hand.

What could Roy Spadros possibly wish to write us about at this hour? Most urgent probably meant the old monster scared the boy half to death. "Make sure you give the boy something for his trouble and tell him all is well."

Pearson nodded. "Yes, mum," he said, then left.

Tony snorted, then handed the letter to me:

Anthony —

Word has reached me of your mishap, and I am appalled at your reckless actions and the loss of your men. Your mishandling of this situation has cost lives and allowed this villain to make a mockery of the Spadros Family. You must allow me to take over this interrogation to learn the truth of the matter.

I also must speak with your wife at once. I await your invitation.

I shook my head, astonished. Whatever Tony told Roy must have been just the thing to say. I had never seen Roy beg before.

I handed the letter back to him. "What will you do?"

He crumpled the letter into a ball and threw it in the fire. "I don't need him to run an investigation of what has gone on in my home or my warehouses. And I certainly won't allow him to come here and mistreat you again."

So he did know what happened. "Who told you?"

"I suspected you hid something the day you claimed to be stung. So I searched for evidence of your story and could find none. No nests, and the staff reported that my father did not leave straight-away as you said, but questioned you for several minutes before he left. The kitchen staff told me you went to Amelia's rooms with your dress torn and your face injured.

"I got the truth from the doctor after much trouble. When I confronted my father, his reaction corroborated it even as he cast vile accusations and excuses as to why he would strike my wife." Tony touched the side of my face. "Even your bruise held the marks of my father's hand. I realized you were terrified of him and feared harm coming to me if you told the truth." He leaned over, kissing my forehead. "That you would take such a terrible blow then hide it to protect my life — it made me see how much you loved me." He laid his hand on my shoulder. "I'm sorry I sent you away the night you came to me. I was in such turmoil over the things my father said —" He paused for a long moment, as if he meant to speak, then shook his head, dropping his hand to the table between us. "No. There was no excuse for my behavior."

I took his hand, my eyes stinging, my heart heavy. "I wish I could be the wife you deserve."

I meant it. Tony deserved so much better.

Tony sat up straighter and leaned towards me. "Never say that! You **are** the wife I deserve. You're the most precious thing in my life." He took my chin and turned my face towards him. "Do you not believe in my love for you?"

"I do." That was the problem.

I turned away, close to tears. I had to think of something to tell him, or I feared I might confess everything. "Yet … I always feel asked to be someone I'm not. A grand lady, an elegant Family woman … someone respectable. The minute they think I can't hear, the whispers begin. No one's fooled by this pretense." I glanced at Tony. "I'm a Pot rag, and that's all I'll ever be."

He gaped at me. "Who whispers about you?"

I snorted, feeling bitter. "Everyone. Everywhere. In the shops, in the street, even at the Grand Ball. Oh, yes, they curtsy and they smile, but when they think you can't hear …"

Tony took my hand in his. "Oh, my love, you mustn't listen, or it'll destroy you. Do you think no one whispers about me? I'm the son of the man most hated and feared, certainly in Bridges, perhaps in this entire country. People fear me. They fear what I may be, what I may become. They whisper that I have a pleasant demeanor to hide some secret horror, that I keep a torture room as my father does —"

I gasped at the thought of Tony torturing anyone.

"— that I engage in acts even worse, whatever their twisted minds concoct. But I'm not my father. I refuse to become him. And I refuse to listen to them." He glanced around as if searching for something to sway me. "You must refuse to listen too."

***

The next morning, a letter came:

> Master Joseph Kerr and Miss Josephine Kerr present their compliments to Mr. and Mrs. Anthony Spadros but regretfully must decline their kind invitation to dinner on the 14th of February due to serious injury.

As I suspected. I was surprised that Joe thought such a severe break — to the thigh, of all places — might heal enough in two weeks' time to leave that contraption of his.

The *Golden Bridges* — a disreputable tabloid, but often the only source of real news — ran a short but alarming article:

TENSION BETWEEN FAMILIES?

> Our Inside Reporter relates a scene between Regina Clubb and Judith Hart at the Clubb Women's Center:
>
> IR: The two went into a curtained room, presumably to have luncheon. Much discussion took place, loud enough to be heard at nearby tables, although the content is not known.
>
> Judith Hart emerged visibly upset, and left at once. According to the maids who this reporter spoke with later on, she left her meal untouched.
>
> GB: What is the meaning of this spectacle?
>
> IR: It's too early to say, but rumor has it that the Clubb Family plans formal protest against the Harts.
>
> GB: Whatever for?

IR: Trespass, spying, and property damage caused by this Red Dog street gang, which some say is inspired by the Hart Family.

GB: A proxy Family battle? That seems too subtle for Charles Hart.

IR: Yes, and foolhardy for him to use his Family colors on such attacks.

We plan further investigations into the relations between Hart and Clubb.

Bold reporting. I wondered how long it would be before threats forced the *Golden Bridges* to move their presses in the dead of night, as they had done so many times before.

But then I thought of another matter. Morton — Master Blaze Rainbow — claimed to work for the Harts. After pretending to be both a Diamond Pot rag and a Red Dogs trey leader.

Was the true Red Dog Gang's original plan to use vandalism to cause problems between the Families? Who might benefit from such tactics? I pondered this for a while without success.

Morton said his employer — whoever that was — wished him to learn who framed the Red Dogs for murder and kidnapping. A major problem for them, because the frame-up seemed to be succeeding, although no one had come out and said it as yet.

When I tried to contact Morton using the Hart quadrant address on his business card, I learned there was no such address. Where did Morton really live? Who did he actually work for? What was his motivation for giving me that story about Helen Hart? Whose side was he on?

The Dinner

"So now we are eight," I told Tony over breakfast. We sat beside our round white table, the garden shrouded in mist outside the large windows around us.

Tony shook his head. "I feared as much, when I heard the news and saw Miss Kerr's distress." He shrugged. "No matter. Eight is an auspicious number. I'm sure the party will go well."

"I hired a quartet for entertainment. I chose several pieces of art to play tableaux after dinner. Even with only eight, we should have enough combinations to please everyone. Plus I've ordered a red Bordeaux to go with our roasted beef."

He smiled at me. "I'm proud of how you've progressed in this matter. You arranged everything yourself this time. The staff tells me all is ordered in sufficient amounts."

I smiled back, feeling pleased.

At the time, what I really wanted was to find a few moments of peace. To be happy. To feel safe. To be of help to someone, anyone. I had lived with Tony six years, and in many ways looked to him to know how to live in Bridges society. And now, Tony was proud of me, and that meant a great deal.

***

I spent the rest of the week alongside Jane and the staff scrubbing, polishing, and decorating. But at last, Queen's Night was at hand, and all was in readiness. The musicians arrived with their instruments as good smells wafted up from the kitchens.

I went to my study, taking the name cards from my dark cherry-wood desk. Roy let me keep it even though it didn't match the gray-white trimmed in palest blue decor.

The desk was mine, and I loved it.

I folded each name card so that they made little tents upon my desk top. Then I brought the folded cards to the dining room.

Candles gave the room a soft yellow glow atop the electric lights of the chandelier. The veranda was lit, giving our guests a place to take in the air after dinner if they wished.

The musicians had set up in the breakfast room and tuned their instruments as I went round the table placing the cards as so:

Tony at the head of the table and I at the foot, as was the custom in Bridges. To Tony's right, I placed Dame Anastasia Louis; to his left, Gardena Diamond. Next to Anastasia, Major Blackwood, then Kitty Clubb would sit next to me. On my right would be Jonathan Diamond, then Lance Clubb would sit next to Gardena. Being eight made for an awkward table, two men and two women sitting beside each other, but there was no help for it. I was to have Joe beside me, and Josie between Jonathan and Lance, which would have made a perfect scene.

Rosemary and holly sprigs graced the center, gathered around short fat beeswax candles. The tablecloth was white damask; the plates, silverware, and crystal, our best.

Tony came round the corner. "Ah, there you are!" He held a bouquet of roses such a dark red as to be almost black: the roses of Spadros. He handed them to me.

"For me? I'm no matriarch." The eldest mother of the family received flowers on Queen's Day, not a young childless wife.

Tony cupped my face in his hands. "In this house, you're all I see." He kissed my lips, lingering, then touched his forehead to mine, the scent of roses filling the air. "We'll soon have children, never fear."

This felt odd. "What of your mother? Is she well?"

"My father will tend to her. I believe he will become the most pleasant of husbands."

This was mystifying, to be sure. Roy Spadros was a violent,

brutal, sadistic man, who caused injury to Tony's mother as often as he could. What changed?

Tony put his arms around my waist. "I never thought when I first saw you that we would be speaking such things."

"Well, we were only twelve years old."

"But you were such a wild thing, cursing and shouting like a zeppelin pilot. Frankly, you frightened me." He paused, gazing to one side as he smiled to himself. Then his shoulders straightened. "But your passionate defiance of my father at every turn made me see I could be bold as well. Become separate from his dominance."

Tony relied on me? Used me as his guide, his inspiration? It felt humbling.

He slowly caressed my cheek, slid his hand behind my neck. "I love you so much." Then he gave me a peck on my lips and chuckled. "I suppose I should see who I'm hosting for dinner."

I giggled, rubbing my hands together, wishing everyone would arrive soon so they might see the scene I created.

Tony ambled around the table, surveying the names one at a time ... then stopped, his face going white. "What's this?"

I laid the flowers on the sideboard. "What's wrong?"

"How could you invite Gardena Diamond?"

"Tony, she's here all the time. She and Jonathan call at least once a month. They were here just a few weeks ago. You spoke with them." He stood motionless, staring. I moved towards Tony, becoming concerned for his health. "You don't remember?"

Tony didn't speak for several seconds as the color returned to his face. When he next spoke, he sounded furious. "This is different. Inviting the Diamonds for dinner is completely different from them calling on us. Did Julius Diamond approve this?"

Julius Diamond was Jon and Gardena's father. He hated Tony so much that he wouldn't even shake my husband's hand. "I assume so. They accepted our invitation. Why? What's wrong?"

Tony said nothing.

"Jon's our friend. You spent much of the Grand Ball sitting with him in front of half the city. Why shouldn't we invite them?"

"You don't understand anything! Having them here for dinner? It just can't be." He paused. "We've never invited them here. A formal invitation sends a message to the whole city. Did you clear this with my father?"

"I never thought I needed to." Was that why Roy wrote us? I began to feel afraid of what I might have done. And worse yet, that I didn't understand why. "What message? Was I wrong to invite the Clubbs?"

"No," Tony said. "That's different."

"Why is it different? I want to understand why you're so upset."

"We're not at war with the Clubbs. We **are** at war with the Diamonds. We've been at war with the Diamonds since ... for ten years now —"

I wondered at that. "Aren't we at peace? I thought the war only lasted a year —"

"We're only at cease-fire. There's never been an alliance between their Family and ours from the time of the Coup. The whole city will wonder: is this a prelude to peace? Are these younger Diamonds emissaries?

"If anything — anything! — should happen to Jon and Gardena while they're in Spadros quadrant, so much as a hair on their heads harmed, the cease-fire could be broken. And we're not ready." Tony turned away, his hand to his forehead. "We're nowhere near ready. My father will be furious."

"Should I cancel the dinner?"

Tony shook his head. "It's much too late for that now." He stared at Gardena's place at the table. The color drained from his face, and he almost sounded afraid. "I will **not** sit beside Gardena Diamond tonight. I — I can't. You must move her at once."

What the hell was wrong with him? "Well, I wanted her to sit beside Lance Clubb. But if it'll make things better, I can switch her with Kitty." I paused, and took a breath. The fault was mine; neither anger nor sarcasm would solve this. "Dame Anastasia may take offense if I seat her away from the host."

Tony gave a weak smile. "That she might." He looked as if he might be sick. "I must contact my father."

As he left, I took a deep breath and let it out. This was not going as I expected.

As I switched the name cards, I realized the musicians witnessed all this. At my glance, they began fiddling with their papers as if they heard nothing.

I almost laughed.

The doorbell rang, and I heard Pearson open it. I hurried past the quartet, slowing to a walk as the door came into view.

Kitty and Lance Clubb were blond with blue eyes and a sprinkling of freckles across their noses. Their hair was heavy and straight with a golden hue. Kitty's gown was dandelion gold, while Lance's suit was saffron, with a cream-white cravat.

Lance Clubb seemed younger than I, even though he was a year my elder. But he won the approval of Gardena Diamond's father Julius, and I planned to introduce them tonight.

Kitty, a rather plain woman, was two years older than Lance and lacked his shy demeanor: she strode up to me at once.

I held out my hand to her. "What a pleasure to see you both!"

Kitty was unmarried, yet older. Should I curtsy to her, or she to me? Fortunately, Kitty solved the problem by curtsying to me.

Lance kissed my hand. "I hope Mr. Spadros is well?"

Music wafted into the room. I felt relieved that the musicians had finally begun to play. "Mr. Spadros is quite well; a matter arose which needed his attention. He'll be here shortly. Come, I've arranged rooms for your refreshment."

Pearson brought Lance to Tony's study, while I brought Kitty to mine. Attendants waited to help them with their coats and hats, and mirrors were set up. A screen was placed inside each door to prevent guests from being displayed to those in the hallway.

The doorbell rang. Major Blackwood was a round, vigorous old man, brown of skin and white of hair. As always, in uniform, several small badges of rank on his left chest. "Splendid to see you again, my dear," he said, bowing deeply. "Always a pleasure."

Major Blackwood was well known on the party circuit but had never visited Spadros Manor. He was neither of the aristocracy nor aligned with any Family. But he helped me two weeks ago, and this invitation was his reward.

Tony walked up just then, looking much improved. "Major

Blackwood!" They shook hands. "Welcome. It's so good to see you. Pearson, would you show the Major to the dressing room?"

"Certainly, sir."

Tony turned to me. "Who's here so far?"

"Lance and Kitty." I hesitated. "I hope you're well?"

Tony nodded. "I never imagined my father would leave the situation with the Diamonds out of your training."

I shrugged. Roy Spadros had neglected more than that. I had no idea how the illegal drug Party Time — a major source of our income — was even made until Tony tried to explain it to me a few weeks ago. "Who knows why your father does what he does?" I patted his arm. "I'm sorry I made such a mess of things."

Tony kissed my forehead. "We'll have to muddle through."

Pearson walked past us just as the doorbell rang.

With a sleek bouffant of white-blonde hair, an erect carriage, and gray eyes, Dame Anastasia Louis swept in, bedecked with jewels, furs trailing behind her. She was well past seventy, with a heritage running back to the kings of England, pre-Catastrophe. But age had only improved her, giving her a stature that made younger women look like foolish girls beside her.

"My dear friends." She gave her hand to Tony to kiss, and I curtsied when she took mine. "I'm so glad to see you."

"And I you," said Tony. "I hear your business is doing well."

"I could say the same."

Tony laughed. "That you could."

The casino brought in over $3,000 this past quarter. The shipments of Party Time we distributed were lucrative as well. This in a city where a penny could get you many things. I had never even seen a dollar before I was sold to the Spadros Family.

Dame Anastasia was rich, beautiful, and fond of us. Plus, she was our next-door neighbor (although she lived a mile away). I took her arm. "Let me show you to the dressing room."

"I've missed seeing you," she said, as we strolled down the hall. "It's been weeks since you've visited. I hope all is well?"

"Yes, very," I said. "I apologize for not calling; we've been quite busy. Did you know Mr. Spadros is renovating the casino?"

She patted my hand. "Come visit me for tea sometime this

week. I have something to speak with you about that I think you'll find most interesting."

At the time, I thought she had advice about investing in her "miracle" gems. "I would be happy to." A maid opened the door for us, and I escorted Dame Anastasia around the screen. Kitty sat with a cup of tea, but set it down and rose when we entered. "Dame Anastasia Louis, may I present to you Miss Kitty Clubb."

Kitty came forward, curtsying low. "It's an honor."

Dame Anastasia took Kitty's hand. "The pleasure is all mine." The doorbell rang and she turned to me. "Thank you, my dear, I'll allow you to greet your guests."

I left my study, closing the door. Tony stood in the entryway, shaking Jonathan Diamond's hand, then hesitated for several seconds. His back was towards me, but Gardena stared up at him, lips slightly parted. Then Jon jostled her elbow; she glanced at me. Tony glanced back, startled.

What was this all about? I walked over to greet them.

Jonathan Diamond was a tall, handsome man of six and twenty. His younger sister Gardena, poised and beautiful. Like most in the Diamond Family, their skin was so dark as to almost be black. Jon's black hair was tight-coiled and cut short. Gardena's raven curls cascaded down one side of her neck, elegantly displayed beneath a royal blue hat which matched her gown. Jonathan wore a black suit with a cravat matching Gardena's gown, pinned with the symbol of their Family in white.

Jon and his sister came past Tony to greet me, Jon kissing my hand. "How lovely you look!"

I gave him a mischievous grin. "I could say the same of you."

He laughed.

"I'm so sorry we're late." Gardena sounded embarrassed. "Father was being difficult."

I could only imagine.

Tony walked up to us and spoke to Jon. "May I show you to your dressing room?"

Jon turned to us. "Until next we meet."

I waved at him then took Gardena's arm. "You survived your father's wrath, I take it?"

She giggled. "He is a bear. But Jon persuaded him to relent."

I squeezed her arm in mine. "I'm so glad. I have a young man who eagerly awaits your introduction."

Gardena let go of my arm and stepped back. "Truly?"

"Yes. I saw him and your father shake hands on it at the Grand Ball."

Gardena's face filled with joy as she put her hands to her mouth. Then she threw her arms round my neck, kissing my cheek. "I'm so grateful." Then she straightened. "Oh, dear. Who?"

"None other than Master Lancelot Clubb."

She put her hand to her chest. "Oh, my." I didn't think Lance was handsome, but Gardena seemed flustered. "How do I look?"

"You look gorgeous." I ushered her into my study. Kitty and Anastasia rose when we entered. "Dame Anastasia Louis, Miss Kitty Clubb, may I present Miss Gardena Diamond."

Gardena stared at Anastasia, her voice dripping with venom. "You. You dare come here, tonight of all nights?"

Anastasia appeared unperturbed. "My dear, I was invited."

Gardena pointed at Anastasia, and her hand shook. "How dare you claim Queen of Diamonds while my mother still lives? How dare you mock my family's grief? You should feel ashamed of yourself!" She fled to the corner and stood facing away.

Gardena's mother Rachel never recovered from the death of her father-in-law, and required tending. It never occurred to me how Gardena might feel to meet Anastasia on Queen's Day.

"Excuse me." I said to the other ladies, and followed Gardena. She stood stiffly staring at the wall. I put my hand on her shoulder. "Are you well?"

Gardena's eyes flashed angrily. "It's not right for her to use my mother's name this way!"

I came round, held her hands. "This is my fault. I didn't consider how it might upset you to see her here."

"I worry so for her, Jacqui. I should never have come. I should be home with her now."

"Nonsense. She would want you to be happy. Am I right?"

Gardena smiled at that, wiping her face with her handkerchief. "I don't wish to spoil your party."

I glanced at Kitty, who watched us, and nodded at her. She came over with some hesitation, and I took Kitty's hand and placed Gardena's in it. "This is Lance's sister. It would please me if you became friends."

I closed the door before heading to the dining room. The musicians were taking a break now that all the guests had arrived and were preparing for dinner.

Jane stood in the dining room directing placement of the serving platters on the long tables by the wall. I approached her. "Is all well?"

"Ten minutes, mum, and all will be ready."

"Thank you. I'll alert our guests."

I went to the sideboard. Tony's roses stood in a vase; beside them stood the dinner bell. I walked past the musicians, then into the hall, ringing the bell three times. I placed it on a small table there in the hall and waited for our guests to emerge.

Tony came out of his library: face pale, collar damp, his hair moist around his forehead. Tony's father Roy Spadros was a fearsome man; I hoped Tony didn't regret his decision to loosen ties with him. I did not want things to go back to the way they were, Roy appearing at any moment to do with our household as he wished.

Our guests began appearing in the hallway, one by one. Once they were all in the hall, I went to Gardena, who appeared much improved, and I led her to Lance. "Gardena Diamond, may I present Lance Clubb."

Lance and Gardena both blushed. Lance took her hand and kissed it. "I'm most honored to meet you."

For once, Gardena was speechless. I jostled her arm. "And I you," she said.

Tony offered his arm to Dame Anastasia, and I took Major Blackwood's arm. Jon gave his arm to Kitty Clubb. I glanced back. Lance offered his arm to Gardena, passing in front of Jon and Kitty, as was proper for a Family heir to do.

At least that went well.

Then I remembered poor Joe, alone and injured. I sighed.

Major Blackwell peered at me. "I hope everything is well?"

"We're two short. A friend suffered serious injury and couldn't attend. His sister cares for him now. I would've liked to have seen them tonight."

Major Blackwood nodded. "Injury is a terrible thing." I thought for a moment he was going to start into one of his bawdy party stories about the Army, but his manner seemed grave. "I will light a candle for your friend. May he play this difficult round with dignity and honor."

This surprised me. "Why thank you, Major."

He patted my hand in a fatherly manner. "It's of no consequence."

We entered the dining room, everyone sitting as they found their places. The waiters began handing out bowls of soup and filling wine glasses. Everyone sat, hands in their laps, until Tony began to eat, then they ate as well.

Jon placed his hand over his glass. "Just water for me."

"And I," said Kitty Clubb.

My surprise must have shown, because Lance said, "Kitty has been accepted by the Dealers."

Murmurs of congratulations went round the table.

The Dealers: a female-only religious group which formed soon after the Catastrophe. Dealers took no intoxicating substances in order to play their hands to the best of their ability. In that way, they were like the Grand Order. But the Dealers handled copies of the Cards themselves, so it was a great honor to be asked to join.

Major Blackwood said, "I remember my father telling me of how his family took him to the Cathedral as a boy to receive the Dealers' blessings." He spoke as if the memory of his father's story was a pleasant one.

"It's a pity the Cathedral was destroyed," Kitty said. "I hear it was beautiful."

Destroyed? Why in the world would she say that?

Lance said to me, "What is it?"

"Forgive me," I said, "I don't mean to offend, but the Cathedral's not destroyed. I grew up there."

Everyone stared at me except Kitty, whose face lit up. "Really? What's it like?"

The high ceiling glowed in the candlelight. The setting sun crossed the one unbroken stained glass window. Lovely ladies in flowing gowns walked that window, flowers and Card symbols arrayed around them.

"Quite beautiful." I sighed, missing my home, my Ma. "But it's been a long time since I lived there."

"How is it that you grew up there?" Kitty said.

"I suppose it sounds scandalous, but my Ma owned it. She bought it shortly before I was born. But she grew up there, too, and her mother before her."

Kitty gazed at one of the candles. "I never realized that it still stood, or that anyone remained."

"We never left," I said.

Jon shook himself. "What do you mean, we?"

Without thinking, I said, "The elders call us the Dealers' Daughters, the ones who survived." I realized this might not be the best subject to discuss over dinner. "I'm sorry, I'm hoarding the conversation. How is the weather there in Diamond?"

Jon smiled. "Quite nice, for this time of year."

"It's lovely and warm," Gardena said, "and the sun came out this afternoon." She glanced at Tony. "Quite unlike here."

Tony bristled. Jon frowned at Gardena.

Was Gardena angry at Tony for inviting Anastasia?

Kitty said, "Why do they call you the Dealers' Daughters?"

"I wondered that myself," Tony said.

Anastasia said to Kitty, "My dear, are you familiar with the history of Bridges?"

"I suppose so," Kitty said.

"Then you might understand that not all that went on during that time was pleasant," Major Blackwood said, "or suitable for dinner conversation."

I felt relieved he had spoken. "Kitty, perhaps I can answer your questions later."

The waiters began taking away the bowls and replacing them

with plates filled with roast beef, roasted parsnips and carrots, and three small grilled fishes.

I began searching for a topic which might be uncontroversial.

Why was Tony saying nothing? He knew this wasn't a strong area for me. He gazed downward, off to his right, as if in a reverie.

I turned to Lance and Kitty. "I hear your parents are launching another yacht." Surely that subject might not cause distress. "What's it to be named?"

Lance leaned towards me with a wry smile. "They haven't decided yet. We're considering the *Asking Bid*."

Laughter around the table. Last month, I spoke with our Inventor about the failing Magma Steam Generator. At the time, I thought the Clubbs might be interested in gaining us as allies.

An asking bid was a question: where are you strong?

The only possible answer would be who our Family trusted the most: which Family, gang, or faction might be willing to work with both us and the Clubbs. I could answer, but I didn't want to. After Tony's outburst, I felt afraid of what else I didn't know about politics in the city.

Tony smiled. "A wonderful name. Pity we don't get the chance to do much yachting; perhaps we might all take an outing with the Harts sometime."

Lance leaned back. "That might be arranged."

Jonathan Diamond snorted quietly beside me, and I smiled at him. That Lance chose this time to say what he did meant the Clubbs didn't care who knew they offered us alliance.

This was getting more interesting all the time.

But Lance's request to court Gardena was in truth a Clubb offer of alliance to the Diamonds. Was Lance making a move to consolidate power under Clubb rule? What of the story in the Golden Bridges about the discussion between Regina Clubb and Judith Hart? Were the Harts being pushed out?

We were only at cease-fire with the Diamonds. Did Lance just ask us to pick sides in a new war? Did Tony just give him the wrong answer?

Gardena's plate was still full. I leaned to my left and whispered, "Are you well? You've hardly touched your food."

"I'm fine," Gardena said, spearing a piece of carrot with her fork. "Truly I am."

"Very well," I said. "If you're sure. I can have the servants make up something else for you if you prefer."

"That is kind, but unnecessary." She ate the carrot, and brought her wine to her lips but barely tasted it.

"Gardena is much like a bird in her habits," Tony said. "Points one way, then hops another."

Major Blackwood laughed. "I wasn't expecting that!"

"Nor was I," Gardena said. She was not amused. "Yet I could say the same of you."

Then I noticed Tony had hardly eaten anything either. He loved roast beef; what was wrong?

Lance peered at Gardena as if measuring her. She blushed, blurting out, "Tell us more about the Cathedral."

I stared at her. Did she not understand I didn't want to talk about that? "What would you like to know?"

Gardena seemed startled, staring back at me as if she had no idea what to do or say next.

Soft music filled the silence as we ate.

"I still don't understand what you meant about the history of Bridges," Kitty said a few moments later. "Do you mean the war?"

This woman was sheltered, to be sure. "Yes, the war."

Jon said, "I wonder why the Cathedral was never rebuilt, somewhere else. I mean, if no one intended to restore the Pot."

With a shock, I remembered Joseph Kerr's words when we were teenagers in the Pot ... *"One day this place could be good .... No more cold, no more rags."* Perhaps the Pot really could be restored someday. The idea inspired me. "The Dealers believe that the site of the Cathedral was holy, special, set apart for a purpose. They don't wish it rebuilt somewhere else."

Kitty nodded. At least she knew about her own religion's history. "**Was** holy?"

Gardena frowned. "Can't you see she doesn't want to talk about it?"

"Let the woman alone," Tony snapped. "I for one would like to know."

Tony didn't know what his own ancestor had done?

Gardena glared at him.

Anastasia leaned back in her chair.

Major Blackwell shook his head, eyes on his plate.

Lance sat perfectly still, watching everyone else. For an instant, he reminded me of Tony's masterful ability not to show emotion when he wished not to.

I let out an astonished laugh. Tony wasn't hiding how he felt tonight. "Well, Mr. Spadros, you asked, so I will tell you."

The music stopped.

I turned to Kitty. "During the Alcatraz Coup, after the Opposition dynamited the bridges, mobs ran through the Pot, burning and looting as they went —"

"My dear," Major Blackwood said, "you don't have to —"

"Yes sir, I do," I replied, "for my husband has commanded."

No one spoke.

"Now, Kitty, when the men, mostly the Hartmanns, grew tired of their sport, they converged upon the Cathedral to lay hands upon the women there. Many a child was dealt in by force that night, and borne from those who survived."

Kitty and Tony blanched, and the table grew silent.

I straightened, feeling a renewed sense of dignity. "So those of us from the Cathedral are known as the Dealers' Daughters, and the ground is no longer holy."

I looked at the pale and sober faces in the room, those at the table, the servants, some with frightened tears in their eyes, and I smiled. *Joe is right. We are truly not like these people.* "But it was a hundred years ago. Please, don't be distressed. Would anyone like more wine?"

The Conversation

The rest of the evening, the others strictly limited the conversation, and no one was put upon to speak on any topic. Gardena and Tony both seemed angry, but I couldn't tell whether with themselves or each other. We had our dinner, then went to the veranda for drinks.

I instructed Pearson to pay the musicians well for their service, then led the guests to the parlor for coffee and dessert. The art books lay forgotten; no one seemed interested in playing tableaux that night.

The mood improved as the night went, and soon it was time for goodbyes. Kitty begged my forgiveness, which I was glad to give. She seemed so innocent of life; I wondered if it was good for her to seclude herself in this way. Lance thanked me for the evening, and for the introduction to Gardena. How he felt now that he saw her performance at dinner, it was difficult to say. Major Blackwood told me I performed admirably; I wasn't sure Tony would see it the same way. Anastasia reminded me to stop by for tea soon. I told her I'd send a note when I planned to visit.

And then it was Jonathan and Gardena, Tony and myself.

"Shall we return to the veranda?" Gardena said. "I wish a word with Mr. Spadros in private."

Jon frowned. Tony shrugged. I said, "Certainly."

I took Tony's arm and we strolled down the hall. Perhaps Gardena wanted to apologize for her part in the unpleasantness between them.

No one said anything as we entered the dining room. The table was cleared, the candles blown out, and the lights turned off. But the veranda was still lit, giving the room a ghostly glow.

Tony opened the glass-paneled door for Gardena, glancing back at us. "This should only take a moment."

Jon and I sat on the side of the table nearest to the veranda doors, turning our chairs to face each other. Tony and Gardena went outside; Tony pulled the doors shut.

"Well," I said, "that could have gone better."

Jon smiled to himself. "You did fine."

It felt good to see Jon again. The last time I had seen him was in my parlor two weeks ago, when I prepared to rescue David Bryce. So much had happened since then. I felt as if I was a different person ... and I wasn't sure I liked the feeling. I had never kept anything from Jon before. But now ... now, there seemed to be a distance between us.

"You seem different," Jonathan said.

"Oh?"

"I've never heard you speak like you did at dinner before."

"Oh," I said, smiling to myself. "What part of it seemed different to you?"

Jon leaned against the arm of his chair. "I don't know — your bearing. It was as if you came into some strength you didn't know of before. What's happened?"

I couldn't tell him, so I shrugged. "I was ill recently. Perhaps that's it."

Jon nodded slowly, eyes downcast. "That does give you time for thought." He took my hand. "I'm glad you're well now."

Gardena and Tony stood a few feet apart, faces pensive. Tony seemed to be explaining something, but quietly, as if deeply disturbed, almost melancholy.

Tony rarely showed emotion to anyone. Seeing him this vulnerable in front of Gardena ... it made me uneasy.

I felt Jonathan watching me. The expression on his face reminded me of the little boy I saw on Market Center, the boy who looked so much like Tony's grandfather. "Jon, may I ask a personal question?"

Jon smiled, leaning his arm on the table, his expression open and earnest, his manner comfortable and easy. "My love, you may ask anything your heart desires."

He always could make me smile. "I saw a young boy a few weeks ago, and he reminded me of you."

I hesitated. Did I want the answer?

Yes. There was nothing Jonathan could have done which would make me think less of him. "Do you have a son?"

Laughter burst from him. "Not that I know of!" He seemed astonished at the thought.

Tony and Gardena stood silent, faces downcast.

"Well, how about Jack? Was the boy his son? His name was Roland ... that's Jack's middle name, is it not? ... and he looks so much like you. He truly could be your son from his appearance."

Jon chuckled, but it seemed forced. "Jack once told me that he has never met a woman who distresses him in that way. I very much doubt this boy is his son."

I sighed. "Well, then, I don't know." I turned my chair to face the veranda, leaning my elbows on my knees. Their conversation was taking more than "a moment." Gardena said something, and Tony's mouth hung open, his eyes wide. Gardena nodded.

Jon said. "His name was Roland? How old?"

Gardena said something quiet but earnest. Tony replied in the same way. "Four, maybe."

"Oh!" Jon said. "My oldest brother's son is four now. It must be him."

Gardena's eyes went empty, and she spoke. Tony's face when he replied looked wistful, longing, nostalgic.

"I suppose it must." I was focused on Tony and Gardena outside as I spoke, but then I realized I was neglecting Jon. "I hope you're feeling well these days?"

Gardena's face tightened: annoyance, as if having to repeat something she had said many a time.

Jon relaxed, turning towards me. "I'm quite well, thank you."

Tony was in anguish at whatever Gardena said. Tony's reply was vicious, and for an instant, I saw his father Roy in his eyes.

Gardena recoiled, then slapped Tony, hard, and pointed at him. *You are a coward.*

Jon stood. "This is just one reason why my father doesn't want her to visit. Stay here." He went outside, closing the veranda doors behind him.

Why was Tony so upset? What could he possibly have said to make Gardena **slap** him?

Jon faced away from me, but spoke to both of them angrily. Tony and Gardena stared in my direction, appalled.

Could they possibly have forgotten I was here?

Tony and Gardena exchanged words. Jon stared at Gardena, shocked. Whatever she said, Tony's face turned red and his hands balled into fists. His stance frightened me.

Jon grabbed Gardena's arm, opened the veranda door, and dragged her inside.

Tears filled Gardena's eyes. "Jacqui, I am so very sorry." Her voice held compassion ... and remorse.

Why? What had she done? "But —"

"We should go," Jon said. "Thank you for inviting us." They went round the corner and were gone.

Tony stood outside, alone, the glare of the electric light behind him putting his face in darkness. I went to the door and opened it. "Tony? Are you well?"

Tony shook his head, face downcast, his shoulders slumped.

"What happened? Why did she strike you?"

He didn't move. "Gardena Diamond is a high-strung woman who's had too much to drink."

I took his hand and brought him inside. His cheek was red. "Gardena hardly touched her drink. Why did you argue?"

Tony didn't answer for quite a while. Then he sighed. "It's a long story, Jacqui. Next time, please consult me before you have people over."

I stood there, not knowing what to think or feel. It seemed as if I chose the exact wrong group of people to invite.

Tony turned to leave.

"Wait," I said. "I was wrong to invite who I did, but I was innocent of your Family's machinations. You even said as much.

You, however, spent the entire evening trying to spite Gardena, with no regard for either my feelings or the people I invited. I don't know what happened between you two, but this is wrong."

Tony didn't meet my eye. "I'm sorry." He walked away.

I turned off the veranda lights and went through the preparation room. In the storeroom, boxes stood beside the stair to my left. The door out to the stables stood open; the air was cool and smelled of rain.

A third of the way up the stair, a small figure sat slumped upon the steps.

Moving to the other side of the stairwell, I tiptoed up, curious as to who it might be. A stair creaked. The figure wheeled to face me in the darkness, quilt flying aside to reveal a pale face and eyes, dark hair. "Who's there?"

I crouched before him. "I mean you no harm."

"You're her. Our lady. Mrs. Spadros."

I sat beside him. "You're Amelia's boy."

His head drooped. "Yes, mum."

"What's your name?"

"Pip, mum."

"How old are you?"

"Ten."

Born about when Air died. "Aren't you cold out here?"

He shook his head. "It's not bad."

Crickets chirped outside.

"Why are you here, and not in your bed?"

Pip turned away to lean on the support. "They always argue. If I'm not around, they don't so much."

Peter and Amelia, arguing? "Why do they argue so much?"

Misery laced his voice in the darkness. "Because of me. They say it when they think I can't hear. If I wasn't here, they could get away from here. But they can't."

I remembered what Pip's father Peter said, after Roy Spadros tortured Amelia …

"If we could leave, we would, but Mr. Roy would follow us, no

matter where we went. We thought it would be better here, that Mr. Anthony could protect us. But —"

Pip spoke as if repeating something he heard once, then took to heart. "It would be better if I never was born."

Even in my worst days — after Air died, after I was brought here, the many terrifying days and nights — I never wanted to die. It never even crossed my mind. What happened to this boy?

"I don't think it would be better if you never were born."

He sniffled. "Really?"

I sat next to him. "Really. You seem a good boy, always helping. I saw you playing with Rocket out in the meadow the other day." I had to ask. "Does anyone hit you?"

Pip sat hunched over, his arms on his knees. "Sometimes."

I shook my head. "It's not right for a man to hit a little boy."

"My Daddy never hit me, mum, never!" He sounded shocked. "Daddy's good to me." He paused. "But ... Mommy doesn't like me." His little body crumpled, and he began sobbing. "Mommy hates meeeee."

I pulled him to me and held him as he cried. I almost asked why his Ma should hate him, but he probably didn't know any more than I did.

In the Pot, for an adult to hurt a child in any way warranted death. How was this going on in my own home?

After a time, he wiped his face with his sleeve, pulling away to sit hunched over again.

"Pip, when people are very sad, sometimes they don't act right. Sometimes they say and do things to hurt people, even people like you who didn't do anything wrong. It's not right for them to do these things, but it's not because you're bad. It's because ... because they're so sad."

Pip nodded, and something in the set of his shoulders told me he never considered such things before.

"Would you like to sleep in the men's quarters?"

"Go away from Daddy?" He paused. "I don't know."

"Well, I'll ask if that might be possible. But you don't have to go if you decide you don't want to." I patted his shoulder. "The beds there are better than the stair."

A smile came to his voice. "Thank you, mum."

"I'm going to go walk now. But I want to walk by myself. Will you promise not to tell?"

"I will."

"Thank you, Pip. Sleep well."

I tiptoed down the stair, peering out of the door. No one stood there, so I slipped out, closing the door behind me.

I walked among the horses, listening to their soft sounds as crickets chirped around us. The stars were bright, and I leaned on a post. A horse came over to sniff my hair, then retreated.

Pip was just a boy. What could have possibly gone on between them to make Amelia beat him?

Amelia never told me how she and Peter got here or why they stayed, even after Roy tortured her last month. She probably felt afraid to share her troubles with me.

Amelia took great pride in her position as my lady's maid. But something in the way she spoke of it suggested she might feel as little choice in the matter as I once thought I had.

Some small animal rustled in the straw beside me as I passed.

That afternoon in Jack Diamond's factory basement showed me I did have a choice. David and I could have died that day, or still be held by Frank Pagliacci and Jack Diamond, undergoing some horrific torture. I chose to fight back.

But how could I fight Roy Spadros? It seemed impossible.

I leaned against a post, watching the trees sway in the distance. Could Joe really get us out of Bridges?

I didn't want to even consider it until Joe was well. To have my hopes dashed again ... I didn't know if I could take it.

To know he might still love me was enough for now.

I closed my eyes, remembering Joe's strong fingers in mine. I'd almost forgotten who I was, but Joe's words and Kitty's innocent questions reminded me.

Darkness ... candlelight ... ancient voices chanting ... Ma's arms round me as I lay curled upon her lap. I felt warm, safe.

"We are the Dealers' Daughters, ever grateful for their sacrifice, bound to keep faith until the land is restored. May we prove worthy of our mothers' courage, showing the Dealer's love to all who enter."

The memory seemed a thousand years ago.

One of Tony's men patrolled the street, far off to the right. His cigarette's light gave his face an orange glow. The wind blew chill.

Shivering, I returned to the stair. Pip was gone, so I crept up the stair, through the sheet-covered shapes in the storeroom, and into the hall. Blitz Spadros, our night footman, held a candle as he walked the hallway, and he smiled and nodded when he saw me.

Tony lay in my bed, asleep. His roses stood in a vase on my dresser, their thick perfume filling the air. After a few minutes' struggle to get out of my finery and jewels, I lay beside him, placing my hand so our fingers barely touched.

My husband was an ordinary-looking man, but I loved to watch him sleep. His guard vanished; his face took on a peace which no one else ever saw.

I kept revisiting the scene on the veranda … last month in his study. The way Tony's voice changed when he spoke of Gardena, the way he looked at her, the way he lay his heart open to her ….

Tony loved Gardena.

Tony was in love with Gardena.

In the Pot we had no such thing as marriage. Until recently, my feelings for Tony had been what I might offer a brother, or a friend, such as Jonathan. I grew up in a brothel; a person might have many relationships in the Pot, even at the same time, without causing offense. But I could see how this might upset a quadrant-man such as Tony, who had been raised in a different way.

But for them to argue so as to come to blows made no sense. And then for him to offer such a bold lie, casting the entire blame on **her**? Something deep ran between them, something old and powerful which turned love to hate, at least on her part.

You are a coward.

Perhaps this deep secret was the reason Jon and Gardena's father Julius Diamond hated Tony so.

Tony lied to me, cast blame on others, provoked Gardena to

violence. None of this was like him. Something happened. No, something horrible was happening **to** him, something he felt too terrible to tell me. Had the fear of his father's wrath for my inviting Jonathan and Gardena pushed him too far?

Tony lay facing me, his cheek pink, his side bruised brown and yellow from the beating he took during the ambush six weeks ago, his black hair tousled. I felt deep compassion for him. I couldn't think of a way to let him know he had my support no matter what calamity had befallen him.

I put my hand over Tony's. He mumbled, "no … no," his face in deep distress.

Tears wet my pillow. I knew all about nightmares.

The News

The next morning, Amelia came in as usual, and over my morning tea, I watched her.

Why would she beat her son? Why would he think she hated him? Why did Peter not intervene?

The *Golden Bridges* had a disturbing article: Hart merchants were discussing a protest against the Hart Family for non-payment of bills. A spokesman for the Harts said the purchases were made without their knowledge or consent.

Could Charles Hart be in financial difficulty? At the Grand Ball, he seemed relaxed, even jovial. Why wouldn't he pay what he owed? What would it mean if his quadrant rose against him?

And Tony had spoken for them.

Tony seemed tired at breakfast, and he spoke little. I didn't ask about the events of the night before; he didn't mention them. He left after breakfast, telling me to run the morning meeting without him. But it was a simple matter, just giving the staff their orders for the day. I sat and smoked for a while after he left. As I rose from the table, I decided to visit Dame Anastasia for tea, and hear her interesting information. Before the business with David Bryce, I called on her almost every week.

On the way downstairs to the meeting, I heard our chef shouting, "How can I work in this disorder?"

"If you would clean after yourself, Monsieur," a woman said, "the disorder wouldn't exist."

"Damnable woman!" Monsieur roared. I heard him stomp up the stairs to the courtyard.

I chuckled, recognizing the woman's voice. When I went past the kitchens, Anne — a sturdy brown-haired spinster in her middle thirties — winked when she saw me. Whatever disorder Monsieur detected in the kitchens, I couldn't see it.

After the meeting, I went to Pearson. "I have a situation I must discuss."

He followed me up to my study, closing the doors behind us. "How may I help, mum?"

I took a deep breath. "Pip Dewey."

Pearson's expression didn't change. "What about the boy?"

"I believe you know very well what. The child's situation is unacceptable. I don't know what has gone on, but —"

"You're correct, mum. You don't know what has gone on."

I stared at Pearson in surprise. He spoke gently, but his words bordered on insubordination. I turned away. "Who is it you fear, I wonder." The list was very short. "The boy may stay in the men's quarters, if he agrees, and a place can be found. If someone has concerns about the matter they may speak with me." I faced him. "Is that suitable?"

Pearson stood for a moment, his face unchanging. "That is quite suitable, mum."

"That is all." He turned to go. "No, wait. Someone needs to speak with his father."

"I'll do that, mum."

"Thank you, Pearson."

The door shut behind him.

At least I had done something useful today.

Pearson didn't seem to think Pip's abuse was worth notice. The people here ... none of this made any sense to me.

Shaking my head, I sat at my desk, surveying my calling list. I had sadly neglected my social duties during the past two months.

Most of the women I visited were cold, and I heard many a one call me foul names in secret — or even to my face — "Pot rag whore" being the kindest.

It amused me. Pot rag was a foul title, to be sure, but whore was the second highest calling someone in the Pot might have. Where they thought to give insult, I saw it as praise. But though they meant insult, I had to pretend I wanted to call on them. We held the quadrant. But if I offended the wrong women, it could cause their men to look elsewhere for leadership.

I collected my notes, the list I made a few weeks earlier, and the pile of cards left while I was ill, and began to sort it all.

I didn't care about these women; they didn't care about me. Why did they play this game? Joe was right: everything these people did trapped themselves, confined themselves so that they could hardly move without causing offense. At times, I felt I could hardly breathe.

But Roy said I must do this. Molly and Tony agreed. I opened my calendar and set to work.

***

The afternoon was overcast yet warm, with a gentle breeze, so I walked the mile to Anastasia's home, my day footman Honor three paces behind.

This was new. I normally walked without escort so close to our home. But with the attack on Tony on New Year's Day and the events since, Tony decided I was to go nowhere unescorted.

Who was a fit escort confused me. No man seemed to be sufficient except family members or servants. Tony was driven almost to terror at my visit to the Inventor's Laboratory below our home, even though the Inventor himself accompanied me, an elderly man of the highest honor. Yet a young, attractive male servant walked behind me without arousing any comment. None of it made sense. And while Skip Honor was a pleasant enough fellow, his presence felt like another bar in my cage.

Dame Anastasia didn't mind Honor's presence; she asked her butler to show him downstairs for tea with the other servants. Then she brought me to her parlor and we sat. Anastasia collected clocks of all kinds, and they ticked merrily as we talked.

"Thank you so much for coming last night," I said. "I hope you enjoyed yourself."

She smiled. "Dinner was delicious and the entertainment lovely ... although I found your friends rather impertinent."

This irritated me when I remembered Gardena's tears. But perhaps Anastasia didn't understand the situation. "I'm sorry. I'll have to have you over again under a more pleasant environment."

"I would be delighted."

The maid came in, bringing us tea, small sandwiches, and thin slices of cake. "Will there be anything else, m'lady?"

"That will be all."

The maid curtsied and left, closing the door behind her.

I picked up my teacup. "How may I help you?"

"On the contrary, my dear, I have something to speak to you about which I hope you'll find beneficial."

She wore her signature necklace: twenty large round-cut diamonds in a chain, a teardrop dangling in the center. Rumor had it the necklace was worth tens of thousands of dollars; she had guards with her wherever she went. The diamonds sparkled in the sun as she talked.

She wished me to collect old debts from a list of men, which she handed over. "I hope you can do this in the next two weeks."

It seemed rather short notice for such a long list. "Is there a reason for the deadline?"

She nodded. "I didn't want you to hear about this from someone else. I'm moving to another city."

The news stunned me. "Moving away? But why?"

She waved her hand. "This all looks lovely, but I'm close to bankruptcy. The cost to mine these so-called miracle gems is enormous. Now that they are so popular, the mining company is charging me double. Even these improved prices are only covering my bills."

"But why move away?"

"Business these days ... it's just not what it used to be. I feel like I'm losing my touch." Her head drooped. "I'm getting too old for this. I need to think of my future." She gestured. "All this ... plus the Family fees every month ... I'm moving where I can live more simply."

I was seventeen years old. I stood next to Tony a second after the announcement of our engagement. None of the hundreds of people in the hall moved. Disdain, shock, and horror filled every face as they stared at me. Roy stood there, glowering at me as if it were my fault. My face burned with humiliation.

The elegant woman rose, gliding forward to take my hand. "Congratulations, my dear."

Dame Anastasia went to the mantle, where a bank lock-box sat. She set the box on the table, took a small key from her pocket, and unlocked it. After removing her necklace, she placed it in the empty box, locked it, and handed me the key. "Yours: a token of my esteem and gratitude for doing me this service."

I was astonished. "Surely I can't accept this for payment. It's too much. It's too much even as a gift."

"It's no gift! Well, yes, it is, somewhat. Payment and gift both. I'm an old woman; I have no real need for this. And I don't think I could sell it, even if I wanted to." She gazed at the box. "It was one of my most beautiful creations … but I won't be able to afford guards for it when I leave." She paused for a moment. "It'll look stunning on you. The thought of you wearing this at some dinner or ball," she patted the box, "fills my heart with joy."

"When do you plan to take your trip?"

"As soon as possible. I have a buyer for the manor. I have to settle some business dealings before I can leave, but certainly within the next few weeks."

"Do you have to leave so soon?"

She gave me a fond smile. "You are a dear. But I'm moving, not dying; you and Mr. Spadros are welcome to visit anytime."

The maid came in with a fresh pot of tea.

When the maid left, Anastasia said, "There is another matter. Frank Pagliacci."

Finally, someone with information on that murderous scoundrel. A bit late, now he was dead, but her information might give me some clue as to how to approach the problem of Jack Diamond. "Tell me what you know of him."

She let out a breath, looking away. "I've been day-leasing my horses. It brings in some income. Two weeks ago, Frank Pagliacci leased a horse from me. He had done so before, and in the past, returned the horse in good order, so I leased him my best palomino. But he never brought it back. So I sent a letter asking for its return. He wrote a few days later saying it ran off."

A few days later?

"My men found the poor creature whipped almost to death outside a brothel in the Diamond Pot. The men there had bandaged its wounds and were taking care of it, but it's too hurt for me to sell for what I wanted."

I felt alarmed. "He leased the horse two weeks ago. And you received a letter from him when? The dates may be important."

"Let me check my records." She left for a few minutes, returning with a ledger. "He leased the horse January 30th —"

The day we rescued David Bryce.

The day I shot Frank Pagliacci.

" — I sent the letter to him on the first of February. He replied on the third."

I stared at her in horror.

Frank Pagliacci was still alive.

The Danger

Frank Pagliacci was still alive. How? "Might I see his letter?"

Anastasia took a letter from several she had marking the place and handed to me.

The writing seemed different from the false note which started me on Frank Pagliacci's path. It was a man's heavy hand, yet a fine one, showing education and skill at writing. I handed the note back to her. "Thank you."

"Was this information helpful?"

"Very." But it felt surreal. Frank Pagliacci ... still alive? "Where does he live?"

She handed me an envelope. "I send letters to his box at the post office on Market Center."

Not much help there. "What does the man look like?"

Color rose in her cheeks. "He's quite handsome, that one. A charmer. About your age, tall, with brown hair." She paused, then shook her head. "But I can't have anything more to do with him, not after what he did to my horse." She shuddered. "Something is deeply wrong with the man."

I hoped she never learned of the terrible things he had done. Kidnapping, murdering boys ... who knew what else? "I'll begin work at once on your debtors. I know just the person who might be able to help."

On the mile-long walk home, Honor trailing three paces behind, I considered my situation. I didn't miss when I shot Frank Pagliacci. But a serious hit would have left the man dead before he reached a doctor. Between the terrible fall from the overseer platform and the delay before his men got to him, I felt astonished he survived. But he did, and it was only a matter of time before he contacted Jack Diamond and they continued their spree of kidnapping and murder.

Frank Pagliacci said he captured David to lure me. Then after capturing me, he planned to kill the Spadros Family one by one as they tried to rescue me. A foolish plan, but I suppose one an amateur villain with a desperate need for revenge might concoct.

But Jack Diamond's involvement didn't make sense.

Jack Diamond hated the Spadros Family because they supported and protected my father after he murdered Jack's friend. But from all accounts, Jack Diamond was mad. Obsessed with cleanliness, refusing to dress in anything but white, even to the soles of his shoes, sleeping all day then not sleeping for days. He flew into a rage at the Grand Ball and even tried to attack Jonathan, his own twin. Yet at other times, he could appear perfectly normal.

Jack's reputation as a murderer and torturer went city-wide. But Jack had no reputation for convoluted plots such as this.

And he had never targeted children before.

But between Frank Pagliacci and Jack Diamond, Jack (when lucid) was the more dangerous of the two. While the Diamond Family was neither as rich nor as powerful as ours, Jack had enormous resources at his disposal. He could reach even into the Spadros quadrant: he left a Red Dog card on my doorstep despite our guards at the bridges and marinas.

Jack Diamond was a menace. When I had proof of his involvement in David's kidnapping and those boys' murders, I planned to meet with the Four Families. I would demand Jack either be confined to a ward or they allow me to kill him.

Spadros Manor appeared in the distance, a white two story building shaped as a U, its arms pointing towards me. I began to make a list as to who might be able to provide such proof.

Eleanora Bryce, David's mother. A man fitting Jack's description came to her home a week before David was taken. We saw two men put a boy-sized struggling package into a carriage in the Diamond Pot: one man in white, the other in brown. Eleanora told me the man in white was the one who came to her home.

The stable-man at the carriage house on Market Center told me these same two men stole the carriage. The man in brown gave the name Frank Pagliacci. I found David's hair in the carriage, as well as a button and fibers from Frank Pagliacci's jacket.

This wouldn't hold up in front of a Family inquiry. Also, the stable-man and Mrs. Bryce were both lowers, easily discredited.

And even though I was the wife of the Spadros heir, I was a woman. Worse yet, a Pot rag, one of the untouchables, despised just for existing. My upbringing in a brothel, my lack of education, and anything else Julius Diamond could learn would be used to discredit me. And to testify against Jack, I would have to reveal my part in all this. The thought of what Tony and Roy might do if they learned of it terrifed me. I had to find solid proof, something no one could gainsay, and I had very little time to do so before Jack Diamond and Frank Pagliacci regrouped.

First, I must send word to everyone involved, warning them that their lives were in danger. I couldn't risk that they'd be targeted without their knowledge. Mrs. Bryce and her son David were in particular danger. David had said nothing since his rescue, but he could not only identify Frank Pagliacci and Jack Diamond but testify against them.

We reached the house and passed the stables. Tony's men stood guard out at the street, tipping their Derby hats as I passed. We walked up the walkway and through the wide front porch. Honor opened the door for me. Pearson stood by his podium, glancing up as I entered. "Ah, there you are, mum. A letter just came for you."

Honor helped me out of my coat, handing it to Pearson. I placed my handbag in my dress pocket and removed my hat, which Pearson also took. "Very good. I'll take it in my study."

I went upstairs to my room, where Amelia sat mending. She stood immediately when I came in. "How was tea, mum?"

Had Pearson not told her about our conversation? "Lovely." I let her change my street boots out for soft house shoes, and then she got me out of my walking dress and into a house dress. I took Dame Anastasia's lock-box key from my handbag and locked it in my dresser drawer.

"I have the blue on blue chintz gown ready for dinner tonight," Amelia said.

I saw no anger at my removing her son from their rooms without consulting her; if I were to guess, she appeared happy. "That's fine, thank you."

The poor child.

Why would Amelia wish her own son gone? I never had a child, but never wanting to see Tony's little sister Katherine? Or for her to think I hated her? It was monstrous.

"Amelia, do you know what happens in the Pot to a man or woman who beats a child?"

She gave me a blank, terrified stare.

"The other adults gather, then beat that person to death." Amelia didn't react, and I took a deep breath to keep my voice from shaking. "So I find it difficult to know the best course here. Shall I dismiss you?"

Amelia came forward and fell to her knees, grasping my skirts. "Oh, please, mum, you can't, not after all I've done for you. I never said anything about your going out at night, or your business, even when Mr. Roy cut me."

"Get up." It was true. This made me angrier. I gritted my teeth to keep from kicking her. "Why does your boy think you hate him? Why do you hit him?"

She turned away. "I ... I become so angry when I look at him, I can't ... I can't think. I know it's wrong, but ..." She covered her face with her hands for a moment. "I can't speak of it, mum ... I can't ... even if I wanted to."

"You've been forbidden to speak of it."

Amelia stared at her hands. "Yes, mum."

This had to be Roy's doing. I clenched the sides of my skirt to keep myself from shouting. "You are not to hit your son again. Is that clear? Or I swear to all the gods above and below, I **will** dismiss you, and let the cards fall where they may."

I didn't wish to speak to Amelia any further, or even to see her, so I went downstairs and into my study. I lit a cigarette to calm myself.

The letter Pearson spoke of sat in the center of my desk. It was from Madame Marie Biltcliffe, my dressmaker.

> Mrs. Spadros,
>
> This notice is to remind you of your appointment for tomorrow, the Sixteenth of February, from 2:00 to 4:30 pm, for the final fitting of your Spring gown. Please advise me at once if this time is no longer acceptable for you.
>
> Your servant, Marie Biltcliffe

I had no such appointment, but inside this note was another:

> Mrs. Spadros, I must see you urgently. It is regarding my son. — EB

This must be from Eleanora Bryce.

Did David finally speak? The boy had done nothing but rock, sucking his thumb, since Morton and I found him in the basement of Jack Diamond's Party Time factory. If David could identify Jack as the man who kidnapped him, that might be enough to persuade Julius Diamond to restrain his son.

Madame Biltcliffe and I had an arrangement where she would pass notes from clients. She often concocted suitable alibis so I might speak to clients without my husband or his men knowing. But I also needed to speak with Madame further about the break-in at her shop.

And the dress did need hemming.

I wrote a note to Madame telling her the time tomorrow was acceptable, sealed it, then leaned back in my chair. Since the ordeal with finding David, all I wanted was to rest and recover. I still felt weak from my illness, and the walk to and from Anastasia's home left me weary.

I lit a cigarette from the end of the first one and gazed outside my window. The patrolling guards reminded me of our constant danger. I must establish my own income, and soon. If anything should happen to Tony, I would be on my own in a city full of people who hated me. Roy Spadros had made it clear any assistance or protection he offered was for Tony's benefit alone.

But I had no real paying cases at present. This business of Anastasia's hardly qualified. Although the necklace was lovely, I would never sell it unless I found myself in dire straits. It was her lifetime achievement; she treasured it above all things.

I didn't understand why she would just give it to me.

Yet the case itself was straightforward and simple. No police were likely to become involved. It could be handled by attorneys, putting myself in no danger whatsoever. And I had the perfect lawyer in mind.

Well, he wasn't a lawyer, not yet. But I felt certain I could persuade the apprentice law clerk Thrace Pike to help me, perhaps without even having to pay him.

I chuckled to myself (until I began to cough) but felt unsettled about another matter. As much as I hated to admit it, I needed to contact Roy. I knew exactly what he meant by his note: it was time for my shooting lesson. We met every month, always when Tony was away.

Roy could have had Molly send me a letter. Instead, he sent notice through Tony, knowing Tony would show me the note. Yet he didn't specify why he wanted to see me. This indicated he believed Tony didn't know of our lessons.

This seemed unlikely. Tony made no comment or question as to what Roy and I might have to discuss, and he knew Roy would want to come here.

Whether Tony knew of our lessons or not, the important thing was that I got them. I should have killed Frank Pagliacci that afternoon. The next time I had the man in my sights, I wanted to be prepared.

Did I dare contact Roy, after Tony denounced him?

No, I didn't dare, not yet. Perhaps I could find someone else to teach me.

The stable-man was a more difficult matter. I felt at a loss as how to warn him of the danger he might be in. I didn't even know the man's name.

I took another sheet from my writing-desk and wrote:

Stable-master, Market Center

Sir:

We met last month about two men, thieves of a carriage: one named Frank Pagliacci. I have reason to believe you are in mortal danger from these men. They have murdered two boys at least, and may be willing to remove all who might identify them.

I can't advise you as to the precautions you should take, but it might be well to arm yourself.

With sincere regards,

A friend.

I put this note in my pocket. I couldn't send it from Spadros Manor; the messenger boy would tell the stable-man who sent it. I would have to find some other way to get the message to him.

When I gave Madame's note to Pearson, he said, "Peter Dewey wishes to speak with you, mum."

Amelia's husband. Pip's father. "Send him in."

Our stable-man Peter Dewey had brown hair and eyes, and was of medium height. He had changed from his usual work clothes into his best suit. He held a clean but battered gray hat in both hands and peered around, eyes wide.

He had never been in this part of the house before.

"How can I help you?"

At this point, he gave a slight start, and focused on me. I didn't rise to greet him. "Begging your pardon, mum." He took a step towards my desk. "It's about my boy." He took another step, and his shoulders straightened as he took a deep breath. "He's too young to go to the men's quarters. He's only ten."

"Why are you letting Amelia mistreat him?"

Peter's whole body jerked as if he had been slapped. "That's none of your affair, mum."

"It **is** my affair, when a boy in my household says it would be better had he not been born."

Peter stared at me, eyes reddening. "When —?"

"Last night. I found him on the stair, wrapped in his quilt."

He began shaking his head. "I'm sorry, mum, he shouldn't have been there —"

"I'm glad he was there. I'm glad he talked to me, and you will **not** punish him for it."

He paled. "I've never laid a hand on him, mum. Never."

"I know. He defends you."

His shoulders drooped. "You can't take my son from me."

"I'm not. He'll be in the same building. On the same floor."

Peter didn't say anything.

I stood up, incensed. "Floorman help us! Think of your boy, instead of your pride."

His head jerked up. "You wrong me, mum. I love the boy —" He stopped, as if he almost said too much.

What was he going to say?

Concern washed away my anger, as I came round the desk. "I only want to help him. He doesn't have to go if he doesn't want to. But give him a chance to live in peace. Whatever's going on, surely he deserves that."

Peter nodded, eyes on the floor. "Thank you, mum."

"I'm sorry for what happened to Amelia. I never —"

He gave me a brief, startled glance, then nodded. "All is forgiven, mum," he said quickly. "I have work to tend to."

"Very well, you may go."

What did he think I meant? What else happened to her? What was going on?

Tony didn't get home until time to dress for dinner. He ate silently, shoulders slumped, and went to his study straight after. I sat smoking and sipping wine as the maids cleared the table.

I needed a post box like Frank Pagliacci had so I might send letters without anyone knowing from whence they came.

I chuckled at the thought; if it weren't for that vile man, I wouldn't need to sneak around like this.

I must warn the stable-man of the danger he was in. I couldn't live with myself if I didn't warn him and something happened to the man. Yet I couldn't let anyone know I sent the message. What would Mrs. Jacqueline Spadros know about plots and murder?

Jane Pearson came into the dining room. "Oh, there you are, mum." She came up to me and curtsied.

"Please sit," I said, and she did.

"I've chosen my replacement, mum. Anne should do well."

"A very good choice, thank you."

"My pleasure, mum. Did you decide about the outing?"

I still had Anastasia's list to take care of; planning an outing for several dozen people would take time. I hadn't even thought of where to have it. "After the 100th celebration, perhaps? One major event a month is plenty."

Jane smiled. "Yes, mum, I agree."

I studied Jane. She took care of the house; she would know everything that went on in it, including what happened to Amelia. Pearson and Peter also knew. But Roy forbade them from talking about it. "I'm sure your husband told you I wish to move Pip to the men's quarters."

Jane glanced away. "Yes, mum."

"Do you think it a good thing?"

She shifted uncomfortably. "It's not for me to say, mum."

"But —"

She sat stiffly, face pale, not looking at me. "Under the circumstances, mum, it seems a wise decision."

Under the circumstances. "Thank you." Jane didn't move. "Is there anything else?"

"No, mum." She pushed back her chair and hurried out.

Interesting, but not in a good way. I drained my glass and put out my cigarette. Then I went to Tony's study and knocked.

"Yes?" Tony sat behind his desk, a book in one hand, his forehead leaning on the other as he looked up at me. "Did you need something?"

"I don't mean to disturb you; I just wanted to make sure you were well." I never knew how he would react when he retreated into his study like this, so I stayed in the doorway.

But he gave me a tired smile and put his book down. "It's

time we went to bed." He came round to take my hand.

"You look weary," I said as we went up the stairs. "Would you like me to rub your back?"

"That sounds wonderful."

Perhaps I could learn what troubled him.

When we got to our rooms, we separated to let our servants undress us. If Amelia was angry at my threats earlier, she gave no sign of it.

It seemed odd to have a maid dress and undress you, but Molly told me the system of service allowed people to have an income. If we all dressed ourselves and did our own washing, what would they do to survive? At the time it made sense, but the more I saw of it the less I liked it.

Once I was in my gown, Amelia curtsied and left. Tony came back in wearing his pajamas. He smiled, and came over to kiss me. "Now, what were we discussing?"

"I was going to rub your back."

"Yes," he said. He took off his shirt, then lay face down on the bed. I knelt on the bed beside him and began to rub his back.

When I was a little girl, long before I got tangled up with the Spadros Family, Ma taught me how to rub a man's back to get him to tell you his problems. "If we were in the Clubb Pot, we'd be selling their secrets, but it's better here," she said. "They know the Dealers' Daughters won't speak of their troubles to others."

At the time I thought the Clubbs must be wicked to tell someone else's secrets. Now the idea of betraying someone like that just made me sad.

"How did your day go?"

"Mmm," Tony said, "well enough. I never thought this would take so long."

"I'm sorry it's taking so long. Have you run into problems?"

He snorted. "Oh, yes, indeed, all day long it seems. When I go to do one thing, they find three more for me. One wall has bees in it, another termites, so both must be replaced. They can't find the material I wanted in black, because it's all been bought. So we had to find another supplier, who wants to import it from Chicago. Which means I have to fill out yet another form." He sighed, relaxing into the cushions. "I wish I'd never begun this."

"My poor dear." I kissed his forehead, brushing his hair away from his face. "Just think of how beautiful it'll be once it's done."

He rolled onto his side. "Come here." He took me into his arms. "You always try to help me." Then he paused. "Even when I don't deserve it."

"Tony … I want to say something." I hoped he could hear it. "I have eyes. I know you love Gardena. It's okay. I'm not angry, or hurt, or upset. We can't help who we love —"

"Shh," he said. "I love you. I married you. I don't want to talk about her."

I lay my head on his arm and put my hand beside his face, gazing into his eyes. I had so many questions that he didn't want to answer. And then he kissed me.

A pang of bitter disappointment: all I wanted was for him to talk to me. I closed my eyes, enduring his touch, and went in search of Joe.

"NO!" Tony screamed.

Our night footman Blitz rushed in, candle in one hand, the other on his holster. Then he peered at us. "Are you well, sir?"

Tony sat upright in bed, eyes wild. He glanced around, then crumpled, hand to his forehead. "Gods, what a terrible dream."

I sat up. "We're fine, Blitz, thank you." Once he left, I said to Tony, "Come here," and I laid his head upon my chest. "What did you dream?"

He didn't speak for several seconds. "I dreamed you were gone." He paused. "I dreamed you left me. You lay there, cold and still, and it was my fault."

I closed my eyes, feeling sad. "Shh … I'm here. All is well."

He wrapped his arms around my waist. "You're all I have," he said, his voice sleepy. "Please don't leave me."

Was he awake, or asleep? I never heard him say such things before. "I'm here, Tony … all is well … just rest." I held him tightly, tears in my eyes as I smoothed his hair.

When Joe was well, if he really wanted to leave with me … what should I do?

"Jacqui? Please love me."

My heart stopped within me for a moment. What was he asking? I had never lied to him in this area: I never once told him I loved him. What should I say?

But his face grew peaceful; he was asleep.

**

Madame Biltcliffe owned a dress shop on 42nd Street in Spadros quadrant. Her shop had a polished oak storefront and large plate glass windows. Inside, it smelled of fresh, clean cloth, and felt warm and inviting.

Madame, a handsome woman of middle age with perfect black hair, came to greet me as I entered. "Mrs. Spadros! So good to see you." She locked the door behind me, turning the front placard to, "Closed: entry by appointment only."

My personal fitting room was ten feet square, with a door-sized curtained opening in the far wall. A small raised area in the center to stand on and mirrored walls completed the scene. Mrs. Bryce sat in the corner on a stool, standing when I entered.

Eleanora Bryce had graying brown hair and dark eyes, and wore widow's brown. Once the curtain fell behind me, she said, "The man in white came round again."

I stared at her, shocked. Mrs. Bryce lived in the Spadros slums, just outside the Pot. How had Jack Diamond managed to get there without alerting the guards? "What happened?"

She sat on the stool, and Madame gestured for me to take my place on the raised area, so I did.

Mrs. Bryce seemed hesitant. "I didn't know what else to do. After you brought David home, I needed help, so I asked a neighbor to watch him. She was appalled at his condition and asked what happened. I told her as little as I could, but word got out, and the men have been watching for strangers. When they saw him, they chased him away with bricks. They say one hit him, but I didn't see it."

"You did the right thing."

Madame brought in a basket filled with scissors, thread, measuring tapes, and so on. Behind her was her shop maid Tenni.

Tenni, a girl of seventeen, looked like me from behind: light brown skin, curly reddish-brown hair. I sometimes switched clothes with her when on cases, so as to lead my men to believe I remained in the shop. Her eyes were brown and mine blue, but from a distance we looked similar. A shop maid's uniform made a fair disguise for me, as no one would expect Mrs. Jacqueline Spadros to dress in such a way.

Madame said to Mrs. Bryce, "Would you step out so Mrs. Spadros can change, please?"

Mrs. Bryce nodded and went into the main store, letting the curtain fall behind her.

Tenni helped me change out of my dress and into the green silk shantung gown. It was a lovely, serviceable dress, with black cording and embroidery upon the front bodice and waist, extending to the floor. The embroidery curved in such a way as to give the illusion that my waist was quite small. I found that part both intriguing and amusing. "I love it!"

Madame's reflection smiled from behind me as she arranged my skirts. "I'm glad it pleases you." She glanced up. "Mrs. Bryce, you may return if you wish."

Eleanora resumed her seat in the corner. She appeared awed and a bit disturbed. "I never —" She took a deep breath. "One day we must speak of how you came to be here."

Before her son David disappeared, Eleanora knew me only as a dirty, half-starved girl in the Pot. The contrast must have been remarkable. I glanced at Madame and Tenni, remembering the servants' faces at my story on Queen's Night. "It's a long tale, not suitable for gentle folk."

Mrs. Bryce stood. "Then it can wait. I don't dare leave David for long."

"I must tell you one thing more. The man we saw with him," I glanced at Tenni, who knelt in front of me, pinning my hem, "the one in brown. He still lives. Tell your neighbors of him as well."

Mrs. Bryce's eyes widened. "Thank you."

"And please give my regards to your son. I will visit the moment I'm able."

She curtsied. "I will." She left through the back curtain; the back door opened and shut.

"Madame, I hope this is not too distressing, but would you tell me again of the break-in?"

Madame glanced up at my reflection from where she knelt behind me. "It was during Yuletide, a few days before New Year's. Mr. Roman across the street sent his shop maid to my home in the morning with the news."

I frowned. "Mr. Roman?" The name seemed familiar.

"Yes, the jeweler."

Ah, a name from the list. "Did either of them see anything?"

"He noticed the broken glass when he came to open the shop. The girl never saw a thing." Madame Biltcliffe worked in silence for a few minutes. "But there was one thing odd." She paused. "It may be nothing ..."

Something about the way she said it made me uneasy. "What? Any detail may help."

"Well," Madame said, "there was a card, as one might use for calling, with a dog stamped on it in red. I had never seen such a thing before."

The Red Dog Gang.

I found that same stamp on the wall outside David Bryce's back stair after he disappeared. A card with the same stamp was left on my front steps. Red Dog stamps and cards had appeared at the scene of petty crimes throughout the Clubb quadrant shop district for weeks now. And the police found a Red Dog card on Herbert Bryce's body after he was strangled to death.

Madame said, "What does it mean?"

I said, "I've seen this stamp before. I'm not certain of all the meanings this stamp might have. But it seems to be connected with a street gang called the Red Dogs." The Red Dog members I had met so far vigorously denied responsibility for the crimes, horrified at being framed for murder and kidnapping.

"A street gang? Why would children wish to break into my shop, ruin the room, then take nothing?" She paused, gazing to the side. "I had forgotten to go to the bank that evening; I had my whole day's take in the cabinet. It was still in the bag, untouched."

These were **not** the actions of a street gang. "Madame, what's in that room? What do you keep there?"

She sat back on her heels. "It's my office and where I store papers. Extra receipt books, writing paper, ink." A line appeared between her perfect black brows. "Invoices. Files. Measurements. I keep a folder on each woman so I may begin work as soon as I get the order. She shook her head. "I don't know what they wanted."

"Were the files touched?"

"Everything was scattered," she said. "It was as if they wished to create as much chaos as possible. Thank the Dealer they didn't open the ink! As it was, it took us hours to put it right."

"And was every page accounted for? Nothing's missing?"

She shrugged. "As far as I know. I would have to go over my ledgers to make sure all the invoices remain there, and check each woman's files to be sure."

Frank Pagliacci's kidnapping of David was personal. His mad boasts when he thought he had me, Morton, and David trapped only confirmed it. "Check mine first. If you find anything missing, even the smallest scrap, notify me at once. It could be important."

She nodded, then began measuring the distance from my hem to the floor at different points. "I learned more about that button of yours."

"Oh! Wonderful! What did you learn?"

"The buttons are carved by hand. Only twenty were made."

This was good news indeed. "And what jackets were made with them?"

"That I don't know. But when we are finished here, I'll give you what I have."

"Madame, when will my dress be ready?"

She smiled. "I can finish it tonight. You may fetch it whenever is convenient. I imagine you'll want it for the Celebration, no?"

I would rather go to the Fire than to a celebration of the destruction of the Pot. But Madame had worked hard on my dress, so I said, "You've done a splendid job. It will be the best gown there."

Madame gave me a paper with her notes about the button, and I gave her the letter to mail to the stable-man on Market Center. As I returned to Spadros Manor, I considered the break-in.

The break-in at Madame's shop was the key. No one would

break into a dress shop office unless they wanted information on a customer. From all the evidence, it was likely the customer was me. The kidnappings, the ambush on Tony, and the theft of our Party Time shipment were all distractions. Perhaps even the murders of those boys were distractions as well. Their purpose was to keep me from investigating the break-in until Jack Diamond and Frank Pagliacci could put their real plan into place.

What did Madame's shop have?

My measurements, the writing paper, records of Madame's transactions with Tony.

Invoices with his signature.

The forged note on New Year's Eve took on new meaning.

Well, their plan worked.

It galled me; I had been so blind.

I wanted to visit David, but there was nothing else to do.

I must tell Tony of the break-in at once.

The Distraction

When I returned to the Manor, I asked Pearson, "Is Mr. Spadros home?"

"Yes, mum, he's in his study. He asked to take tea there."

I went past Pearson to Tony's study and knocked.

"Come in." Tony sat behind his desk, surprise on his face. I must have looked peculiar, still dressed for the street as I was. "I hope your appointment went well?"

I sat across from him. "Madame Biltcliffe's dress shop office window was broken a few days before New Year's Eve, and —"

Tony sat forward. "What?"

"Yes. The room was ransacked. I believe they were after my files. Invoices bearing your signature."

Tony stared at me for a full twenty seconds, the little color he normally possessed draining from his face. "This explains something. I went to my father's home, asking what he thought I could have done differently."

I felt impressed. "It must have been difficult to do."

Tony shrugged. "I'm glad I did. He said something which made no sense, so I asked what he meant. He showed me a letter, in my hand, with my signature, yet I didn't write it. In it were wild tales of torturing my men to death. Unspeakable acts — even my father was shocked." He shuddered. "I wish I hadn't read it."

Good grief. Roy only found real enjoyment from the pain of others, and was known for torturing his enemies to death. For something to shock **him** … it would have to be truly terrible. No wonder Tony was having nightmares.

I recalled the article in the *Golden Bridges* about problems between the Harts and Clubbs. Had any other shops been broken into? "Tony, if they have your signature and your hand, we must contact the other Families, tell them to beware of any notes from us." The last thing we needed was for a war to begin because of a forged note.

Tony nodded. "I received word from Alexander Clubb, asking if a letter from me was legitimate. It was not." He paused. "I'll send word with Ten. They know he is to be trusted."

Ten Hogan was Tony's first cousin, eight years his elder, who the men called Sawbuck.

I leaned forward. "I believe the attack on you, the shipment theft, and the kidnapping of your men was to distract us from this break-in so we wouldn't investigate it." Who would have expected a paper to cause so much trouble? "Madame said her shop was unusually busy after the break-in. More accomplices?"

Tony put his hand to his forehead. "This is incredible. Why are we being targeted so?"

The Clubbs had probably been saying the same thing for weeks now.

Tony rested his hand on his desk. "Thank you for telling me this. I'm not sure what I would do without you."

We sat gazing at each other across the desk. I wondered what it might have been like if we had been given a chance to meet, and court, and perhaps even fall in love, instead of it all being forced upon us. I didn't know what I felt for Tony: friendship, companionship, at times, deep pride in him. He had grown a great deal during the past six weeks.

I remembered Joe's question: *do you love him?*

I didn't know.

I remembered Gardena. If Roy hadn't taken me from my home, would Tony have married her instead? Perhaps that might have been the better choice. "What will you do?"

He glanced aside. "Other than send word to the other Families, I'm not sure what we can do."

This I could help with. And it was a good distraction from things I could do little about. "All messages to another Family should come from a trusted hand. No more messenger boys. Also, the contents should have a specific word signifying it's from us, that few know."

Tony nodded. "Good."

"And no message should be acted upon without confirmation of who sent it."

Tony hesitated. "Sending notes isn't all they might do." He retrieved a ledger from his desk. "I haven't done the accounts —"

I stared at him, shocked. The *Golden Bridges* article about the Harts refusing to pay what they said were false bills now made sense. "Tony ... could they be using our own money against us?"

His face turned red. "I don't know."

I reached across the desk and he put his hand in mine. "Tony ... I don't know what's happening. But you can't keep on like this. I worry for you. You're working long hours. You're not sleeping well —"

He flinched.

"— and you can't keep doing everything yourself. Hire someone you trust to go over all the accounts, even before the break-in at Madame's shop. We must know what they're doing, and what they've done. And we must know it soon, if we're to stop whatever it is they plan."

He didn't meet my eye, but took a deep breath and let it out, then rose, moving to the door. "I must gather my men."

"Tony —"

He stopped, still facing away. "Yes?"

"Would you teach me to shoot?"

He let out a breath and faced me. "Why?"

It seemed obvious to me. "What do you mean, why?"

"Why would you possibly want to learn to shoot people?"

Why would I want to learn to shoot? How did he not know his father had been teaching me to shoot since I was twelve? But his eyes held only confusion. "Well —" Obviously his parents hid my lessons from him somehow. And his men did too, which meant Roy told them not to tell him. I couldn't think of a reason for Tony not to know I could shoot. But until I knew why Roy didn't want Tony to know, I felt afraid to say anything. I didn't want to make the same sort of mistake I had at the dinner. Nor did I want to upset Tony even more than he was already. "You're always so worried about me. I thought —"

He let out a short amused laugh. "No, no, no ... you don't need to worry about such things."

Tony wasn't a good shot. Maybe he felt embarrassed? "If you don't have time, maybe one of your men could —"

"No." He shook his head. "Under no circumstances ask them."

"But why?"

"It's not proper. Besides, I don't want you involved in such things." He smiled at me the way one might smile at a small child. "Just stay near your men, and all will be well."

"But —"

"No. That's final. Don't ask me again."

He left, closing the door behind him. I went to change out of my street clothes and tell Pearson that tea should be delayed.

The Disguise

After Tony gathered his men, they went into his study for quite some time. Since they didn't seem to want or need me there, I went to my study and took my tea there.

I needed to learn to shoot better. Tony wouldn't teach me, and he forbade me to ask his men. There were no shooting ranges in Bridges for women. Perhaps Josie knew how to shoot? I doubted it, but I would ask the next time I saw her.

The more pressing issue was that for ten years Tony's men had hidden something from him. Why would his father Roy (and more importantly, his mother Molly) not tell him I knew how to defend myself?

When Mary came to take my plates after tea, I said, "Would you ask your father to come here?"

"Certainly, mum," she said.

A short while later, Pearson arrived. "How may I help?"

"Which days is Mrs. Molly Spadros 'at home'?" A proper lady had days which were set aside for visitors to call. I did this for over a year after Tony and I married, and sat for many a day waiting for someone to visit.

"I'll inquire, mum."

"Thank you, Pearson."

***

At dinner, Tony said, "I hope Dame Anastasia is well?"

"She means to leave the city."

"I'm sorry to hear that. I know she's been a friend to you."

I felt a melancholy sense of loss. "She has."

We resumed eating in silence for some time, then Tony said, "I'm going to be gone tomorrow."

"The casino?"

He nodded. "The city inspector will be there, plus the architect." He paused, taking a bite of his dinner. "I should be home by tea-time at any rate."

"Dame Anastasia asked me to help with some of the arrangements. Perhaps I'll do that tomorrow while you're away."

Tony smiled fondly. "Good. Spend all the time you need to with her."

He obviously thought I meant to help with such things as paperwork or perhaps packing, but I had a different plan in mind.

***

The next day, the headline for the *Bridges Daily* read:

EXPLOSION AT CLUBB MARINA

A boat at the Clubb Marina suffered total damage after an explosion just prior to midnight. The boat was in one of the day hire berths, and it is unknown what boat it was or whether anyone was aboard at the time. Police are investigating the wreckage to determine the type and cause of the explosion. As of yet there are neither witnesses nor suspects.

Did Morton say he had no berth in Clubb quadrant, or was that just at the Women's Center? I couldn't remember. But I had no word from him in almost three weeks. Although I still felt irked at Morton for abandoning me and David after we escaped the factory, I now felt concerned for his safety.

***

I visited Anastasia after the morning meeting, taking the carriage this time.

While Honor and the coachman cooled their heels by the carriage, I changed into a scullery maid's calico dress. Anastasia bound my hair in a white scarf while I removed my makeup.

My men were forbidden to leave the carriage alone, so one of them would be out front with it at all times. I had to get out of the house and past them somehow.

Anastasia kept glancing at my face. "That bruise on your cheek is a fearsome disguise."

"A blessing from Roy Spadros." In a way, I deserved it. I was foolish to try to seduce a reporter, especially without investigating his background. If I had, I would have known he belonged to the Bridgers, a fanatical religious group. Thrace Pike's enraged pamphlet denouncing me almost got the both of us killed.

Anastasia sighed. "As I feared. Yet it may be of use to us." She turned my chair towards her, and opened a box with makeups of various colors, "from my time in the theater."

"You were in the theater?"

"Oh, yes, as a much younger woman. It was one of many tries the city made to revive some culture after the Coup." She smiled. "I don't believe I was half bad at it. Makeup, I mean. "

"I had no idea."

"It was quite fun. Of course, my father was horrified at the idea of me being anywhere near the theater, but I was rather wild then." She laughed. "I met your friend's mother once there when she was a small girl."

I blinked, confused. "Whose mother?"

"The Diamond girl ... Gardena, is it? Terrible what happened to her mother Rachel. She was a beautiful child." She paused. "I'm not unsympathetic to the girl's feelings on the matter, but she must learn to control her temper."

Anastasia did have a point.

"It's even worse when you consider what people say ... I mean ... oh, perhaps I shouldn't speak of it."

"What?"

She lowered her voice. "They say Rachel's husband Julius still takes his husband's prerogative, even though her mind is like that of a child. Shameful, if you ask me."

Would he really do that? The man could have any woman in the city.

"Done," Anastasia said. "Perfection."

When I looked at the mirror, a much younger woman stared back at me. Anastasia's makeup added a recently bruised eye atop the old bruise on my cheek.

"You will be a young maid, beaten often, seeking help against her lover." Anastasia powdered over it for just a moment, as if I had tried to hide the marks, yet had done so poorly.

I almost feared to appear before Thrace Pike in this manner. "You must show me how to do this." Then I hesitated, remembering the numerous maids in my kitchens. "How can I leave? Surely your staff will know I don't belong here."

Anastasia smiled. "Never fear." She led me downstairs to a side door, then to a gate, where a man stood guard. She put her arm around my shoulders. "This girl is under my protection. Bring her to me at once when she returns."

The man flinched when he looked at my face, then nodded. "Yes, m'lady."

With an old shawl around my shoulders and a covered basket on my arm, I hurried past my carriage, head down, as any young maid would past two strange men. They paid no attention to me.

***

I hadn't made an appointment with Thrace Pike. But when I went to his grandfather's law firm and asked to see him, I was shown up at once.

Thrace Pike's entire office was smaller than one of my closets: dusty, paneled in dark brown, packed full of books and papers. A narrow window let in the pale light of an overcast sky, doing little to improve the room's look.

Thrace Pike, a man of twenty with straw-colored hair and eyes of very dark brown, stood when I entered. He wore the same threadbare brown suit he had worn the last three times we met. Like his window, he was thin, pale, and transparent, barely containing his horror at my appearance. I mentally congratulated Anastasia at her skill with makeup.

"Please, sit down." He pointed to a chair beside his desk, and

I sat. He leaned forward, putting his elbows on his knees, and spoke in a kind manner. "How may I help you?"

I smiled. "You finally don't recognize me."

He frowned, peering at me. "Mrs. Spadros?" He spoke in a whisper. "Dealer help us." He gripped the corner of his desk nearest me, sounding truly aghast. "What happened to you?"

I grinned. "A friend with skill in makeup."

The color returned to his face. "You've had your joke. What do you want?"

"Surely you don't think I of all people could visit an attorney's office dressed in my own clothes? With my usual makeup?" *What a foolish man.* "I'm here on business. Two items of business, to be exact."

"Business." He sounded confused. "But you have an attorney. Why come here?"

"The Spadros Family has an attorney." I placed my hand gently on his. "But this is not Spadros Family business." I gazed into his eyes. "These matters are of importance to **me**. I would be obliged if they didn't hear of it."

After several seconds, Mr. Pike flinched, drawing his hand back, his face red. "Of course not. No one will hear it from me."

"I knew I could depend on you."

At my words, his cheeks grew even redder. He took a deep breath and let it out. "How can I help you?"

I took the list from my basket. "A friend wishes these men to repay their debts." I handed the list to him.

"Is there a reason your friend doesn't use her own attorney?"

"I did wonder that myself, to be quite honest. She spoke of being in financial distress. Perhaps she can't afford the retainer?" I shook my head. "It's terrible to see a woman placed in difficulty."

Mr. Pike nodded, keeping his face quite still. From his previous rants, I believe he was secretly pleased at a rich woman being brought low, being the champion of the poor that he was, at least, in his own mind. "I'll send notices to these men at once." He paused. "What is your second matter?"

I took a deep breath and let it out. I needed to word this carefully. "I believe Jack Diamond guilty of a crime. He would kill me if given the chance. I need information about him."

Thrace Pike's face grew pale.

I hastened to say, "I don't need information in order to harm him. I only wish to gain proof of his offense before going to the Four Families for an inquiry. They will deal with him."

Mr. Pike stood. "I must speak with my grandfather at once."

Ah, the grandfather. At last I would meet him.

I waited there for a quarter hour before Mr. Pike returned. "Please follow me."

I followed him past dozens of tiny rooms similar to his own with young men toiling away. Then we reached a spacious one, where an old man sat behind a desk of mahogany.

Doyle Pike: white hair, skillfully cut and immaculately combed, shrewd hazel eyes. His clothing probably cost more than Mr. Pike's entire monthly salary. He didn't rise to meet me. "Have a seat, Mrs. Spadros."

Thrace closed the door behind us.

"Whoever did your makeup is a master," Doyle Pike said. "I've seen many a beaten woman, and if I didn't know better, I would have sworn you to be one too."

I took the offered seat. I couldn't say it was a pleasure to meet him, so I said nothing.

Doyle Pike peered at me for several seconds, then placed a sheet on the desk in front of me. "Thrace told me what you want. Here are our usual charges."

I didn't touch the sheet. "So you'll perform these duties?"

"Dunning these shop owners is a minor matter, especially if it's for you, as opposed to, say, your husband. But we don't get involved in Family matters. Bad for business."

"I see." I scanned the page; this was more than I planned to spend. "I have a question."

Doyle Pike smiled. It reminded me of a picture I saw at Spadros Manor as a child, in a book of legendary creatures, pre-Catastrophe: the alligator, preparing to bite. "By all means."

I gave Thrace Pike a quick glance.

"My grandson has given up all Bridger connections to work here," Doyle Pike said. "It was a condition of my taking him on."

Really? I turned to look at Thrace Pike, who stared straight ahead, face crimson. "I'm astonished. And your wife as well?"

Thrace Pike didn't move or look at me.

"The whole lot of them," Doyle said. "I disowned his father years ago for getting involved with such nonsense. Good to see young Thrace here finally come to his senses. Not only are the Bridgers bad for business, you aren't going to get anywhere in this city being connected to them."

So Mr. Thrace Pike had been serious when he said he wanted to overthrow the Families.

I rose. "I'm doing this on behalf of an elderly friend, who's in financial difficulty. This is more than I'm prepared to pay."

Doyle smiled. "You're doing this on behalf of a woman who takes in more money in a month than every attorney on this block combined, who it seems has you taken in as well."

I didn't like the sound of that, and perhaps it showed in my expression, for he laughed, picking up the sheet on the desk. "These are our usual charges. You know, for the usual folk. But for Mrs. Spadros, perhaps we could come to an agreement."

I sat. "I'm listening."

He picked up the list of names and ran down it. "I imagine you've already been paid. My guess is, in gems. Am I right?"

I smiled.

"I find I have a lack of interest in gems. But I do have an interest in new customers. For every name on this list, you refer a customer to me, and we can call it even."

"I find I have a lack of interest in providing you with new customers. I would prefer to keep this arrangement between ourselves, and not involve others." Others who might wonder why Jacqueline Spadros referred them to an attorney uninvolved in the Spadros Family Business. "Perhaps a cut of any money recovered. Say, one percent."

Doyle Pike leaned forward, elbows on his desk. "Where were you when I was thirty ... "

"Not even a consideration in my grandmother's mind, I imagine."

His face soured. "One percent it is." He glanced up at Thrace

Pike, who stood gaping at our exchange. "Well, go on, boy, get to it. We need to earn our cut."

Thrace hurried out.

These men must have owed Anastasia a great deal of money. Perhaps I should have asked about this before taking on the case. Maybe her diamond necklace, instead of being too great a payment, wasn't payment enough.

The Investigator

"Now about this business with the Diamonds," Doyle said. "I have just the man for it." He opened his desk drawer and took out a business card. "Name's Jake Bower. Does good work." He handed me the card. "Just a few doors down. Tell him I sent you."

Jake Bower was a blocky man in his forties, dark as a Diamond with a ready smile. He had short, wavy black hair, wore a dark blue suit, and walked with a limp. He reminded me of Julius Diamond, if the man had any humor to him. Jake met me at the door, and after a moment's hesitation said, "Come in."

I went inside. Through a partially opened door, I glimpsed a small room to the left, which held a neatly-made bed and several portraits on the walls. A short, unlit hallway lay straight ahead. To the right, the front room was almost completely lined with dark wooden bookshelves and file cases. A small desk stood underneath the window; an oval table in the same dark wood stood in the center. He gestured for me to sit, and he sat across from me, folding his hands on the table. "What can I do for you?"

"I was referred to you by Doyle Pike."

"And you might be?"

I could imagine his confusion: I wore a scullery maid's dress, yet spoke like an upper. "That comes later. First, tell me of your work and qualifications."

He laughed, long and hard, as if my words delighted him. "You're no scullery wench. Very well. I have no appointments today. If you can't pay me, at least you're amusing."

Good. He took payment in advance, as I did.

"I assume you know what I do. What I do **not** do is work for the police."

Even better. "Are you a Diamond?"

He laughed again. "Not that I know of. My family has been in Merca since before the Catastrophe. But my looks do come in handy. It amuses me to dress up and stroll the Diamond promenades alongside those moneybags from time to time."

Alone? I saw no evidence of a wife. "Master Bower —"

"That's Mr. Bower, if you please, miss." He rubbed the back of his neck. "It's a long story. A reason I have nothing to do with police." He paused. "Just so we're clear. Please continue."

"My apologies, sir." I hesitated, not sure how to proceed. "First of all, this is a Family matter."

"And if I'm not mistaken, involving the Diamonds. Correct?"

"Yes. So anything I tell you must remain here, between us. Do you understand?"

He straightened. "I should not call myself a professional otherwise."

"Even if you were to face a torture room?"

His eyes widened. "I've never considered such a thing. To be in such a room would mean certain death, yet I suppose I would do my best."

I smiled. If we were fortunate, it would never come anywhere close to that. "Excellent. Then next, you should know you have the pleasure of speaking to Mrs. Jacqueline Spadros. I wish you to find information on Master Jack Diamond."

Mr. Bower stared at me in shock. "I'm not sure whether to be more surprised at your face, your name, or your target."

"The face is makeup. The name is inconsequential. Jack Diamond is the true problem."

He took a deep breath and let it out. "Indeed."

I gave Mr. Bower an abbreviated version of the events of this new year: the kidnapping of David Bryce; the murders of the two young men who searched for him; the firefight at the Diamond Party Time factory. "This is personal, and direct, targeted to torment me. I have seen a man I believe to be Jack Diamond twice involved with this Frank Pagliacci. I can remove that villain myself; to get Jack Diamond, I need proof of his crimes to set before the Four Families."

Mr. Bower sat motionless, watching me for several seconds. "What sort of proof do you need?"

"Records of any kind linking him to the locations I saw him and the known dates of the disappearances. Anything which links him to these murders. Witnesses." I shrugged. It would be a miracle if anyone was willing to speak against Jack Diamond, but it would do no harm to try. "There must be something."

He nodded. "That I can do. Anything else?"

"If you can't find anything … perhaps a way to make him hesitate to torment my people further."

Mr. Bower's eyes widened. "Blackmail? It would need to be something quite extraordinary to cause Master Diamond to care if it be released. Unless you want me to go after his family —"

"No," I said, thinking of Jon and Gardena. "Absolutely not. Under no circumstances are you to put them in harm's way."

"Very well."

After that it was merely a matter of details.

***

A group of elegantly dressed women stood talking at the taxi-carriage stop. One woman with curly red hair had her back to me. She spoke in an animated fashion, waving her arms around. As I drew closer, it became obvious by her accent, which was quite strong and distinct, that she was an outsider. When I walked past, I glanced over at the group — and stopped.

"Zia?"

I couldn't believe my eyes. Blaze Rainbow and his younger sister Zia had led me to believe that she was deaf and mute. Yet here she was … talking! The other women stared at me, then at Zia. Zia's face, at first puzzled, turned white.

I took a step towards her. "Zia, where's your brother?"
She turned and ran.
The women called for help. Ignoring their shouts, I chased

Zia down alleyways, along streets. We pushed past promenading families, cart vendors. She stumbled over a sign outside a shop, knocking it over, shaking off the shopkeeper's outraged grasp. Then she turned right into a long narrow alley. I caught up to her, grabbed her arm. "Where's Blaze Rainbow?"

She shook me off. "Leave me be!"

"You're not deaf or mute. Why did you lie?"

She reached down for a weapon. I dropped my basket and put my boot-knife to her throat before she even reached hers, forcing her back up against the wall. "None of that, now. I've no need for killing. Show me your hands." She put them up against the wall. "Where's Blaze Rainbow? He owes me money!"

She laughed, unafraid. "He owes me, too. Your precious Blaze Rainbow is mad. He tried to kill me!"

"What? When?"

"Right after your little boat ride. He's nutty as a fewking loon, going on about Frank Pagliacci."

"You know Frank Pagliacci? What did he say about him?"

"He kept going on 'bout how he was a murderer."

I stared at her. "Frank Pagliacci IS a murderer."

Her nose and eyes reddened, disbelieving outrage crossing her face. "You're a liar!" She moved incredibly fast, swiping my knife down and aside, dodging away as it clattered to the ground. She threw a right hook at my face, but I twisted left. A grating, slipping sound and a crash came from behind. When I turned, Zia lay on the sandy cobblestones, breathing heavily, the stack of wooden boxes by her head tumbling to the ground.

Perhaps I should have thanked Roy Spadros for the practice in dodging his blows over the years.

Zia lay on the ground, face turned away, still panting.

I felt sorry for her. She really believed Frank Pagliacci was a good person. I leaned over to help her up. "Come on, Zia ..."

She threw sand in my face and ran. By the time I could see clearly again, she was gone.

Damn.

A dark patch stained the ground where she lay. I went up the alley and retrieved my knife; a line of blood ran along its edge.

I wiped the knife clean and put it away, silently thanking Josephine Kerr.

"Again," Josie said. "Faster."

She was just one year older but I always felt like a little girl beside her. "I'm trying."

She shook her head, then her knife appeared in front of my eyes as if by magic. She wasn't even sweating. "Trying will get you dead. Do it again. Faster."

The day I pulled my knife as fast as she did, she let me become one of the Watchers. I was fourteen years old and a fast runner. I wanted to run with the gang, but she said no, I couldn't be risked with that. At the time, I felt as if I wasn't good enough.

After the past six weeks, though, I was beginning to wonder if Josie might have had an inkling of what was going to happen to me, even before I did.

I coughed. Grit irritated my eyes. I was dirty, my hair was a mess, and I must have breathed some of that dust in, because I kept coughing. Weary, I undid my hair, shook the sand out, then wrapped it in the scarf again.

What a day.

Whistles and shouts came from the street, accompanied by the sound of feet running my direction.

Damn that woman! Not only did she get me dirty, she set the police on me for good measure.

I grabbed Anastasia's basket, her shawl, and the large red kerchief covering it from where they lay on the ground and ran around the building. It was then I realized I was near my friend Anna's shop. So I hurried down the back alley, pulling my hair free of its white scarf and shoving it under the red kerchief. I couldn't change my dress, but this much I could change.

Shouts and feet came from around the corner behind me as I twisted my hair into a bun. I peeked around the corner. No one was there, so I rushed across the alley and up the stairs to Anna's back door, which she always kept unlocked. I slipped in, locking the door behind me.

I slid down the door and sat. That was too close.

Anna Goren was an apothecary, the woman who sent my morning tea. Over the years, she had helped me identify many strange substances I found during my cases.

Anna's back room was full of various testing mechanisms. A small lemon-yellow table and two wooden chairs stood in the corner at the far end, across from the door to her shop. To my left, a bed and small end table lay in the corner, both piled high with books and papers.

The lock rattled behind me, and I crouched behind one of Anna's machines, which sat quiet. If I peeked out, I could see the open doorway to the front room. Anna hummed to herself as she moved about the storefront. But I didn't dare show myself yet.

My caution turned out to be justified: a few moments later, Anna's front door jingled as someone entered.

"Can I help you?" Anna's high-pitched quavering voice sounded wary.

"Probationary Constable Paix Hanger —" the man said.

The last time I had seen the man, he was a full constable, and working in Spadros. I felt a twinge of guilt for his present situation — demoted and confined to Market Center, I imagined — but this lasted barely a moment.

"— I'm looking for a woman, beaten about the face, dressed as a scullery maid. There's been a knifing; the woman was last seen running in this direction. She's considered armed and dangerous. Have you seen her?"

"I have not," Anna said. "No one's been here for an hour."

"Have you no customers?"

Anna sounded offended. "I am no tradesman; I provide apothecary services to the entire city. Only those bringing in and picking up orders arrive on a regular basis."

"I see. I would like permission to search your shop, in case the woman slipped past you."

"You may certainly **not** have permission," Anna said. She moved towards the doorway. A bookcase stood just on the other side of the doorway; a baseball bat leaned against it. "This is my home, under protection of law — you need a warrant to come any further." She stood in the doorway, her back to me, her lined brown hand on the bookcase just above the bat's handle.

"My apologies, mum." PC Hanger's voice retreated. "If you should see this woman, please notify us at once."

Anna didn't move until the door jingled once again. Then she let out a breath. "You can come out now." She turned towards me. Today she wore a deep purple cotton dress with a white apron. "I heard the lock rattle; I know you're still here."

I emerged from behind her machine. "I'm sorry to cause you trouble, Anna, but I didn't know where else to turn."

She frowned. "How do you know my name?

"Anna, it's me." I took a step towards her. "Mrs. Spadros."

She stared at me as if she had seen a ghost. "Good heavens! Did you really **cut** someone? Are they dead? What happened to your face?" She paused. "Did they hurt you?"

"The makeup is a disguise, Anna, like the dress. I had to come here in secret. And yes, someone did attack me, but she was alive when last I saw her. I need help, and I don't have much time."

A long strand of curly brown hair fell beside her face from its untidy pile atop her head. She put her hand to her heart. "By the Shuffler! I'm so grateful you're not hurt." She fanned her face. "What can I help with, dearie?"

I studied her. Perhaps ... "There are two matters —"

"Anything, my dear. Those horrid police constables won't hear of you from me."

I shook my head; if she were going to do that, she would have when PC Hanger was in her shop. "What have you learned of the Magma Steam Generator? Can it be fixed?"

The Magma Steam Generator two miles deep under Spadros Manor was one many which powered the city of Bridges. Our Inventor told me last month that the drill tube which allowed access to the lava was failing. This meant that the rest of the city's tubes probably were as well. This would bring the city, an immense mechanism, to a standstill, making it unlivable.

She took my arm and brought me to the table. "Sit, please. Would you like some tea?"

I chose the chair which put me out of view of the street. "If you have some made."

She blinked. "Ah, yes. Well, no."

"Don't trouble yourself then." I coughed. "If you might just tell me what you've learned …"

Anna sat across from me. "I've learned little of it, even in the libraries. But I've considered the matter thoroughly." She paused, then spoke slowly, as if measuring every word. "If there is a particular way the tube was supposed to have been tended, by means of a mechanism to keep it from deteriorating, as your Inventor says, then the mechanism should still be there. And if the mechanism is there, the controls to it must be close by. If you might be able to set that right, the problem may take care of itself. I'm not sure if this is possible." She shrugged. "Perhaps someone has already thought of this. But perhaps it might help."

I felt chagrined that I not thought of this simple thing. "Thank you, Anna, I'll pass this along." Inventor Call had probably already thought of it, but perhaps it might help.

She smiled fondly. "No trouble at all, dearie."

"May I borrow a dress? If I go out like this, I'll never get off the island."

"Certainly!" She bounded from her chair and went to her bed. Beside the foot of the bed, right where I had crouched, she pressed on the wall panel. This panel clicked open, turning sideways on hinges to reveal a hidden closet. In it hung several dresses and shawls on hooks. A black hat and a white bonnet sat on a small shelf above the dresses. "Come here." Anna began dusting me off. "Never fear," she said, "I won't let you come to harm." The door jingled again, and her voice lowered to a whisper. "I'll leave you to dress — take whatever you need." She went out to the front room. "May I help you, mum?"

I surveyed the dresses as Anna talked with the woman in the front of the store. I needed something light which I could change out of myself; I still must appear in front of Anastasia's man as a scullery maid. Then I had an idea. Since Anna wore a larger size than I did, I put one of her dark purple dresses on over mine. Fortunately, the hat had a veil.

A dark purple dress and a black hat seemed suspiciously like mourning garb; I wondered who Anna had lost.

The door jingled again. A few moments later, Anna returned. She hurried over, took my face in her hands and kissed my forehead, as she always did. Then she put the hat on me and adjusted my veil. "Now off with you." She wagged her finger. "And don't use that horrid disguise near me ever again."

"I'll send your dress in a day or so."

"Don't fret, dearie, just get home safe."

"I will, Anna." She let me out of the back door, and I waved as I went off to find a taxi-carriage.

***

On the ride back to Anastasia's house, I considered Zia. I could see an outsider pretending to be deaf if she didn't want anyone to hear her speak, but obviously she had no problems speaking in public. Why would Morton go along with it? How was it that his sister was an outsider? Was she even his sister? And why pretend she was deaf? Why would they lie to me?

Zia didn't speak about Morton as a sister would. She held no sorrow over his trying to kill her, for one thing. She either was lying about him trying to kill her or she wasn't his sister at all. Or something was seriously wrong with her mind.

Perhaps Zia was Morton's lover, and they had a falling out over her loyalty to Frank Pagliacci.

But then I remembered Eleanora's words about her visit to the police station, the day I went to her shop:

"What did the couple look like?"

Mrs. Bryce smiled like a young girl. "Nice looking, especially the man!" She fanned herself with her left hand. "They were about your age, and the lady had red hair."

This sounded suspiciously like Frank and Zia.

At least Morton made it back to the boat safely. That was some small consolation.

Did Morton really try to kill her?

I couldn't see him doing that. He was reckless, and at times

99

less than a gentleman. But whether she was his sister or his lover, I couldn't picture him trying to kill her.

**

The taxi-carriage deposited me near a fir thicket several blocks away from Anastasia's mansion. After the carriage left, I hid from view, pulling Anna's dress and hat off. I put her items in the basket, covering them with the red kerchief. I then put the scarf over my hair and the shawl around my shoulders before venturing down the street. Honor and the driver stood talking; they gave me a brief glance then went on as before. The man at the side gate ushered me to Anastasia's rooms without a word.

When her door closed behind me, Anastasia said, "You look as if you've had quite a day."

"I feel as if I need another bath."

Anastasia laughed as she dusted me off.

I began combing the sand out of my hair then stopped, surveying my face in the mirror. "You must show me how to do this makeup — it's quite convincing."

"Oh!" Anastasia said. "I can do better." She went into her closets. Several minutes later, she emerged, carrying a book: *The Essentials of Stage Makeup.*

I gasped in delight. "Wonderful! This will be ever so helpful."

"It's yours," Anastasia said. "I'll get some cold cream for your face." She returned to her closets, emerging with a jar as I finished combing my hair. "What happened?"

While putting the cold cream on, I told her what happened between Zia and me — without mentioning names.

Anastasia said, "You're investigating Frank Pagliacci."

I reached for a cloth and began wiping the makeup off my face. "I did ask about him for a reason."

She shook her head. "You must not pursue this man. I beg you. Stay away from him. He's much too dangerous." She paused, her head down, shoulders drooping. "I wish we had never met."

"I'll be careful."

"His associates are even more dangerous than he is. Promise me you'll avoid him. Those who've crossed him are dead."

Anastasia sounded so afraid that I took her hand. She was an old woman; no need to upset her. "I promise."

"You'll do as you please, of course, as you always do." She paused. "You **must** stay safe; I want to show you the city when you visit."

I continued removing my makeup. "Where are you going?"

Anastasia put her finger to her lips, eyes wide. "No one must know, not even you. If you were to be caught …. No. With my men here, I'm safe for now, but not even they know. I can't chance Frank finding me in a strange city, unprotected."

She's truly afraid of him. Frank Pagliacci didn't seem so frightening that day in the factory, but she seemed to know him much better than I. "I understand."

"When I've arrived, I'll get word to you. I promise."

I chuckled. "I'm seldom difficult to find." Then it occurred to me: if Frank Pagliacci (or Jack Diamond, for that matter) wanted to capture me, they had many opportunities to do so which they never took. What did it mean?

***

By the time I cleaned my face, put on my usual makeup, dressed, and returned home, it was past tea time. Tony came out of his study when I arrived. "I hope everything went well?"

He sounded worried by the amount of time I had been gone. How much longer could I keep deceiving him like this? "Very!"

Pearson began helping me from my coat.

"With the help of Anastasia's maids, we got three whole rooms packed. She was quite grateful for my assistance."

Tony gave a fake smile. "I'm glad." He took my arm and drew me away from Pearson. "Someone's here to see you."

"Me? I have no callers scheduled today."

Tony opened the door of his study. A man wearing a dark brown suit lay on the pale blue sofa. "He was unexpected."

As we walked in, the man raised his head. He was in his mid-thirties, with a crooked nose; short, light brown hair; and pale skin. His face was bruised and his lip was split, but I recognized him at once. "Master Rainbow?"

He nodded. "Forgive me if I don't rise. I feel unwell."

I no longer needed to look for Morton. He had come to me.

The Feds

I rushed into the room, horrified. "What happened, sir? Who's done this to you?"

He gestured for us to sit, so we did. A maid came in, bringing water in a bowl, along with a cloth.

"Bring tea and a pitcher of water," I said. The maid curtsied and left, closing the door behind her.

Morton leaned on one elbow, eyes partially shut, and began cleaning his face.

Tony leaned over to speak in my ear. "Pearson found him on the front porch, unconscious. It was only a few minutes before you arrived. He has just awakened."

"Has the doctor been called?"

Tony nodded.

Morton wore the same dark brown business suit he wore over two weeks ago when we rescued David Bryce. But his suit was rumpled and stained, with his shirt tails out and one pocket torn. His Derby hat was nowhere to be seen. Dark circles lay under his eyes, and his skin had a sallow look.

The maid returned with a tea tray, accompanied by our day footman Honor, who carried a large pitcher and three glasses on another tray. These were all set before us on the long low table.

Morton lay his head down on the sofa and closed his eyes. Tony and I looked at each other anxiously. I had many questions but feared pressing Morton until the doctor had seen to him.

Dr. Salmon, our personal surgeon, came presently, and examined Morton while I stood in the hall. "Pearson," I called down, "we'll have a guest for dinner."

I leaned against the railing, weary. Who would attack a gentleman, other than ruffians? I hoped that Frank Pagliacci's men hadn't caught up with Morton. If so, he was fortunate to be alive.

Tony came out. "The doctor says Master Rainbow suffered a recent concussive blow to the head and two minor gunshot wounds a few weeks ago. He has a serious case of exhaustion, and has not eaten properly in two weeks. He may be infirm for several days." He paused. "He should stay here until he recovers."

The last time I saw him, Morton was bleeding from gunshot wounds sustained in the battle at Jack Diamond's Party Time factory. That ordeal was unspeakable; I still hadn't fully recovered. "It would be unimaginable to turn him away."

Tony gave me a real smile this time. "I hoped you would say so. He has done much to help this Family in our troubles with the Harts. It would seem a shame not to repay him for his kindness."

What would Tony do if he knew all my meetings with Helen Hart were a lie? "What can I do to help?"

Before Tony could speak, Dr. Salmon came out. "He's asking for you both, in the strongest terms."

While still bruised and beaten, Morton seemed much more alert. "Please, sit," he said. With the injuries to his mouth, he sounded like he did the first day I met him in the Diamond Pot.

Fortunately, his teeth hadn't been injured, since he had a beautiful smile. But he wasn't smiling now. We sat in the chairs across from him, I for one curious as to what had happened.

He glanced at Tony. "I'm afraid I've brought trouble to your home. But I didn't know where else to go." He stared at the floor. "I've been betrayed. The Feds are after me."

Tony said, "You may stay for as long as you need to. They wouldn't dare come here, even if they knew you were in my study." He grinned. "They have no friends in this city."

"They believe I'm guilty of murdering one of their Agents," Morton said. "But I'm not; this Agent still lives, and is the one who put me in this state. I only wish to clear my name."

Tony leaned forward, elbows on his knees. "Do you wish us to contact someone? The Harts, perhaps?"

Morton shook his head. "They can't help matters." He paused. "And that's where everyone thinks I would go. No, I was right to come here." He closed his eyes, leaning upon the back cushion. "I never thought it would come to this."

Tony and I glanced at each other. Morton sounded so … lost, as if his life had taken a horrible and unexpected turn. Tony said, "Do you have any family we could call?"

Morton opened his eyes and looked at me. "No," he said. "None. Not anymore."

Could Zia have betrayed him to the Feds? Why would she do that? She mentioned Frank Pagliacci as if she knew him well. Too well for my liking. How could I ask without explaining to Tony how I knew Morton's sister? And how I learned she knew Frank?

Tony turned to Dr. Salmon. "What instructions have you for us? Should we keep him awake?"

"He must be watched constantly overnight," the doctor said. "But let him sleep if he will. If he vomits, or his pain worsens, call me at once. I'll return in the morning. I recommend complete rest for the next week until any pain is gone."

Morton grimaced. "Is it so serious?"

"It is," Dr. Salmon said. "Physical or mental exertion of any kind, even reading, can cause a setback."

Once the doctor left, Morton said, "What's to become of me? I don't wish to place a burden on you. You may be in danger if they discover I'm here."

"Nonsense," Tony said. "We'll take care of everything. It's no burden at all."

And so it was done. Amelia helped me into a house dress "suitable for dealing with illness or injury at home." She knew everything about fashionable and appropriate dress, it seemed. The concept of a special dress for such an occasion amazed me.

But I felt annoyed by her presence. Why should I have to deal with this woman? "Amelia, I'm sure sometime tonight we'll be pressed into taking watch over Master Rainbow. When is the best time?" She had too much information on me to dismiss her without cause. If I didn't keep her close, Tony or Roy would likely assign me someone worse. "Or should I get one of the other maids to play escort tonight?"

Amelia looked tired. I wondered what she occupied herself with while I was gone. "I'll speak with my husband."

I smiled at her dogged persistence to stay by my side. With any luck, she would fall asleep beside me, and I would be able to speak with Master Rainbow undisturbed.

When we went to Morton's room for dinner, he was clean, dressed in pajamas, and propped up in bed. He ate slowly due to the injury on his mouth, drank a great deal of water and tea, and said little. "I hope you will excuse my manners. I had little time to eat or drink, and little chance to sleep."

I wondered what happened to his yacht.

Finally, Morton leaned back on his pillows and sighed. "You have saved my life," he said. "I'm forever in your debt."

Tony smiled. "Happy to help. Now rest. My butler's preparing a rotation of men to wait on you overnight."

Morton glanced around in alarm. "Strangers?"

"They're my most trusted men," Tony said. "But I can have them come in for introduction, so you recognize their faces."

Morton relaxed. "That would be most appreciated." He shook his head. "I'm sorry; after all your generosity, I must seem presumptuous, even paranoiac. But I've been betrayed so often these past weeks —"

Tony nodded, his face grave. "I understand." He reached beside Morton's bed and rang for a servant.

Honor entered, collecting our plates. "This is our day footman, Skip Honor," I said. "I trust him with my life."

Morton nodded. "A pleasure to meet you, sir." Which was odd; surely a quadrant gentleman would know how to address a servant properly.

Honor gave a slight smile. "You're much too kind." He put the plates on a tray, moved the bed tray to the window seat, opened the door, then turned to Tony. "Anything else, sir?"

I said, "Mr. Spadros, I'll stay with Master Rainbow for now, if it please you. Perhaps Amelia might be summoned?" I paused. "I'm not fatigued, and then you may collect your men and instruct them at your leisure."

Tony nodded. "Honor, get Blitz up if he's not already, ask Pearson to see what men are available, and tell Amelia to attend us at once." Blitz Spadros was another of Tony's cousins, our night footman. He seldom slept, so he would be an asset tonight. "Have the men assemble in my study."

"Yes, sir." Honor took out the tray, leaving the door open.

If Honor did those things in the order Tony put them, it might be a while before Amelia arrived. Tony would be distracted, not wishing to leave until she got here, yet wanting to have things settled. As I thought, Tony began glancing at the open door every few seconds, then got up and began to pace.

"I met a mutual friend today," I said, then stopped. How was it that Zia and Anastasia both knew Frank Pagliacci?

Morton raised his head slowly. "Oh?"

Tony glanced briefly in our direction and kept pacing.

"Yes," I waited until Tony faced away from us. "Zia …"

At her name, Morton flinched, as I thought he might, but since Tony faced away, he didn't notice. "I don't remember her last name. What was it?"

"Cashout," Morton said. "How is she?"

Perhaps she wasn't his sister after all. "She seemed well enough. We had a bit of a chat before she had to run."

Morton chuckled, wincing a bit. "I'm sorry you two couldn't chat longer. Perhaps she might've been able to enlighten you as to my circumstances."

Tony went into the hall, leaving the door wide open, and looked over the railing. Then he came back in. "I'll return shortly." He strode into the hallway and called out, "Where's Amelia?"

Pearson's voice came from downstairs and below us; he was in the entryway, by the sound of it. "I'll fetch her at once, sir."

I turned to Morton. "Why did you lie to me? Zia can hear and speak as well as I can."

"She insisted on it. She felt sign language would be a way to talk without you understanding what we said, in case you were false." He paused. "I suppose she was the false one."

Indeed. "What happened?"

He glanced at the open doorway. "I returned to the boat; she and my carriage were gone. I searched for her, but I began to weaken, so I cleaned my wounds and rested until nightfall. I intended to search for her again, but Diamond guards came and I fled on my yacht. Since then, I have moved from one berth to another. The first night, the Feds demanded to know why I attacked their Agent. When I denied it, we fought. I threw them overboard. The next day, they asked if I had killed their Agent, as they received no word since their last communication.

"They and Frank Pagliacci's men have attacked me at every turn, claiming I murdered their own. Last night, after being awake over two days straight, I found myself floating among the wreckage of my yacht. My head hurt, and I felt nauseated and dizzy, but I managed to climb on some boards. The current took me then and I made it to the better parts of Spadros overnight."

In the freezing water? "You're fortunate to be alive."

He stared at his hands. "My yacht was beautiful. And Zia betrayed me." He paused. "She introduced me to Frank Pagliacci. I trusted her." He gazed out of the window to his right. "Perhaps I shouldn't have. My only hope is that they think I'm dead."

Amelia ran in, her youngest daughter asleep in her arms, and curtsied. "My apologies, mum, sir. My little one is ill, and —"

"Master Rainbow, my lady's maid Amelia Dewey."

He smiled. "A pleasure, mum."

Amelia blushed all the way to her hairline. "I'm honored, sir." She curtsied again, then sat, obviously uncomfortable with his greeting her as an equal.

"Master Rainbow has suffered a serious concussive blow to his head, Amelia. We're to watch for any sign that his condition worsens." I turned to him. "But you seem to be feeling improved."

"Good food and drink has helped. And a bath, and rest."

Amelia rocked her six year old daughter. The girl's dark brown hair was plastered to her face with sweat, and her cheeks were flushed.

I remembered Air's brother Herbert at that age. The same dark brown hair and pale skin.

Both Air and Herbert, dead now, because of me.

"What's wrong with your wee lass?" Morton said.

"A fever," said Amelia.

He closed his eyes, leaning his head back on his pillows. He didn't speak for so long, I thought he'd fallen asleep. "I got the fever when visiting at me uncle Johnny's. 'Get the meadowsweet tea' he yelled at Ma, and she put mint in it too." He sighed. "I love the taste of mint."

We sat silently for some time. Finally I heard the men moving about downstairs, and Tony came up with Honor and Blitz. "I've set up a rotation," Tony said, "such that someone he's met will be here at all times, with a new person rotating in every hour." He glanced at the flushed and sleeping child in Amelia's arms. "That will be all, Amelia, you may put her to bed now."

"Thank you, sir," she said, and left.

We left Honor and Blitz there with him and went to bed. There at the end, Morton's accent sounded very much like Zia's. Were they both outsiders? What were they doing in Bridges?

***

Morton slept through the night, and even through breakfast. Dr. Salmon came to see him after that and examined him. "The man has a serious case of exhaustion, and rest will do him well."

We stood in the hallway outside Morton's room. Honor came up the stairs. "I can sit with him if need be while you go to morning meeting."

"Mrs. Spadros," Tony said, "would you run the meeting?"

So I did. There was little to say. The whole staff had been involved in arrangements for yet another ill guest in less than a month's time. "It's imperative you notify myself or Mr. Spadros if anyone you don't know comes here, even a new delivery man or messenger boy. And speak about our guest to no one, even if you've known them since birth. The Feds are after him."

The staff looked at each other in alarm.

"As long as they don't know he's here, we're quite safe." Even if they did; according to our Inventor, this manor house, which used to be a scientific station, could withstand a bomb blast. "But we depend on you to watch for any spies."

Afterwards, Pearson spoke to me privately. "Do you think it wise to tell the servants of the Feds?"

"They must be aware of the danger," I said. "or they won't know what to do and what not to." I learned that quite well this past week. "Let them speak freely of their fears. Don't allow them to send messages, even to merchants. If any seem fearful or troubled, or too calm, remind them they would not wish to invoke the wrath of our Family by betraying our trust. Then take them off any duty which would bring them into contact with visitors."

Pearson gave me a look as if he evaluated me and was pleased with what he saw. "Very good, mum."

"Ask Mary to bring some mint tea for Master Rainbow."

I went up to Morton's room. Tony and Sawbuck sat beside him. Morton was awake, propped up on pillows as before. I knocked softly on the open door. Morton smiled when he saw me.

Tony glanced back at me and smiled as well. "Come in. As you can see, Master Rainbow is improved today. I wished for Master Hogan here to meet Master Rainbow, as we have need to plan what to do." Tony reached out for me and I took his hand. "I'm glad you're here. Close the door."

So I did, and took a seat near the foot of Morton's bed. "I told the staff of the Feds."

Tony and Sawbuck gave each other a quick glance.

"I felt it best that they understand the danger we face so they make no wrong move or become complacent with messengers or guests. Also, I told Pearson to watch for any who seem too afraid or troubled, and move them to duties where they can send no messages to any visitors."

Sawbuck nodded. "That seems wise."

Tony nodded as well, his face devoid of expression. I could tell he felt uneasy. I learned to read him long ago; it seemed difficult for him to hide his emotions from me.

Morton glanced from me to Tony. "It seems a good plan."

Tony rose. "Mrs. Spadros, may I speak with you privately?"

"Why, of course," I said, and out we went.

Once the door closed, Tony whispered, "I did not mean for you to speak your plans to the staff, or to Master Rainbow."

"Tony, if we can't trust the staff, who can we trust?"

He shook his head. "I trust you, and I trust Ten. No one else. I don't believe Crab and Duck were the only spies in this house; I have evidence that some of our servants report to my father on a regular basis."

A shock went through me at that, although looking back, it shouldn't have surprised me.

"And I find it much too convenient, Master Rainbow appearing the first time he did, in the midst of our turmoil. I don't think he is who he says he is."

I nodded. "Although it would be unusual to inflict oneself with injury simply to gain admittance."

Tony chuckled. "Indeed it would be. No, I believe someone is chasing him, and his injuries are evident. What I doubt is that the Clubbs would allow Federal Agents into the city so easily. And what better way to gain entry to our house than to claim estrangement from the Harts and escape from the Feds? The animosity between my father and Charles Hart is plain for all to see, and no Family would fail to shelter a man so pursued." He sighed. "What's done is done. But, my love," he put his hand on my cheek, "you're at your best when you watch, and when you reason. Don't hasten to speak, or to act, until you've thought the matter through."

I put my hand on his and nodded, feeling disappointed with myself. Mary Pearson, our butler's daughter, came up the stair with a breakfast tray. She was nineteen and pretty, with straight light brown hair. Tony opened the door, and we went inside. I fetched the bed-tray for Mary to put Morton's plate and cup upon.

"That smells delicious," Morton said. "I feel famished."

"As well you should," I said, "for it's almost eleven."

Mary put her tray on a side table then brought over Morton's plate and silverware.

Morton glanced up at us. "I hope you won't mind if I begin."

Tony smiled. "Of course not."

So Morton began eating while Mary poured his tea. At the

first sip, his face lit with happy astonishment. "Mint tea!" Morton said. "My favorite. How did you know?"

"You told us last night," I said. "But you were quite fatigued; you may have forgotten."

He nodded. "Yes," he said with his mouth full, "I was."

What did Morton tell the men? He could have said anything and might have no recollection of it.

Mary said, "Will there be anything else, sir?"

"No," Tony said. "I'll ring if there is."

Mary curtsied and left, closing the door behind her.

Sawbuck took a deep breath and let it out. "The men are watching for any attack. They're quite motivated to do so."

This didn't surprise me. Between their compatriots being killed and kidnapped and an assault on a shipment, it was clear Frank Pagliacci and his false Red Dog Gang were trying to make inroads into our territory. No Family man would stand for it.

"Miss Josephine Kerr left her card earlier," Sawbuck said. "Pearson told her you weren't at home."

I said, "Any particular reason you mention this?"

Sawbuck looked uneasy. "I'm alert to anything unusual. She didn't attend the dinner due to having to care for her brother, yet finds time to come here, today of all days."

"She probably fears causing offense," Tony said. "Miss Kerr and Mrs. Spadros were childhood friends, yet I imagine our favor is quite helpful to them from a social aspect."

Morton continued to eat as if we were not there. Doubtless he knew nothing of Josie, although it was odd that the Kerr name brought no curiosity as to our association with them. Although if he worked for the Harts, as he said, perhaps he already knew of it.

The Kerr family built the city of Bridges, ruling it father to son for 400 years until overthrown 100 years ago in the Coup which we were about to celebrate. Most people in Bridges associated the Kerr name with decadence, greed, and descent into squalor as just reward for their crimes. Few realized Polansky Kerr IV lived in the Hart quadrant, although his grandchildren seemed welcome among the unmarried gentlemen and debutantes. Joe and Josie were even invited to the Grand Ball this year, although not even the *Golden Bridges* made note of it.

I sat watching Sawbuck, Tony, and Morton. If we were to plan, we should do so. If we were not to plan here in front of Morton, should we not go elsewhere?

Ah. Tony and Sawbuck must have planned to each present a topic related to the events since the attack on New Year's Day to see what Morton knew.

Tony smiled at me. "Has Madame Biltcliffe learned anything more of who broke into her shop?"

Morton had a puzzled expression, as if unable to connect what this had to do with his predicament.

"No," I said, "but I haven't had a chance to visit her of late."

Morton knew Frank Pagliacci. When Tony learned this, he would become even more suspicious and ask Morton all sorts of questions. I couldn't take the chance that in Morton's injured state, my involvement in this might come out. I caught Morton's eye and pretended to yawn, covering my mouth with my right hand then bringing it up as if to smooth my hair. As I moved my hand past my face so it blocked the view of the other two men, I winked at Morton, who smiled.

"I see yesterday's events have fatigued you as well," Morton said, his eyes drooping. "I wonder if we might have this conversation another time."

"Of course," Tony said. He and Sawbuck rose.

"Oh," Morton said. "Is someone tending to my shoes? They were quite expensive."

Tony smiled, a flash of amusement crossing his eyes. "My manservant has taken care of them. They're under your bed."

Morton let out a breath, relieved. "Thank you."

I moved Morton's bed-tray to the window seat then followed the two men out of the room. Morton turned to lie down as I left.

Tony closed the door. "Let's go to my study. Pearson can send one of his sons to check on him later."

When we got to the study, Tony gestured for me and Sawbuck to sit in the chairs across from his desk, while he sat behind it. It was an interesting arrangement.

Tony said, "What do you wish to tell us?"

I felt confused. "I?"

"I fail to see how you're so fatigued at eleven in the morning as to yawn in front of a guest. Therefore, I presume you have something to discuss that you wish Master Rainbow not to hear. Or have you forgotten your manners entirely?"

I paused to find some topic suitable to distract Tony from this line of discussion. "I feel concerned with this tactic of yours. While bringing up topics relevant to the past month may shed light on Master Rainbow's knowledge, it may reveal too much to someone we know little about."

Tony snorted, yet I felt surprise and admiration in his demeanor. "I told you she would see through it. Did I not?"

Sawbuck chuckled. "You did." He reached in his pocket and handed a five to Tony.

I gaped at them. "You **wagered** on me?" I burst out laughing. The audacity of this man!

Tony leaned back, grinning. "So what do you suggest?"

A fair question; it took a moment to concoct an answer. "Master Rainbow has confided in me in the past. I believe he may even have some regard for me. Allow me to speak with him on whatever subject you wish. You may pose the questions, I'll relay them. In his unguarded condition, he may let something slip."

Sawbuck's eyes narrowed. "There's a danger to this."

Did Sawbuck suspect **me**? "Well, yes. If I were you, I would have a man standing outside, in case I should scream. Perhaps two. Although Master Rainbow isn't much taller than I, wrapped in his bed, and in a weakened state." If I seemed too eager, Tony wouldn't do it. "Perhaps it's a bad idea —"

Tony grinned, rubbing his hands together. "No, it's perfect. We can listen at the door. He'll never suspect you."

I felt sad. I would never betray Tony, but I couldn't let Morton betray me, even unintentionally. "Then I suppose we should get started on the questions."

The Deception

After an hour of conferring with Tony and Sawbuck, I felt tired of sitting, so I took a brief walk and a smoke in the garden. Tony's men stood guard at intervals in the distance where the land rose to give them a better view. The ones closer by tipped their hats when I came outside. Bells chimed in the distance, marking noon, yet the sun barely shone for the clouds that covered it.

Sawbuck seemed to suspect everyone. I recalled our ride to the Kerr's home on New Year's Day, when Tony spoke of his older brother, the true Spadros heir, poisoned when Tony was two years old ...

"From the first time Ten learned about my brother, oh, I was two or three so he must have been eight, or perhaps nine. When he heard of it, he said he would watch over me, that he would never let anyone hurt me. He has kept his word."

Twenty years the man had watched over Tony. What might he do if he considered me a threat?

When I went back inside, Tony met me in the hall. He handed me the questions, which I placed in my pocket.

Pearson walked up to us. "Your mail is on your desks."

"Thank you, Pearson." I turned to Tony and took his arm as we strolled towards his study. "Since you'll be gone tomorrow, perhaps I'll go pick out my Summer gown."

Tony laughed. "I have yet to see your Spring gown, which I paid a great deal for."

"Surely, it's on display by now. You never go into town, or you would've seen it. It's most lovely." I gazed up at him with my best smile (Ma taught me that one) and he smiled back, his pupils wide, his cheeks reddening.

Flirting with Tony was a risk; he would want me for my wife duties tonight. But it was worth it. I needed an excuse to go to Madame's. Then I could go to Market Center and see what Thrace Pike recovered from Anastasia's debtors. She'd be leaving town soon, and I wanted to have something to give her.

"Oh, very well," he said. "Go have your fun. Perhaps after we visit the Kerrs we can drive past and see this wonder."

"Thank you." I went to kiss his cheek, but he turned, kissing me full on the lips there in the hallway, his hand upon my back, pulling me to him.

Oh, my. Where did this come from?

When Tony spoke, his voice was earnest and strained. "When you go to Master Rainbow's room after luncheon, I wish you to remember this."

Was he jealous? "Have no fears about Master Rainbow; I don't find him attractive. But it's sweet of you to say such things."

Tony drew me into his study, then closed and locked the door. "I love you so much." He kissed me as I leaned on the door. He had never done this before ... in daylight, in his study ... I found it interesting.

After a time contemplating the matter I pictured Joe there, and the whole scenario changed: that soft brown hair, those beautiful green eyes. I kissed Joe, feeling his hard body pressing so perfectly against mine. "Ohh," I said to Joe, "how I love you."

With a shock, I realized I came too close to saying Joe's name, and the thought of what might happen if I did terrified me.

Tony picked me up then and brought me to the sofa. But the spell had been broken; I couldn't find Joe again in the awkward position and Tony's desperate passion.

I almost wept, I missed him so.

Finally, Tony buried his face between my breasts as he cried out, and collapsed atop me, panting. Then he laughed. "I always wanted to do that."

I turned my head, gazing at the room. This used to be his father Roy's home, his study, his sofa. Every piece of furniture, every minute here must have added meaning to Tony, reminders of deeds and emotion.

Tony had spoken of leaving Bridges, making the Business "worthy of respect." In his eyes I had seen his agony at doing the things expected of him as the Spadros heir. Heard the love for Gardena in his voice. At times, he might feel as trapped as I did.

I held him to my chest and smoothed his hair, feeling deep compassion for him. I loved Tony as I might a brother. A beloved younger brother. But it was getting harder and harder each day to pretend I desired him. I forced my breathing steady as grief squeezed my heart. What could I do?

***

Later, I went to my study to tell Mr. Pike and Madame Biltcliffe of our meetings. I wondered how to send the letter to Mr. Pike, who wouldn't be apt to hide the correspondence. I couldn't send it as Mrs. Jacqueline Spadros; if the note should appear later it could be used in all sorts of unsavory ways. I decided to continue to use my false name Eunice Ogier. That way, if Mr. Pike did lose the note, it couldn't be traced to me.

On my desk lay a letter:

> Miss Gardena Diamond presents her compliments to Mrs. Jacqueline Spadros, and hopes to have the pleasure of her company for luncheon at the Diamond Women's Club on the Twenty-First of February, 1899.
>
> RSVP

I didn't know how to feel about going to the Diamond Women's Club. I understood why Gardena wanted to meet there: it was the only way for her to return my dinner invitation. I would never accept an invitation to her home because her older brother (the mad and murderous Jack Diamond) would be there. I feared for my safety near him. Of course, his twin brother Jonathan would likely be there as well, if for nothing but my protection. Even so, Tony would never allow it even if I wished to go.

But their Women's Club should be safe enough; men were never allowed inside, or even permitted to loiter outside. The guards at each of the Clubs were there to enforce this.

Although I would like to meet Gardena for luncheon, I wasn't sure what we would talk about. That my husband seemed to be in love with her? That she struck him in his own home?

But I needed to know what all this was about.

I went back to Tony's study, and he sat at his desk reading his mail. He gave a warm smile and came to me. He had changed his clothes and righted his hair. I wondered what his manservant Jacob Michaels thought, seeing Tony appear in his rooms before luncheon in such disarray.

Probably the same thing Amelia said when she helped me change and redo my hair. "Oh, to be young and in love."

I handed Tony the note. "Gardena wants me to come to luncheon in Diamond. At the Women's Club."

He set it aside, then took my face in his hands, kissing me. "Then, my love, you shall go."

I felt relieved that he didn't protest or show fear of what she might say. In spite of his words about her instability or hidden motives or spirited nature, in spite of her slapping him and calling him a coward, he trusted her. He accepted her words, because he trusted her judgment. In his heart, he knew it to be true.

But it wasn't true; he'd never shrunk from any duty, no matter how painful he found it.

I thought back to what he said about Gardena the night of the dinner. Why would he say such things about someone he loved and trusted?

Then, he was trying to distract me, or divert some blame from himself. And today, he wanted to make me happy.

I considered his nightmares, his sleepless nights. He loved us both, and it tormented him. It was tearing him apart.

I put my arms around him and lay my face on his chest. The only feeling I could pick out was sadness.

***

After luncheon, I went to Morton's room, Tony and Sawbuck following at a distance.

Morton sat in an arm chair by a small table near the window, his back to the corner of the room. Today, he wore a white shirt, brown cotton pants, and dark brown slippers.

"Forgive me if I don't rise; I become dizzy when I do."

I went to him, offering my hand, which he kissed. "There's nothing to forgive." In my palm was a note, which I passed to him, then sat in an arm chair at the other corner of the window, close enough for conversation yet out of arm's reach. This way, if anyone should come in, it would be clear we sat separate.

I had written the note earlier, and secreted it in my sleeve:

My husband and cousin listen. FP is alive.

He stared at the note, then at me, alarmed.

I nodded. "I'm glad to see you're well enough to sit here."

Morton began ripping the small paper into bits. "This is the most difficult part of recovery. I'm well enough to sit up but allowed little to do." He collected the pieces into his hand. "Would you bring me a glass of water?"

I rose. "Certainly!" I brought it to him, and resumed my seat.

He swallowed the torn pieces then washed them down with the water.

I felt touched by his trust; poison on the paper would have solved any problem of what he might say. Either he was very trusting, very foolish, or very brave. "Perhaps I can read to you sometime, since you're not yet allowed that pleasure."

"That would be diverting." He paused. "I hope you and your family are well?"

"Yes, indeed."

He sat for a few seconds. "Well, we can talk about the gloom outdoors, the price the miracle gems go for this afternoon, or the various types of tea. Or you can ask your questions."

What was he doing? "Whatever do you mean?"

"Madam, I may be injured, but I'm not a fool. You've been escorted and watched most closely since I first met you. Do you now expect me to believe you're here in my bedchamber for conversation? Or my attractive charms? I'm not so deluded." He let out a short laugh, but it was a merry one. "Or to read me stories like a child? No, you were sent here to learn something. I have nothing to hide. Ask what you will."

I stared at him, astonished, then realized he was right. If he went along too easily it would be suspect. "Very well ... have you met a man named Frank Pagliacci?"

His expression moved from astonishment through fear to understanding. Then he said, "The name seems familiar. I've heard it before. It's an odd name, to be sure."

"What of a group called the Red Dog Gang?"

"Is this one of those slum gangs? Of children? How would I know of that?" He chuckled. "I wasn't raised in such ways."

"Tell me more of yourself, then, of your upbringing."

He smiled, relaxing. "My parents were immigrants; they moved shortly after marrying. But quite well-off; I had a tutor, and while my home wasn't as grand as this one, we had a butler and maids and all the trappings of refined living. My parents died of fever when I was twenty, and as the only child, I inherited. I have been a gentleman ever since, living on their estate."

"And where is your estate?"

"Ah, I spoke of it in a general sense. The properties were sold long ago. I was unmarried and without desire to be responsible for their upkeep. I live off the interest income, downtown in the artists' area. I enjoy life there; I have a maid who keeps house, and I come and go as I please."

The address he gave was indeed in the artists' area of Hart, although there was no such building. The rest of the story could be total fabrication. Something about his mannerisms made it difficult for me to tell when he lied and when he spoke true. Perhaps his parents being outsiders had something to do with it.

"You said Frank Pagliacci's name sounded familiar. Can you remember where you heard it?"

He let out a breath, glancing away. "I was in a restaurant. Someone mentioned the name. I don't recall exactly."

A knock came at the door, and Tony entered without waiting

for an answer. "Master Rainbow! How are you?"

Morton gave him an amused smile. "I'm well. Did you enjoy our conversation?"

Tony stared at him.

"As I said to Mrs. Spadros, sir, I'm no fool. If I had such a lovely wife, I wouldn't allow her in here alone unless I stood by."

Tony burst out laughing, extending his hand. "I like you, Rainbow." He pulled up a chair and sat facing us both. "We could use a man like you here. Most of my men are young, and have little experience of life."

Most of Tony's men were older than he was. I found it interesting that Tony would make such an offer. I wondered what Sawbuck (who surely was still listening at the door) thought of it.

Morton said, "I thank you for your kindness, sir. But I would hardly know where to begin in such a Business, even if I weren't in the employ of the Harts."

"What do you do for them, then?"

"Ah, at present I'm little more than a messenger. I've worked as an investigator in the past, simply from boredom, and at times I retrieve information for them. We have no contract, and I've sworn no oath, if that's what you're asking." He smiled, but it was unpleasant. "And I'm not an enforcer."

That reminded me of what my friend Vig said a few weeks ago, although with much more anger. I hoped Vig was well; while he sent me a note after our argument that night, I hadn't seen the man or been to his saloon since.

Tony seemed taken aback. "Well, of course, I wouldn't expect a gentleman such as yourself to be one." His expression became calculating. "But it would be interesting to have a friend in Hart."

He didn't consider the Kerrs friends, then, despite his words.

Morton chuckled. "A spy, sir? I've never done such work." He glanced at me. "It would hardly be honorable."

I almost laughed. It echoed my words to Morton in the Diamond Party Time factory's basement when he tricked Frank Pagliacci's guard into helping us then shot the man. Morton's reply? "Fuck honor."

And he knew I would recall that. But at the time, a little boy's life was at stake. And it occurred to me that we held Morton's life just as surely as I held David's that day. Morton could barely stand. "Perhaps we could come to some agreement that Master Rainbow would find suitable." I said. "Since he's sworn no oath."

***

We decided Morton was doing well enough that we would be "at home" from now on. The next morning, Pearson came to my study telling me Miss Josephine Kerr had come to call.

Which was odd. She visited the day before. Why this urgent desire to see me after our heated conversation a few days ago? I began to wonder if something was wrong. Had Joe taken a turn for the worse? "Seat her in the parlor."

Tony had advised me to think when having the urge to act. After Pearson closed the door, I sat and thought, heart pounding. I wanted to rush in, grab Josie, and shake her until she told me Joe was safe and well.

But Sawbuck didn't trust her.

I remembered Tony's words: *I trust Ten, and I trust you.*

Who did I trust?

The moment of panic passed. I didn't have enough information. I needed to determine exactly how much to tell her about what went on when I told people I was with Helen Hart.

I took a deep breath, stood up, and went to the parlor.

Josie rose when I entered. She seemed perfectly composed, which made me feel much better.

"I hope all is well?"

Josie gave me a amused smile. "Yes, all is well. As well as can be expected, I suppose, under the circumstances."

I gestured to the sofa. "Please, sit. Would you like some tea?"

"No, thank you."

I sat across from her. "Is your grandfather well?"

"Perfectly well, thank you." She paused. "And before you ask, so is Joe."

"Am I so transparent?"

She chuckled. "A bit." Her face softened into fondness. "And I love you for it."

I felt humbled by her trust in me, which I wasn't sure I

deserved. I spoke quietly. "I'm sorry for any harm or worry or concern I've caused you. I forget how you must have suffered during the past six years."

Josie nodded, her face grave.

"I know how this looks. I'm a married woman, and your brother's terribly injured. Yet when he spoke unbecoming words instead of being a friend to him, I allowed him to shame himself. I can only pray he remembers none of our conversation."

Josie said nothing.

"I let my feelings for him cloud my judgment. I have no desire to prolong his pain by letting him believe there's any future for us together. I belong to the Spadros Family, and if they knew any of this, they would kill him." My stomach knotted. "I fear it would be neither gentle nor quick."

Josie nodded, gazing at the table.

"I know what you must think of me. Lying to everyone about where I've been. Using your friend's name as she lay bereft and in agony, while I did, in your eyes, things I should not. But —"

Could I trust Josie? I'd known her all my life. The way she'd been acting lately was strange — flying into rages, especially — but Joe had never been so badly hurt before. She must be under tremendous strain.

Joe trusted her with his life. And I trusted Joe.

"I need to explain what happened since they took me away."

I sat beside her. In whispers I told her how I was grabbed by strangers at random times from the age of twelve. They dragged me to Spadros Manor, where I was stripped, beaten, and forced to learn the Spadros Family Business. I revealed how Roy forced me to marry Tony at gunpoint. I told her about my investigation business: how it began, why I did it, how I developed my network of informants, how I kept it secret. Then I told her about Eleanora's request, and my work with Morton to rescue David.

I never used Morton's real name. It wasn't that I didn't trust her, but the fewer people who knew about Blaze Rainbow, the better. I couldn't involve the Kerrs in any conspiracy involving the Feds. While they were under the Harts' protection, it would be unfair to put them at risk. "So it was out of ignorance I used that story. I trusted the man, and I should not have. I hope you can forgive me."

Josie relaxed. "I do. I too am sorry for not trusting you. So much time has passed, and people can change in ways you would not believe."

We sat silently for several minutes. Morton's room was above us, and his bed creaked as he moved.

Josie stirred. "Joe keeps asking for you."

So this was why she came. I shook my head. "I don't think it wise to visit alone. It would be best if I kept my distance until he's completely well. And I ... I dread seeing Marja again. I did nothing to cause her daughter's death, and I know she doesn't blame me ... but I feel responsible." Grief twisted my heart, and my eyes stung. "I brought Ottilie here, and now she's dead."

"Don't worry about that. Marja's no longer working for us."

I felt horrified. "Is she —?"

Josie stared at me, appalled. "Of course not! She works for my uncle now. My grandfather may be many things, but he's not Anthony Spadros."

I felt offended at the comparison, but she had a point. The Spadros Family's way of dealing with problem people was not to move them but to eliminate them altogether. In that sense, Tony was very much like his father.

But then I felt surprised. "I never knew you had an uncle."

Josie smiled. "I never knew either. He changed his name to avoid the unpleasantness of being a Kerr. But he's a kind and honorable man."

The door upstairs opened and closed. I heard a murmur of talk, but not what was said.

"You have company?"

"Yes, my husband's friend is visiting."

Whatever they spoke of must have been amusing, because Morton laughed. He had a rather distinctive laugh.

Josie glanced at the clock on the mantel and rose. "I must go; the doctor arrives soon. I promised Grampa I would take down the doctor's instructions. Joe has trouble remembering details."

I walked her out to the front porch. "I'll speak to my husband again about visiting. Has he come by yet? He said he meant to."

Josie shook her head.

I patted her arm. "Don't fret. You've lost none of our esteem." I took her arm, and we strolled to her waiting carriage. "We're renovating the casino, and it's taken a great deal of his time. He asks about Joe and his welfare."

"That's good to know." She climbed into the carriage. "Come visit soon."

Should I go? It seemed safe enough. No harm could come with Tony there; if Joe were to act in an unseemly manner, we could simply leave. "Yes, we'll be by shortly. I'll send a message as soon as I know the date." I waved to her as she left.

As I stood watching her carriage drive away down the street and disappear into traffic, a great swell of gratitude brought tears to my eyes. Joe was well. Not healed by any means, but safe. Oh, gods, he was safe. And Josie and I were still friends.

At the time, that was all that mattered.

The Idea

I went into my study, lit myself a cigarette, and poured a glass of bourbon to celebrate. But then I remembered Frank Pagliacci and Jack Diamond, and a weight fell upon my soul. How might I deduce their plans?

Anastasia, Morton, and Zia all knew Frank Pagliacci, and quite well, it seemed. Yet none of them mentioned Jack Diamond.

Did Frank Pagliacci keep his involvement with Jack a secret from them? If Frank wanted to make himself appear more imposing, claiming allegiance with a Family member would be the method of choice.

Unless …

I thought about how Pagliacci boasted that afternoon in the factory. Could he fancy himself greater than a Diamond heir? This could cause conflict, which might lead to their downfall. Or, if the man truly craved attention above all things, cause him to make a mistake which I might exploit.

But I felt as if I missed something. The last time I felt this way it cost two boys their lives and a third his sanity. I couldn't take the risk of missing something again. I took out a sheet of paper and began to write:

Item One: Red Dogs break into Madame's shop

Item Two: False notes — possibly false invoices

Item Three: Spies in brown (Duck & Crab)

Item Four: Kidnapping and murder

Item Five: Attack on Tony

Item Six: Impersonating a DA — false office

Item Seven: Whipping a horse

Item Eight: Boat explosion

I stared at this list, trying to see some pattern in it. After a time, I added:

Item Nine: Impersonating the Red Dog Gang

I perceived two patterns. First, deception. False notes, false invoices, and impersonations, all surrounding a "very good-looking" man. Second, violence. Attack, kidnapping, murder, whipping a horse, explosion, and whatever happened to Crab and Duck which affected Tony so. And whatever they did to little David Bryce.

Deception and violence. Frank and Jack. It made sense. But I had never heard of Jack being involved with something like this before. Whipping horses? Exploding boats? Strangling boys?

I leaned back, eyes closed. Something didn't seem right.

I recalled my feeling that the kidnappings, murders, and attacks were distractions to keep us — or more to the point, me — from investigating the break-in at Madame's shop, which yielded the materials for the false notes and invoices.

So what were the false notes and invoices for? Sowing discord, yes, they tried that. Using our money to finance their schemes: both devious and insulting. But once Tony's accountant reviewed the ledgers, we should have some idea of what they planned. What else might they do? There must be more. The plans seemed too simple, the distractions too great.

And the boat explosion. What did it mean?

I finished my glass and poured another. Morton and Zia could identify Frank Pagliacci. They were both in danger.

Morton was safe as long as he stayed here, surrounded by our men. Zia seemed unlikely to take any warning I cared to give, even if I wanted to try to find her. At that moment, she was probably telling Frank I knifed her. I recalled the dark stain on the sandy cobblestones in that alley.

At the time, I hoped she wasn't hurt too badly.

If the boat explosion was an attempt to silence Morton, it made no sense for Jack to have done it. He seemed not to care at all who knew of his crimes. As a Diamond heir and a keeper of the prison, he had the full might of the Bridges justice system behind him. Why go to the trouble of killing someone in such a dramatic yet inefficient way? A knife to the throat was more Jack's style, and much more certain of success.

And I didn't like Morton's idea that the Feds might have been behind the bombing. Although most people in Bridges hated and feared the Feds, this wasn't their style at all. While they might track a person down, it would be to bring them to Hub to stand trial, not to murder them in their sleep.

So that left Frank.

An idea occurred to me so forcefully that I rose from my chair: a distraction was a side bet, not the main play.

Frank Pagliacci was assigned the distraction.

Jack Diamond wasn't sane enough for long enough to create this plot, nor to execute it.

Someone else was in charge here.

I paced the room for an hour trying to think of who might be in charge. This new man must be someone I hadn't heard of yet. Who might have enough influence over Jack Diamond to reliably control him? It was clear from the events at the Grand Ball that he didn't even listen to his own father.

I sighed and rang for Pearson.

He came in at once. "Yes, mum?"

"Would you see if the Inventor is available to come here and speak with me?"

"I'll inquire, mum." He closed the door behind him.

After a quarter hour, Pearson announced Inventor Maxim Call's arrival.

Inventor Call was wiry and brown, with thinning white hair and piercing blue eyes. "Well, girl, I'm here. What do you want?"

I curtsied. "Sir, I wished to speak to you on the matter we

discussed at our last meeting."

He frowned. "Young lady, I'm old. I don't remember what I ate for dinner last night, much less a discussion we had for a few minutes last month."

Really. "The Magma Steam Generator? Under the house?"

"Oh! Yes! Now I remember. Your husband gave me a fierce dressing-down about my bringing you there, until I told him if he wanted me to stay he'd better show some manners. Used to be a good quiet studious boy," he shook his head.

I chuckled, imagining the scene.

"Well, what did you have me dragged up here for?"

I hesitated. How did Anna put it? "If there is a way to cleanse the Generator and restore the pilings, and it was done on a routine basis for 400 years, there should be some mechanism in place. The mechanism surely has controls to it, which should be nearby. If those might be found —"

"Then all we need to do is learn how to use them."

I felt deflated. "You've thought of this already."

"Indeed we did! We searched the place years ago, never found a thing." He studied me. "But it was a good thought."

"I can't take credit. I asked a friend for advice, and she gave me this answer."

"Really? I'd like to meet this woman."

"Her name's Anna Goren; she's —"

Maxim Call held up a hand. "I know who Anna is." He stood silent for a moment. "I asked Anna to marry me once. She was the most talented woman I ever met. Beautiful as well. Anna could have become an Inventor, but she couldn't stand anyone to direct her work, or limit her in any way." He paused. "How is she?"

"Very well. She has an apothecary shop on Market Center, which supplies half of Bridges."

His eyes and nose reddened. "That's my Anna." He paused, gazing at the floor, then smiled to himself. "It gives me great pleasure to hear she's well and happy." His shoulders straightened, and he stood taller, as if gaining new courage. "When you see her again, give her my regards, will you?"

"I will." I thought of the hidden compartment in Anna's shop.

"Could the controls be hidden somewhere?"

"Why would they do that?"

"I don't know. It's just something which came to me."

Maxim Call considered this for a moment. "Perhaps we're looking in the wrong place."

"Sir?"

"Well, perhaps the controls aren't in this piling at all. Perhaps the controls were powerful enough to work on multiple pilings at once. Why, there are six pilings in this quadrant alone! I'll have my boys look for hidden compartments here, of course. But I think we need to start searching the other pilings as well." He nodded to himself as he began wandering off towards the door. "Very interesting idea."

After he left the room, I chuckled. What a strange old man. "Glad I could help!"

The Truth

I went to Madame Biltcliffe's dress shop that afternoon and did pick out the cloth for my Summer dress, but it only took ten minutes to do so. Then I changed into Madame's mourning garb (with veil) and was off to Market Center.

Thrace Pike seemed surprised to see me, until I explained why I sent a note under another name. He appeared relieved, even glad, to see me with my bruise covered and no additional ones showing. In truth, the bruise Roy Spadros left on my face when he struck me last month was almost gone and easily hidden.

Mr. Pike had puzzling news: each debtor had returned his notice saying that the gems had no curative powers whatsoever. "They seem honest men, who wished to learn the truth about the gems before selling them to others."

"Why not just sell the gems at the going price?"

"They feel this price is falsely elevated. To sell will leave their customers holding worthless merchandise. It's integrity which holds them back."

I wondered if this integrity was a smart move.

He must have seen my opinion on my face, for he said, "If they sell gems which turn out to be worthless, no one will trust their judgments in the future." He seemed pleased to be explaining something to me, which was amusing.

His reasoning, however, made sense. But another matter puzzled me. "So if they believe they're being defrauded, why not return the gems? Why not go to the police?" Personally, I wouldn't go to the police, but surely a merchant might.

Mr. Pike shook his head. "I don't know."

***

My coachmen ignored me as I left the public taxi-carriage veiled and dressed in Madame Biltcliffe's mourning garb. Instead of going into her store, I crossed the street, entering Roman Jewelers. Glass cases displayed fine gems and jewelry of all sorts in the brightly lit room. A shop maid stood behind the counter. "May I help you?" An olive-skinned, portly man in his fifties with graying dark brown hair sat behind a desk in the room beyond.

"I'm here to see Mr. Roman on a business matter."

Mr. Roman took one look at me and put down his pen. "Come right this way." He ushered me into his office, turned to a black wooden file cabinet trimmed in brass, and took out a folder. "I'm so sorry for your loss, mum. Here is our standard estate sale packet. It has forms to inventory the jewelry you wish to sell —"

"I'm sorry, but I'm not here to discuss an estate sale."

He gave me a chagrined look. "My apologies! Please, take a seat." I sat across from him while he closed the door and took his seat behind the desk. "What can I do for you?"

"I'm here on behalf of Dame Anastasia Louis —"

At her name, the man paled, then rose, drawing away from me. "Who are you? What's your name?"

"I can give you a name, but it wouldn't be my real one. Why do you think I came here veiled? Please, sit. I bear you no ill will; I'm not with the police. I'm investigating this matter and only wish to ask you a few questions."

He gave me a quick appraisal then sat, the color slowly returning to his face. "Very well. What do you wish to know?"

"I know the reason you gave Mr. Pike as to why you aren't paying your debts. But I had some further questions."

He nodded, his eyes taking on an evaluating look.

"Did Dame Anastasia make any claims as to the use or benefit of these gems when she sold them to you?"

"She did." He reached into a drawer.

I felt for my pistol in its calf holster, but he produced a flyer:

THE MIRACLE GEM

Dug from the earth

Blessed by the sacred healing mineral springs of Old Montana

Cut and polished by master craftsmen

Benefits physician-certified

A long list of various colored gems and their uses proceeded forth. The flyer also contained a description of various elixirs, oils, and creams using these gems, "for milder cases," at a lower price.

"How many gems did you contract for?"

"One of each, so that I might see their uses for myself. I asked for a trial period, which she agreed to, then gave them a fair trial with myself, family members, and friends. None experienced any benefit whatsoever, even when used as directed."

This seemed odd, especially in light of the article in the *Bridges Daily*. And the gems were certified by this Doctor. Could all these men be mistaken? "Why didn't you return the gems?"

"I tried to a week ago. The clerk told me this wasn't acceptable, that I must pay for the use of the gems since I did not pay on delivery. When I protested, her guards escorted me out. A man came to my home that night and said —" His face turned red, and he looked away. "She's obtained information on a matter I don't wish to become public. This man threatened to use it against me should I speak of this or go to the police. But I no longer care. Tell her what you will. I refuse to pay for worthless gems. If she lies on their usefulness, what else has she lied about?"

What indeed.

Mr. Roman said, "What are you going to tell her?"

"I? Nothing as yet. For you see, she has paid me in gems."

The man nodded. "Ah. Bring them to me. I'll be glad to appraise them for you, at no charge."

The thought of Dame Anastasia Louis forging her signature diamond necklace was ludicrous. "Who was this man?"

"He didn't say. A Diamond man, dressed entirely in white."

Jack Diamond? In downtown Spadros? How could he have

come here?

"I do have a question," Mr. Roman said. "Why would you, of all people, work for her?"

I blinked in alarm. "What did you say?"

"You don't stay alive as long as I have in this city without being able to see who people are behind their masks and veils. You're a young woman, in no grief, yet veiled as in mourning. You carry yourself as an upper, yet your voice is roughened by tobacco and you smell of alcohol. Even if I didn't recognize you by that, and the dress of my friend across the way —"

I stared at him, shocked.

"— I would know the ring you wear anywhere —"

I peered at my hand, in its glove, the outline of the ring plain.

"— seeing as I made it." He smiled to himself. "Well, I suppose helping a neighbor is as good a reason as any." He paused. "Don't worry, my dear, no one will know you were here."

I felt relieved. "Thank you very much, sir. I'm sorry to have alarmed you." A thought struck me. "Why did you not tell my husband of this … Diamond man?"

He gave me a slight smile. "But I did."

No wonder Tony was so upset at having Jonathan and Gardena Diamond to our home.

I walked a block down, crossed the street, into the alleyway, and up to Madame Biltcliffe's back door. But after I gave Madame her dress back, I didn't change into my own. I had one more place to visit: Anastasia's factory, where the gems were being cut and polished. Fortunately, Madame allowed me to use Tenni as a decoy for a while longer.

I wanted to learn how this all worked, why her costs were so high. I wanted some evidence that she told me the truth.

The factory was in the Spadros quadrant, a large brown building with "Manufacturing Associates" on the front door. Lights blazed on every floor, and armed men stood watch at every entrance. Horse-drawn trucks came and went, workers carried boxes to and fro. I stood across the street, trying to decide how to approach this. If I asked for Anastasia dressed in Tenni's shop maid uniform, they would surely ask my name. Perhaps I would try another tactic.

I walked across the street and approached a man counting boxes. "Sir, do you know if they're hiring?"

"I'm sorry, miss, I don't know. Just making a delivery."

I went past a guard to the front desk where a young man stood behind a counter. He was corpulent, with big ears and a bigger nose, hair greasy, skin pock-marked, with thick round spectacles, but he stood as if he owned the place. Perfect for what I had in mind. I went to him and curtsied. "I was wondering, sir, if you're hiring here."

He gave me a self-important smile. "No, miss, sorry. This factory is set to close soon. We're just finishing up the last of the orders. Only a few days yet to go and then we'll close, and maybe a day to tidy up. We have all the help we need right now. But my, aren't you a sweet one for asking."

I gave him the smile my Ma taught me to use when you're buttering up a mark. "What all do they do here? It seems so busy to be closing."

His cheeks reddened, and he stood straighter. "Well, we make gemstones. Gorgeous ones, best in the city. The exact replicas of any sort of gemstone imaginable. It's truly amazing what scientific achievement can do these days. You can't tell the difference between them and the ones dug from the ground."

I didn't have to feign surprise. "Really? That must be so expensive. And difficult!"

"Not at all," he said. "We have a special patented process. In fact, no one I know of has even thought of creating gems in this way. It's a true miracle." He glanced around, then leaned his arms on the counter. "Do you want to see?"

I gazed in his eyes in rapt anticipation. "Oh, I would love to!"

I took his arm, which smelled of sardines, and held it snug. He brought me to a room with boxes of paper masks and hair covers. We put them on, and thin white coats which tied. "This keeps the gem dust from our clothes and lungs," he said with a tone of authority. Then he handed me goggles, which I put on.

I giggled. "This is fun!"

He escorted me around the factory, hardly taking a breath between sentences as he explained every detail of the process. Even if I wanted to speak, I couldn't have.

But I truly didn't want to: I felt amazed at the display before me. Huge machines held bubbling liquids, and extruded bars of clear material, which went to cutters and polishers. Beautiful cut gems of all colors came out the other end.

I smiled up at him. "This is so wonderful!"

"Hey!" A middle aged man pointed at us. "You there. You aren't allowed here on the floor."

"Yes, sir," the young man said. Then he turned to me. "He's a right bear, he is. But no worry; he can't do a thing to us. Let's go back out."

We took off our goggles, hats, coats and masks, and he escorted me outside in the courtyard.

I gazed up at him. "Oh, it was the most beautiful thing I've ever seen. I hope you won't catch trouble?"

"No, no. He can't do anything to me," the young man said, with much bravado. "He has no real power; he's just jealous that you're with me. Some men can't get a woman, and they have a fierce hatred and jealousy for anyone who can. But the real reason he can't touch me is that I'm related to the owner. She's my great-aunt, Dame Anastasia Louis herself."

I made my eyes wide as a schoolgirl. "Really? You're an important man, then."

He grinned, as if to a small child. "I am." He put his arm round me. "She's going to make me famous, she said, teach me everything she knows. Did you know she was a famous actress? She did a show that was the talk of the town. Played the Queen of Diamonds, because she was the understudy and the woman who played the part suddenly took terribly ill and later died! Her role was controversial. It was quite the scandal back then, seeing as she was an aristocrat and all — and she didn't look the part, she had to wear special makeup, but she didn't care. From all accounts, she performed magnificently! Even the President of the Feds came to see her at the show in Hub! What an honor for our family."

What an idiot you are. I snuggled up beside him, there with workers going all around us, and gazed up at him with wide trusting eyes. "There's one thing I don't understand, though. Doesn't making gemstones cost a terrible large amount?"

"Oh, not at all! It's fairly amazing; each gem costs us less than a penny, once you factor in the materials, the shipping them in, the labor. And then last week the price was $10 each!" He laughed. "And then you know all the elixirs and such?"

I nodded, lips parted, as if I had never heard such wisdom.

"They sweep the floor every night, and all that gem dust gets washed and separated out, and it goes into the next day's mix. Costs us nothing extra!"

"Oh my," I gushed. "How wonderful for you! You must be a very rich man."

He preened. "Well, I do all right. All the workers get equal shares, so as long as the business does well, we do well. But I'm just starting out. In a few days, we'll be off to set this up in another town. Our business partner is injured, well, there's rumors he and my great-aunt are to be married soon, which is only proper for a woman, to be married and have her husband run the business, but he'll be along as soon as he's recovered."

"Oh? Injured? How terrible!"

"Yes, it is, isn't it? Shot in the leg by a competitor! You wouldn't believe how many people are jealous of our operation. But to shoot him? Utterly despicable! Why, this man is of the highest caliber, a true gentleman. 'My boy,' he said, and he actually put his arm on my shoulder — imagine! A great man like him, putting me as his equal — he said, 'when we're done here, I'll get rid of these lowlifes lording over you and promote you to where you can do some good in the company.' Can you believe it? I'm going to run a factory of my own, get my fair share of the profits: the upper crust, so to speak. It's wonderful that my great-aunt met this man!"

He paused, his face changing, as if he had an idea. "You want to come with me? I'll marry you right proper. You don't need papers to marry on the zeppelin, once you're free of the aperture."

I glanced away, trying not to laugh. *We've been talking for twenty minutes and he proposes marriage?* "Why, sir, I don't even know your name. And I could hardly leave my elderly widowed aunt. I care for her nights."

"Well, we could bring her too," he said. "And my name is Trey Louis. What's yours?"

I tilted my head to look up at him. "Eunice Ogier."

"Ah, Eunice, what a lovely name. And a lovely girl you are, too." He paused. "You come meet me at the zeppelin station on the first of March at 3 o'clock. Gate 19. It's the last zeppelin leaving before the show, leaving at half past three, and I'll be glad to be rid of this place. Get there at three, and I'll buy two more tickets — one for you, one for your aunt — once you arrive."

I leaped away from him, jumping up and down clapping. "Oh, just wait until I tell my auntie!"

Fear crossed his face. "Now you can't tell everyone, love, especially not with Dame Anastasia's name used. No one must know. She plans to leave quietly."

"I understand. Not a soul." I put my finger to my lips. Then I took his hands. "Oh, Trey," I said with passion, "I'm so happy! I'm to marry a rich man. Who would ever have thought?"

He beamed at me. "I'll show you the best time, my sweet. You and your auntie. You'll see." He glanced at his watch. "I better get back. How about a little kiss for your affianced?"

"Oh," I said, fanning myself. "I wouldn't want you to think me a loose woman, kissing you here in the street." I moved close to him, and embraced him, nuzzling his cheek with mine. "Give you something to think of between now and the wedding."

The same middle aged man bellowed from the door. "Louis! Where the hell are you? We got deliveries here!"

"My love, I must go," he said, and ran off.

I left the area as fast as I could before Trey changed his mind.

Was I wicked, to tease him so? Perhaps. But I had learned more truth in a half hour than I might in weeks of investigating.

Dame Anastasia was running a scam.

The Ploy

Soon I was back home, and so was Tony. He was taking his coat off when I came inside. "How was your visit with Miss Kerr?"

Pearson must have told him. "She was anxious about our good graces," I said. "And Joe has been asking about us."

Tony nodded. "Tomorrow we can pay a proper visit."

"I'll write her at once. After luncheon, perhaps?"

"Yes, that would be good."

After changing into house clothes, I returned to my study and wrote to Josie.

Then I brought out my list and studied it again. I was beginning to see another pattern: this "business partner" of Anastasia's, who she was to marry, sounded suspiciously like Frank Pagliacci. And Frank seemed to also be Zia's lover — at least in her mind.

When a man is proven to be a kidnapper and strangler of boys, it shouldn't be surprising to find him a cad as well.

I wrote notes to my informants asking for any details on Anastasia they might glean. I handed the stack to Pearson and went upstairs to dress for dinner.

While Amelia fussed with my dress and hair, I considered Anastasia's scam. A penny a gem, sold for ten dollars — a sweet little set up. It sounded as if the workers were in on the scam as well. Splitting the profits gave them sure motivation to keep quiet.

Then to lie about the benefits … unless this whole list of men were mistaken, this Dr. Gocow must be in on the scam as well — if he were even real. I touched the moonstone hanging between my breasts, wondering how much Tony paid for it.

I needed to talk with my contact at the newspaper. How did these articles get into the *Bridges Daily* if they were false?

***

The next day, the *Bridges Daily* had this as its top story:

STABLE-MASTER MURDERED

> The Bridges stable-master was found strangled in his bed upon arrival of his taxi-men this morning. Market Center police have evidence of multiple persons involved in the murder.

> Memorial services will be announced after the police investigation has completed.

Shock, recriminations, and vows to fight crime filled much of the rest of the article.

Melancholy swept over me. What more could I have done? I gave the letter to Madame Biltcliffe — did she send it? Did it reach the stable-man? Did he take the warning, or toss it aside?

The fact that this man died of strangulation — just like those boys — chilled me. Had Frank Pagliacci healed enough to resume his killing spree?

Amelia came in. "Mum, I must have dropped this on the way up. I'm sorry."

I took the envelope from her and opened it. Large, child-like printed handwriting on cheap paper greeted me:

> j-bird they wan to kill yur ma to. i walk pass the pokit pare home from work at 7 then down the side.

> marja

J-bird was Marja's name for me when I was a little girl.

The Pocket Pair was my friend Vig Vikenti's establishment.

How did Marja know that I would know where it was? Very few people knew that I even knew the man, much less visited him.

I looked at the envelope but other than my name on the front, it held no other information.

"Amelia, ask Pearson to come here."

"But mum, you're not dressed."

"I'll get my robe."

She went out, closing the door behind her. I threw the note in the fire, watching it burn. I got my robe then sat back at my tea-table and finished my toast while I waited.

The door opened. Pearson peered at me. "Yes, mum?"

"The letter which came this morning. Who brought it?"

"One of the usual messenger boys, mum. Do you need me to call him back?"

I handed Pearson the envelope. "Find out who sent this, or at least the location it came from, as quietly as possible."

"Yes, mum." Pearson was the perfect man to choose if you wanted something done discreetly.

They want to kill your Ma too.

"What time does the morning paper print?"

Pearson hadn't moved, which surprised me when I realized it. "Early, mum. It's here at half past seven. Even if the truck came here first —"

The *Bridges Daily* office was on Market Center. I nodded.

"— perhaps five? Or earlier, if they're to have them all wrapped and ready." He paused. "I never considered the matter before." For the first time in my life, John Pearson sounded surprised. "They must be up half the night."

So Marja hadn't seen the paper yet — she heard this last night. *They want to kill your Ma too.*

"Mrs. Spadros," Pearson said, "are you well?"

"Find out where this letter came from."

Amelia was in the midst of doing my hair when Pearson returned. "The boy said he got it from a warehouse in Spadros, mum — a food distribution center on 17th and Broadway. It was in a letter-basket he picks up every morning for an extra fee."

Right near Vig's bar. "Thank you, Pearson."

He bowed and turned to go.

"Wait. Who owns that warehouse?"

"I don't know, mum. Would you like me to find out for you?"

"Yes, but quietly."

Marja either worked at this warehouse or close by. She overheard someone planning to kill the stable-man and my Ma.

Did she stumble upon Frank Pagliacci and his crew?

I could see them wanting to kill the stable-man. He could identify them. But why target my Ma?

I remembered the rage in Jack Diamond's eyes as he knelt by his friend's corpse ten years ago. Did Jack think he could get at my father through Ma?

It was absurd. Ma didn't love Peedro Sluff, and he had never once spoken of her. But Jack didn't know that.

And there was another possibility.

Morton, David, and I cowered behind the boxes as Frank Pagliacci boasted. "I have you; when they come for you, I'll kill them, one by one."

But that didn't work: we defeated him and his men. Was this another ploy to capture me?

Frank Pagliacci might have fooled me once, luring me to Jack Diamond's factory, but it wouldn't happen again. Roy said if I went to the Spadros Pot he would kill Ma and everyone in the Cathedral. Perhaps Frank didn't know that.

How did he know about Ma?

It didn't matter. I had to get Ma out of Bridges altogether, somewhere safe from both Frank and Jack.

***

Morton still slept a great deal, but was able to come down the stairs for breakfast, with help. "This sausage is quite good," he said. "My compliments to your chef."

"Monsieur will be pleased," I said. "I favor it as well."

Tony laughed. "We might have to buy a whole extra hog just for breakfasts, should —" He stopped, his face stricken.

Should I come with child.

Tony's eyes met mine. "Forgive me."

Morton glanced between us. "Is something wrong?"

"Nothing," I said to Tony. "Think nothing of it."

I gazed at the gardens through the large windows around us. I still took my special morning tea … and Tony obviously thought my "inability" to bear children distressed me.

I felt a sudden hatred of my life: forced to lie in every area in order to have an existence other than what the Spadros Family dictated for me. But could it ever be any different?

I turned to Morton. "How are you feeling, sir?"

"Weak still, but improving." He paused for several moments, then straightened in his chair, his demeanor relaxed, contented. "It's good to be here. I never imagined the Spadros Family to have such pleasant circumstances, or such congenial company."

Tony smiled. "I do imagine our fearsome reputation."

Morton appeared flustered. "I meant no offense, sir."

"None taken. I'm not my father, Master Rainbow. One day he'll be gone, and I mean to have good and loyal men by my side when that happens. I hope you'll consider my offer."

Morton stared at his plate, hands in his lap. "I'll consider it."

I saw why Tony thought Morton wasn't who he said he was. For a moment there, the true Blaze Rainbow showed through, a man who evidently juggled conflicting alliances.

Why did Morton hesitate? Was this a ploy to see what else we might offer? What did his employer give that we did not?

***

That afternoon, Tony and I left Morton asleep in his bed and went to visit the Kerrs. A young girl of perhaps eighteen ushered us into their parlor. There we waited for some time until the maid wheeled Joe in.

The large bandage on Joe's head still remained. The cuts and scratches on his face and arms were healing, and he smiled that beautiful smile as he entered the room. He had a bandaged calf, a metal brace on his thigh (with much plaster) and steel going into the leg itself. This was supported on a metal platform which emerged from his brass and wooden wheeled chair. Josie and their grandfather Polansky Kerr IV came in behind him.

"Hello!" Mr. Kerr said. "So good to see you!"

"I'm so happy you could come," Josie said.

We rose to greet them. Tony appeared shocked at Joe's condition. "I hope you're well?"

Joe nodded. "Much improved, sir. Forgive me for not rising to greet you."

This took Tony off guard. "Well — of course!" He moved to shake Joe's and Mr. Kerr's hands and kiss Josie's.

We all sat. Joe peered at me, his face somber.

Mr. Kerr said, "I hope you and your family are well?" A gentleman of eighty and seven, he was well-dressed, well-groomed, and appeared in perfect health.

"Indeed," Tony said. "We're quite well, thank you."

"Would you like some tea?" Josie said.

"Certainly," I said.

"Daisy, fetch Mr. and Mrs. Spadros some tea, please."

The maid curtsied and left, returning with a tea-tray so quickly I wondered if she had it sitting outside the room. She began to pour for us, mine first.

"What news of the outside world?" Mr. Kerr said. "I hear your Family does quite a bit of shipping from your quadrant."

Tony chuckled. "My father's in charge of that. I hear little other than what is in the *Bridges Daily*."

"Do you not travel?" Josie said.

Tony shook his head. "Being the Family Heir, I'm allowed little travel, except of course, in our quadrant. I suppose I'm too highly valued to risk in a zeppelin."

"A pity," Mr. Kerr said, and the way he said it made me feel this was the truest thing anyone had said so far. "I find travel opens new viewpoints and opportunities seldom found at home."

Tony smiled and took my hand. "Perhaps someday Mrs. Spadros and I will travel." He turned to me, gazing in my eyes. "Would you like that?"

To leave Bridges was my fondest wish. "Very much so." I glanced up to find all three of the Kerrs watching me. I forced myself to laugh. "Surely it's not so uncommon as all that."

"It's quite expensive, I hear," Josie said. "Only the aristocrats do much traveling these days. Although we do get our fair share of tourists here in Hart for the races."

"You know," Tony said, "I have never been."

Joe's face brightened. "Oh you would love it," he said. "Quite diverting. And the food is magnificent."

"Perhaps I might persuade Mr. Hart to extend you an invitation," Mr. Kerr said.

Tony turned to me. "Our fourth anniversary is soon. Perhaps we might go then, to celebrate."

A spasm of anger crossed Joe's face.

Tony, focused on me as he was, didn't see it. He turned to Mr. Kerr. "And perhaps you would like to visit the casinos? We're in the midst of renovation, but even so there are many games open."

Josie turned to her grandfather. "Oh could we go? Please?"

Mr. Kerr smiled. "It's difficult to deny my grandchildren anything, it seems. Very well, we shall set a date." His voice remained light, but I could see the pain in his eyes. "After the celebration, perhaps?"

Tony regarded him for a long moment, then nodded. "We've imposed upon your hospitality long enough." He rose, and went to Joe, so I did as well. "Best wishes for your recovery, sir." He turned to me. "Come, Jacqui, we must be off."

I wasn't sure what was going on, but I said nothing. Tony turned to me once the carriage was in motion. "I'm sorry to leave so suddenly, but I got a — a terrible feeling. And I had a thought: my ancestor destroyed his." He paused. "If our positions were reversed, and I had the heir of the man who destroyed my family in my home — I feared taking tea with them."

"Tony!" The idea was monstrous. "These are my friends I've known my entire life. They had us for luncheon New Year's Day. If they wished to poison us, wouldn't they have done it then?"

"You know Master Kerr and Miss Kerr. But your friend is gravely hurt — and what do you know about the grandfather?"

I recalled the fear in Joe's face. *My grandfather is a monster.*

Tony shook his head. "I just — I felt something was terribly wrong. You're welcome to visit as you like, but I — I don't think I'll go there again."

The Blackmail

Nothing during the visit seemed wrong to me. Could Tony's lack of sleep and worry about the issue with Gardena — whatever it was — be making him paranoid?

I turned to Tony, hoping he might speak further on what troubled him about the visit, but he stared out of the window.

Tony's brother was poisoned by an assassin. Perhaps this made Tony wary of anyone who had cause to hate him.

We approached the bridge to Market Center. After a while, my thoughts drifted to how I might get Ma out of the city.

If I had money for a zeppelin ticket, the matter would be simple. But I didn't, so the alternative was smuggling her out. And the only way to smuggle someone out would be to appeal to the Clubbs, who would want to know why I wanted a Pot rag smuggled out of the city.

Gardena seemed to like Lance, and the Clubbs seemed to want to be our allies. That didn't mean I would automatically trust them with my mother's life.

Whatever I did, it had to be something that Roy never learned of. He had never expressly forbidden me from contacting Ma, but I had never dared to before. I always feared he would kill us both.

Why did I not go to Tony? My mother wasn't at my wedding because Roy led Tony to believe Peedro Sluff was my only family. To reveal she was alive would mean I had lied to Tony for the past ten years. What else might I have lied about? He would begin asking questions about a great many things. He'd at least want to know why I lied, and I couldn't tell him his father had threatened me every step of the way to the altar. Roy made it very clear he would kill me if I did so. Could Tony really protect me from Roy?

I couldn't take that chance. Tony must never learn that Roy blackmailed me into marrying him until I was somewhere Roy could never find me.

***

The next day, I went to luncheon with Gardena, uneasy about what she might have to say. I wished that she and Tony had never had their conversation, or rather, had taken it out of my presence.

We passed through the side bridge to Diamond at once; evidently, she had sent word in advance.

Light gray cobblestones paved the streets, and the curbs were painted white. Many of the buildings were either black brick mortared in gray, painted white, or of silver wood with silver fittings. The lamp posts were delicately spiraled wrought iron painted white with faceted crystal lamp covers which I imagined looked lovely when lit.

Thousands of gentlemen and ladies, many as dark as the Diamond Family, pushed prams, promenaded, or entered shops. The Diamond quadrant ladies seemed to prefer bright colors; the streets looked festive just from their clothes.

The streets teemed with traffic. The Diamond Family's horses and carriages were white, with silver and white tackle. Our black carriage and horses stood in stark contrast to theirs.

My carriage stopped in front of the Diamond Women's Club, and my outriders halted beside us as Honor helped me out to the street. An attendant in Diamond livery, white with silver buttons, came up. "Mrs. Spadros, you're expected. Welcome."

I smiled. "Thank you." I went to the stairs of silver wood with silver banisters and a silver-gray carpet. An attendant opened the silver wood door.

The entry was carpeted in the same silver-gray. An attendant stood behind a white podium. "Ah, Mrs. Spadros, right this way."

I didn't expect to be greeted so warmly.

The luncheon room was large and white, with picture

windows covering the far wall. Tables with white tablecloths were set up throughout the room, but the room was empty. Gardena sat at a table in the center of the room, her mother Rachel beside her. Gardena's attendant pulled out her chair as she rose to greet me. Rachel Diamond seemed intent upon the napkin in her lap.

"Gardena, what is this? Do we have the entire room today?"

"I thought it would make your men feel more comfortable if the Club were closed for today, rather than being full of people."

I smiled. "Thank you for thinking of my men."

"You hold your servants in high regard." She took my hand. "And care for their comfort. It is something I love about you."

She wore a cream-colored gown trimmed in tan. It made her skin seem even darker than it was, and the shade gave her face a rosy glow.

"You look gorgeous," I said. "Is this your Spring dress?"

She blushed. "Thank you. It is."

"Mine is still being displayed." I laughed. "My dressmaker is quite the entrepreneur."

"Come, sit." She patted the table next to her.

An attendant stood by with my chair, so I sat. "It's nice to see you, Mrs. Diamond."

"So nice," Rachel Diamond said, in a singsong voice. Then she raised her head. "Who are you?"

"This is Mrs. Spadros, Mama," Gardena said.

"Oh, yes, how wonderful to meet you."

We last saw each other not six weeks ago, but Gardena shook her head, so I let the matter drop.

I took a sip. "I hope your family is well?"

"Yes, as well as can be expected."

"Is something wrong?"

"Jack has taken to his rooms these past few days. Jonathan has felt rather poorly as well; the doctor prescribed a trip to the country, with fresh air, meals on the veranda, and daily walks. So I miss seeing him. My older brothers are all busy with their families, and rarely visit. My father keeps to his study, so the house seems rather empty. But I shall visit Jon this weekend."

"Gardena, why does Jon take all those vials? What's wrong?"

"It's nothing; he's always had a delicate constitution, and the city air is often foul." She patted my hand. "Jon will be pleased that you asked after him. I shall send your love when I visit."

"I wish I could visit, but I doubt Mr. Spadros would allow it."

Gardena gave a pensive sigh. "All in good time." But then she smiled. "Would you like some wine?"

"That sounds lovely."

Rachel Diamond sang, "Lovely."

Gardena gestured to the waiter, and he brought our wines. Gardena drained her glass.

I had never seen Gardena drink much before. "Did you have a chance to speak with Lance the night of the dinner?"

"I did briefly. And he called on me yesterday afternoon."

"Wonderful! I'm so pleased."

"It was nice to see him. He's caused controversy amongst my brothers, though. Cheh-zah-ray says the Clubbs are the most dangerous Family in the city, much too dangerous to ally with."

"Cheh-zah-ray?"

Gardena blinked. "Yes, my oldest brother. I saw him on the dais before you greeted my parents at the Grand Ball. Have you not been introduced?"

"No." I remembered the man who glared at Tony that night. "And I've never heard such a name. How is it spelled?"

"C-E-S-A-R-E. Cesare. It's Italian for Caesar, after my father's grandfather. Did your family not teach you Italian?"

My cheeks burned. "I was born in the Spadros Pot, Gardena. I said so at our dinner."

She blushed. "Forgive me. I meant the Spadros Family."

It seemed I hadn't been taught many things I needed to know. We sat in awkward silence, while Rachel Diamond hummed tunelessly to herself.

Gardena's manner seemed formal, almost strained. I wondered what she could possibly have to tell me that she was so nervous about. And she hadn't asked at all about Tony, even when I brought his name up. "May I ask a personal question?"

A blank, terrified stare crossed her eyes for a brief moment, then she said, "Of course."

What did she have to be afraid of? "Perhaps this isn't a good time to ask. You brought me here for a reason."

"Can't I bring you to my quadrant because we're friends?"

"Of course. I'm happy to be here. But you seem upset, and I want to be of service. How can I help you?"

She looked away. "Don't ask about Anthony. Or why we fought. Or why I struck him. Please." She turned her head toward me, and pressed her closed hand to her lips. "It would break trust, and endanger lives. In any case, it's his story to tell." She took a deep breath. "I would like very much for you to know. I begged him to tell you. But I can't speak of it. Not here. Not now. Please."

She spoke as if she knew Tony well. But she didn't know such a simple thing: he hated being called Anthony. "Then I'll remain silent. It hurts, though, to see you both in such pain and not know why." I pondered whether I should I reveal how much Tony loved her. But whether she saw it or not, my words would only bring grief. "I only want what's best for you both."

Gardena took a deep breath and let it out. Then she smiled a fake smile. "You're right; I did have something I must share with you. I need advice, and I don't know who else to turn to."

"If there's any way I can help, I will."

She didn't speak for several minutes, her head drooping. The waiters stood aside, covered plates in hand.

Finally, she raised her head.

"I'm being blackmailed."

"I don't understand," I said. "What have you done?"

She took a deep breath, and when she spoke, she sounded small and old and weary.

"I killed my grandfather."

The Crisis

I stared at Gardena in shock. "You did **what**?"

She began to laugh. "Oh, if you could see your face!" She signaled for the waiters to bring our food: lamb, spring greens, and new potatoes.

"Is this a joke? Because if it is, it's in very poor taste."

Gardena shook her head, contrite. "I wish it were."

Once the waiters refilled our wine glasses and retreated, Gardena cut her mother's food as she told me her story.

Hector Diamond was a kind and gentle man, at least to Gardena and her family. He was a younger son who took over the Business late in life. His main passion was mechanism, and he became the Diamond Family's Inventor, the youngest to rise to that rank since the Coup.

Hector and his brilliant soon-to-be daughter-in-law Rachel were friends immediately upon meeting. Rachel became one of his Apprentices, and after her marriage to his son Julius, they spent hours in their basement working on one contraption after another. Gardena spent much of her childhood playing there while her mother and grandfather worked.

"I can't tell you what they made," Gardena said. "That's secret. But their grand achievement was to have been an automaton with the electrical patterns of a human brain. It might be truly alive, and think for itself. Just imagine the possibilities!"

Her mother and grandfather decided to use their minds as

patterns for this automaton, and all was going well. But a storm came up, and something went terribly wrong.

"Fortunately, none of us children were in the room at the time," she said. "But we heard a great noise, and the lights went out, then a roar from my grandfather and a sound of smashing. My father and brothers ran downstairs to see my grandfather breaking all he had built. My mother stood in the midst of it, her face blank and staring.

"It took all of them plus many servants to restrain him. He was tied to his bed. My mother would do whatever you asked, but then stay still until you told her to do something else.

"As time progressed, they both regained a bit of their sanity, but have never been the same. During my grandfather's calm periods, he spoke of futility and wishing for death. Many a time, he begged me to kill him. The only time which seemed to bring him joy was when we took tea together. He loved mushroom sandwiches, so I made him some."

I put my hands to my mouth in horror.

"The cook was a wretched woman, who beat us when my parents were absent, so I made it appear her doing." Gardena stared at her plate; the lamb fat had begun to congeal. "My father killed her." She turned to me. "Who would know what I did?"

Rachel hummed a children's tune in the silence. I leaned back and took a sip of my wine, stunned by the revelations. "Tell me what's happening now."

"Last week, I received a letter which said, 'I know what you have done.' At first I didn't know what it meant, but the letters continued every day, with greater threats. Then," she glanced away, "I received another, which said, 'mushroom sandwich.'"

Why wait all these years, then blackmail her now?

"Each letter was brought by a different messenger boy. Each said he got the letter from a different part of the city, but they all said the man looked like a Diamond." She laughed. "In other words, he could be just about anyone in the city."

I laughed. "But not Charles Hart."

Rachel Diamond gave me an amused glance which was so … aware … that I shuddered. How much did she understand?

Gardena laughed. "Or Roy Spadros." But then she sobered. "His last letter said he plans to send letters everywhere if I don't pay him a great sum, more than I have: the police, the newspapers, my father." She paused, looking away. "I fear my father the most. He will never forgive me for what I've done."

I glanced at Gardena's mother, who was trying — and failing — to eat her lamb with a spoon. "Should we be speaking of such things in front of her?"

Gardena sighed and switched out her mother's spoon for a fork. "I've cared for her daily for many years. Sometimes it seems as if she knows what you say ... but I don't really think she does."

"But what if she says something to your father?"

"Oh," Gardena said, "I don't think Papa would believe her."

That look Rachel gave me ... "I suppose you know best." I took a bite of lamb; it was quite good.

How to handle this crisis so her father wouldn't learn the truth, yet the blackmailer might be silenced? "Arrange a meeting with this blackmailer in a public place. Have your brothers there and capture the man. They can discuss this with the man at leisure, and your father need never be notified."

"What should I tell my brothers?"

I shrugged. "The truth: a man is blackmailing you. You need not say why, or tell them whatever you wish. I'm sure you can think of something." She had eaten nothing. "You'd best eat, or you'll lose your reputation; the bird eats thrice its weight daily."

Gardena chuckled at the reference to my dinner party, but began eating. After she had eaten about half of her plate, she said, "Will you come with me? When we catch this man."

The idea made me uneasy. "I don't know, Dena ..."

"I promise, Jack won't be there. He has a horror of sitting in wait; he thinks it tedious. Please come with me. This whole thing is all too frightening. I wish you to be with me, as support."

Why didn't they **do** something about him?

"It can't be in Diamond quadrant, Dena, it can't ... please ... make the meeting on Market Center."

Gardena nodded. "I would be so grateful. But what do you need? I've taken of your generosity twice now, and this seems like a poor return."

I stared at my plate. "I don't know if I ..." Could I trust her with this? I glanced at Rachel; she was intent on her napkin again.

Don't let Jack hurt my Ma.

But I couldn't say that. Gardena believed Jack to be sick, not dangerous. I didn't want to get in an argument about her brother or reveal his crimes, not in the midst of Diamond quadrant.

I stared at my plate, feeling ill. Sharing this with Gardena, who didn't understand the danger ...? But who else could I trust? If Jon wasn't away, I would have gone to him. He would help me in this without question.

I took a deep breath. "I must get my mother out of the city."

Gardena gazed at me without moving. "I've never heard you speak of your mother before." Then she frowned slightly. "Why must you get your mother out of the city? What's wrong?"

The irony didn't escape me. "Her life has been threatened."

"What's happened? Are you sure? This is horrifying!"

If only she knew. "I have good evidence. I wouldn't ask something like this for anything less."

"I'm sorry. Of course, you know best." She sat silently, eyes far away. "I overheard Cesare and Lance talking about shipping Pot rags to Dickens as workers. Would that do?"

Pot rags. "Is that what you think? That I'm just a Pot rag?"

She put her hands to her mouth. "I'm so sorry, Jacqui. Of course not, you're not like that."

I shook my head. She just didn't understand. "I appreciate the thought, but my Ma would never leave for that; she's an owner."

And I remembered how the Clubbs sold the secrets of others. Could I trust Lance Clubb?

Gardena said, "Perhaps he can make her a supervisor?"

I laughed. My mother ran the best brothel in the Spadros Pot. "Now that's something she certainly can do." Then I sobered. Ma would be giving up everything she had worked so hard for.

"I'll speak with him about it," Gardena said. "If I do that, will you come with me?"

I took a breath and let it out. I would have to get a message to Ma; she still might not want to leave me here. It was so risky. If the letter were intercepted, it could mean both our deaths ... but it was the best chance I had to get her to safety. "Very well, but it must be truly secret. No one must know my mother is leaving the city. I'm serious; she might be killed."

Gardena stared at me in horror.

"And your brothers mustn't breathe a word I was there to meet your blackmailer. Mr. Spadros would be quite upset if he learned I placed myself into such danger."

Gardena smiled fondly. "He would." She sat up straighter. "It's settled, then. I shall write when it has all been arranged."

When I left the Diamond Ladies' Club and approached my carriage, I realized I could have gone to Anastasia any time to smuggle Ma out of the city and she would have done it. I had a terrible vision of an empty lock-box.

I don't trust Anastasia anymore.

"I should like to visit the bank on Market Center."

"Of course, mum," Honor said.

It was a short ride to the bank, my outriders clearing the path through Diamond and across the bridge to the island.

Gardena had done a terrible thing. But it wasn't what caused friction between her and Tony.

I believed Gardena told the truth about her grandfather, but ... something didn't ring true about the blackmail. I felt that whoever blackmailed her did so for another reason.

What was Gardena involved with?

***

I entered the bank, a sandstone edifice several stories high. Of course, I had been to the bank many times, but never had a lock-box before. I felt unsure how to proceed, so I went to the teller, who acted as if accessing a lock-box was an everyday occurrence. After a brief wait for the manager, I produced the key to box #7 and was ushered into the vault area.

Rows of boxes ran along an enormous golden hall, to the ceiling; there must have been thousands of them. But we didn't go inside the hall itself, but into a small glass antechamber. "Wait here," said the manager.

In the antechamber sat a round table of polished wood with

carved wooden chairs. It also held a drawer made completely of glass, set waist high in the wall closest to the box room. The table was lit from above, as if the purpose of the room was to display it.

I waited while the manager approached a technician dressed in white who stood inside the hall. They spoke briefly, then the manager returned, standing outside the open antechamber door.

The technician used a system of levers, gears, and pulleys to move a large arm over and down, to the bottom row. The arm then slid inside a small cubicle in the far wall and emerged holding a box. The technician guided the arm completely around, then deposited the box into the glass drawer. The drawer slid forward; there lay box #7. "Astonishing!" I said.

The manager smiled to himself.

The necklace lay inside, just as when Anastasia put it there. The jewels sparkled brightly, the metal showed the same patina of our finest silver.

I let out a breath, relieved. At least in this one thing Anastasia had spoken true. I ran my finger over the beautiful necklace then locked it away.

***

When I exited the bank, Honor raised his hand to help me into the carriage, but I said, "I'll be along shortly."

"Yes, mum," Honor said, but I felt his eyes on me all the way down the block. The day was warm and pleasant, with a slight breeze, and I strolled along like everyone else on the promenade. I turned into *The Bridges Daily*'s offices, giving Honor a brief smile as I did so.

The thin man in his thirties leaning over the counter reading a worn, dog-eared novel quickly straightened when I entered the shop. "Mrs. Spadros! How may we help you?"

"I wish to place an ad for the Celebration program."

"Right this way." The man led me past an array of busily typing men to an office. The glass-paneled door read:

Mr. Paul Blackberry
Clubb Desk

Mr. Blackberry, a portly man with long graying sideburns, nodded to me as I entered. "Surprised to see you here. Must be important!" He gestured for me to sit across the desk from him. I noted the numerous faces of those pretending they had work to do which allowed them to pass by the large windows so they might peek in.

"It is," I said. "What have you learned of Dame Anastasia?"

He lit a cigar, and puffed on it. "The records aren't all that clear back when she came here, but —"

"What do you mean? Hasn't she lived here her whole life?"

"Goodness, no! She and her father, Sir Rounder Louis, arrived back in the late 40's. From Chicago, if these reports are correct. Must have been a teenager, and from all accounts, she was a wild one." He grinned. "You would have liked her."

I laughed.

"She drank, smoked, ran off to the theater, even played a role — I'm sure you've heard of her stint as 'Queen of Diamonds' —"

I nodded. Trey said as much. I wondered why she never mentioned it. Trey certainly seemed proud of her.

"— and generally carried on like this for years. Her father was no help there; a notorious gambler and loan shark. Some say even his knighthood was a fable. But after a few years in Bridges they were seen at every Grand Ball, dining at all the Family parties. After a while she settled down and took up various amusements, all with hints of impropriety. From all accounts, though, she's a good jeweler, or at least a successful businesswoman."

"Whatever happened to her father Sir Louis?"

"Up and disappeared one night. There were rumors of some scandal, and Dame Louis wore mourning garb for a while, but then she went on as before."

"You make it sound unseemly."

After putting on spectacles, he picked up a pile of ancient newspapers and set them on his desk, paging through them. "Seen with dozens of men," he peered over his spectacles at me, "young men, mind you — over the past thirty years. Sometimes several at once. Then there would be some uproar, and the faces would change."

The men guarding her were indeed young.

"And there's something odd."

I leaned forward. "What?"

He rested his hands on the desk. "I've talked with several jewelers. She's never been seen in person by one of them. Not at a convention, nor a workshop, nor even a showing."

"That is indeed odd." I wondered what it meant.

Then I remembered the faces at the window behind me and reached into my pocket, handing him a folded paper. "I'm supposedly here to place an ad for the Celebration program."

He gazed at me, sympathy in his eyes. "I'm sorry, Jacqui. This must be a difficult time for you."

A much thinner, much younger reporter in the Pot. The same bushy sideburns, only dark brown back then. "May I take your picture, miss?"

I smiled. An easy mark, I thought. "Sure."

Picture taken, I went to hug him, and picked his pocket.

I shrugged. "No worse than any other." He never got angry, though he did ask for the wallet back. But I was only five; I got better at pickpocketing as time went on. "It's good to see you, sir."

"Let me walk you out," he said, rising, and came round to open the door for me, the faces outside scattering.

I chuckled at that.

We strolled through the sea of typists past Mr. Durak's open door. The man lay face down on the floor.

I rushed into his office, which stank of alcohol, and knelt beside him. The man was breathing, but slowly. Tear-stains streaked his brown face. His graying brown hair was disheveled, his collar, askew. I looked up at Mr. Blackberry. "Call a doctor."

The faces outside the plate glass windows peered back at me, puzzled and concerned.

Mr. Blackberry rushed out of the room, roaring, "Don't you louts have anything to do? Get to work. You, call the doctor."

I rolled Mr. Durak on his side should he be sick. Drunken men were a common sight back home in the Pot, but I never expected such here.

Mr. Blackberry came in and shut the door. "How is he?"

"Out cold." I settled back on my heels, holding Mr. Durak steady with my right hand. An empty bottle of whiskey lay on the floor under his desk. "What's going on here?"

The desk creaked as Mr. Blackberry settled on a corner. "Ah, my dear, his wife turned in her cards in the fall, and poor Acol's not been the same since. Never wore mourning but a week. Comes in and leaves on schedule, but does little but drink. We forced him to go to your charity event; thought it would be good for him to get outside."

"I had no idea." Seeing Mr. Durak — a solid and reliable man — in this terrible state seemed most unsettling. "I saw his interview with the banker. About the gems."

Mr. Blackberry frowned. "Dame Anastasia set that up. The gals were all aflutter about the man she came in with. I never saw him." He gestured with his chin at Mr. Durak, who snored softly. "His secretary said he gave her the interview already dictated, but only he spoke."

"Do you think he concocted it?"

"I have no idea. If true, it's suicidal, if you ask me." Mr. Blackberry put his hand to his chin. "A pity."

I remembered our brief interaction at the charity event last month. Nothing seemed wrong. "Has he no children?"

Mr. Blackberry shook his head. "His wife was incapable. His first wife died in childbirth, oh, back when I was a cub reporter, the babe along with her." He paused. "This time hit him hard."

I had a sudden vision of Tony, alone and grieving, and I shook my head. "He deserves better."

The doctor and his assistants came in then and we left the room so they could tend to Mr. Durak. Then Mr. Blackberry escorted me to the door.

"Sir," I said, "make sure he's taken care of."

He nodded. "I'll get him home and in bed once the doctor says he can be moved."

"Thank you." I squeezed his hand, but close, so none saw it. "Dealer's blessings with you."

He smiled. "And also with you."

Honor stood outside the door, relaxing when he glimpsed me. "Is all well, mum? I saw the doctor's carriage."

I strolled past, and he fell in step beside me. "A man took ill, but he's being cared for."

"Very well, mum. Spadros Manor?"

"Yes, thank you."

In the carriage, I shook my head. Anastasia (and likely, Frank) had dragged Mr. Durak into this scheme of hers ... or was it theirs? ... and used him to defraud the city.

I wondered whose idea creating these false gems was. The little I knew of Frank Pagliacci indicated poor reasoning skills. Whether this came from lack of intelligence or carelessness, it was difficult to say. The process as described to me by Anastasia's great-nephew Trey, though, spoke of a plot well-crafted. The factory and processing alone would have taken years to set up.

Would Anastasia have planned the kidnappings, the attack on Tony, the false letters, the break-in at Madame's shop? No. What possible motive might she have? By all appearances, she held regard for us, not hate. She had no reason to extract the sort of vengeance from us that Frank spoke of at Jack Diamond's factory. And if she wished to harm us — or me in particular — she had only to say a word to the right ear.

The horses trotted down the busy street, shops passing by as we went.

There seemed to be more than one plot here. Jack and Frank were being directed by someone else. Anastasia had her simple yet ingenious scam, which might just work. Zia's hopes were probably much like Anastasia's: marriage, home, and family.

Back then, I didn't see any reason to care about Anastasia's scam, other than concerns for the safety of anyone associated with Frank and Jack. So she defrauded some merchants. What was that to me? The fact that she involved Mr. Durak did upset me, especially her doing so while he grieved his wife.

But I couldn't understand the violence. What did whoever directed Jack Diamond and Frank Pagliacci stand to gain from that? What pushed this ringleader to move from breaking into a shop and causing a mess to kidnapping and murder?

Jack Diamond in Spadros, harassing merchants and widows. What could cause him to do that, when he normally would have (by his reputation) simply murdered them? Frank Pagliacci strangling a grown man this time. Why change his targets?

And why was the group so afraid of being revealed?

None of this made any sense.

We went over the bridge to Spadros quadrant. Sailboats passed under us, sending pale gray ripples over clear water.

I suddenly remembered Roy's letter to Tony:

You must allow me to take over this interrogation to learn the truth of the matter.

Tony never answered that letter. And when Roy learned that these men used our money to finance their schemes, he would be furious. He must have his men feverously searching for them.

I laughed. Jack and Frank must be terrified! Being pursued by Roy Spadros would produce a crisis for anyone. No wonder they were trying to cover their tracks.

Perhaps the tide had finally turned in our favor.

The Betrayal

When I returned home, Pearson had a letter for me:

I have news. — JB

JB had to be Jake Bower, the investigator I hired to learn about Jack Diamond's movements since New Year's.

I poured a glass of bourbon and lit a cigarette. The thought of going to meet Mr. Bower made me weary. All I wanted was a few days to rest, to forget about Mad Jack Diamond and his deranged ruffian Frank Pagliacci. Which seemed unlikely to happen.

Where could Frank Pagliacci be? Besides Anastasia, none of my other informants had any word of him. Clearly he hadn't fled the city. Was Jack hiding him? Jack had taken to his rooms; might Frank be hiding there also?

No. With Jack and Rachel ill and Jon out of the house, Julius wouldn't allow a stranger to stay with them. Gardena would have said something about a visitor, especially one as badly injured as Frank must have been. And I couldn't see Jonathan allowing a stranger to go to their Country House.

Why did Julius put up with Jack's behavior? That was another mystery. He had to know that ...

Wait, I thought. Jack, by all accounts, was as fearsome a creature as Roy Spadros. Perhaps Julius used his son's madness to keep order in the city, or to frighten the other Families from acting against them. It was the sort of sly move that wouldn't surprise me, coming from a Patriarch.

These men were utterly ruthless when it came to controlling their territories. But could a man stoop to betraying his son, exposing his son's malady just to promote his own schemes?

***

I got my "rest" after all. For two days, Tony was entrenched in his study with an unassuming young man who I presumed was the accountant he hired. Even though engaged, Tony came out every half hour to ask me some question or another. The constant interruptions were maddening; I could go nowhere and got little done, other than my weekly kitchen inventory with the maids.

But then Tony went back to the casino. Dr. Salmon came to check on Morton — the first time he visited since Morton's arrival without Tony or one of his men hovering.

After the doctor visited Morton, I asked if we might speak privately. We went to my room, and sat at the tea-table.

"I hope all is well?"

I said nothing.

"My dear, something is wrong, or you wouldn't have asked for me. Please, I want to help you."

I took a deep breath. "Sir, I believe you have betrayed me."

Dr. Salmon's lined face grew pale, and his eyes widened.

"I asked you to keep silent about Roy Spadros and his attack on me. I specifically asked you not to tell my husband, yet you did. I trusted you not to notify Roy about the attack on my husband, yet somehow he knew. You report to my husband. You report to Mr. Roy. Who else do you report to? How can I trust you with anything?"

Dr. Salmon's voice shook. "I'm your doctor. I report to no one. I didn't tell Mr. Roy about the assault, I swear."

I realized: this man is **old**. And deeply afraid.

"Mr. Anthony beat me," he whispered.

Tony did **what**?

He spoke as if to himself, his eyes empty. "I brought him to this world, and his father before him — yet he beat me. He so fiercely wanted to learn what had befallen you that I feared for my life." He paused. "He swore no harm would come to you." He leaned forward, peering at me. "Has he hurt you?"

Tony beat Dr. Salmon. I turned away, shame flooding over me. "No."

If I would have told Tony that Roy hit me, this would never have happened. But I felt so afraid ... of Roy hurting Tony, of Tony asking why Roy would hit me ... which would lead to telling him of my failure with Thrace Pike last month. That was humiliating enough without Tony going into a frenzy about it. "I'm so sorry. This is all my fault."

Dr. Salmon didn't speak for some time, and when he did, he sounded sincere. "I wish I knew how to help."

Find me a way out of this city? All I could hope for at this point was to get my mother to safety.

But there was something he might help with. "Doctor, may I ask something unrelated?"

"Of course."

"Mrs. Rachel Diamond. Do you know of her case?"

He nodded. "Mr. Julius Diamond sought counsel from every doctor in the city before his father died."

"Can anything be done for her?"

The doctor shook his head. "She's suffered electrocution of the brain. There's little to be done in such cases."

Something occurred to me. "They were working on a machine, trying to put their brain patterns into it when the accident occurred. Do you imagine her thoughts might be in the machine still?"

Dr. Salmon burst out in laughter. "Oh, my dear, your mind is exquisite. You should take up the writing of fantastical novels! Such a thing is absurd." But then his face sobered. "No, Mrs. Diamond is gravely injured, and has been for some time. I'm sorry. I doubt she'll ever recover."

I felt somewhat embarrassed, as well as sad. I remembered Gardena's grief, and her mother Rachel, a beautiful woman who used to be an Apprentice, trying to eat lamb with a spoon. "I just hoped ... that maybe ... she might get well."

***

The doctor released Morton to do light reading and stroll in the garden, which he felt anxious to do. I accompanied him, just to get a chance to plan what to do next about Frank Pagliacci.

Since our discussion up in Morton's room, Tony seemed to regard him as one of his men. Yet Tony and Sawbuck had been in meetings at least once a day without either of us, to what end, Tony didn't say.

"I feel," Morton said, "that your husband doesn't trust me."

The sun shone pale and wan through the clouds, yet the day was warm. I carried a parasol, but doubted I would need it. "Does it matter?"

He glanced back at Amelia and her daughters, who "by coincidence" were out strolling that day. "I suppose not."

We walked a foot apart and in plain view of the house. What did Pearson think was going to happen? "Why did you leave us, there at the factory?"

Morton let out a breath. "There were so many men, and they thought you were no threat. I reasoned that if I drew them off, you and the boy might escape."

"But why take the carriage?"

He seemed confused. "I was hurt; you were unharmed. If I tried to hire a taxi, the driver would insist on taking me to a doctor, and the police would have been called. The boy needed attention in any case, and I felt certain you had someone you might bring him to who would be discreet."

I nodded. True, every word. "I'm sorry to doubt you. I ... I don't think I was doing much reasoning at the time."

Morton smiled. "You did fine."

"There's one other thing. Why did you use that story about Helen Hart? It's come to cause me trouble."

He turned to me. "In what way?"

"A mutual friend heard the story. Mrs. Hart was extremely ill, and could never have been out boating."

"Oh," Morton said, chagrined. "I had no idea. My apologies. It seemed the best plan under the circumstances."

"Well," I said, "I've taken care of it." I still felt annoyed, but even Josie said the matter was kept secret. I took a deep breath and let it out. "What are your plans?"

"I have a choice: to stay or go. Which I do depends on your husband. I have nowhere to go now that my yacht is destroyed. I dare not return home; I'm sure it's being watched. My plan is to stay as long as I can and see what I can learn of who's betrayed me to the Feds."

"What of Zia?"

He snorted. "Zia." He shook his head. "She is, of course, the most likely candidate, yet has no motive."

I then told him the details of my encounter with her, and her defense of Frank Pagliacci. I had forgotten about it up to this point, what with all that had gone on.

Morton shook his head. "I've never known Zia to be enamored of men. She's always seemed too shrewd, too skeptical, too distrusting of their motives." He paused. "But perhaps this man has fooled her."

It certainly seemed that way. She spoke like a woman in love, whose lover was being falsely accused in a way too vile for her to imagine. "Zia's not your maid, and I can't believe a sister would ever be so false. What is she to you, really?"

He looked away. "For a while, she was my employer. Then my — I suppose the best term would be business partner. Now?" He shrugged. "I don't know whether it would be better for her to be dead or alive. I can't prove she lives, but she's disappeared after telling the Feds I attacked her."

I stared at him in horror. "Zia was a Federal Agent?"

He nodded. "I wish I never met her; she's betrayed me, and possibly them as well. Now I'm hunted."

Anger rose in me, and chagrin. *I had her on the ground and I let her get away!* "If I knew she was a Fed, I would've killed her the day we fought and saved everyone the trouble."

Morton flinched, but said nothing.

"How is it that you joined the employ of ... were partnered with ... a Federal Agent?"

He kept his eyes on the ground as we walked. "I've known Zia for some time. She was known to my family and came from the same city as my parents. She inherited a great deal of money and hired me to do some work for her. We've worked together ever since." He paused. "She would leave for long periods of time, and her explanations of what happened were incomplete. Perhaps this was when she did her work for them."

I always pictured Feds as grim-faced men in dark spectacles, not as a pretty young woman with red hair who threw sand when cornered. "I'm stunned."

"You might imagine what I felt."

We walked along for a while, the laughter of Amelia's children far behind. Her kiss on his cheek, his obvious distress when he realized she was in danger, his reaction when I spoke of killing her ... "Did you love her?"

He snorted. "Hardly. As I said, she ever distrusted men's motives, and regarded me more as a nuisance than anything else." He paused. "Don't misunderstand me; I enjoy the company and charms of women as much as the next man. But I've never wished to be tied to one. I prefer to go where I please, and when."

I felt much the same way.

We approached a table and chairs set up under an arbor, and we sat. "And what of your employer? Your Red Dog trey?" I felt concerned about Clover, the young "ace" with the eye-patch, and the other boy, like Stephen, the "chip" who I had never met.

Morton shrugged. "Clover's a smart boy, although you wouldn't know it from talking to him. When Stephen was murdered, we met up once — for me to send your dress — and I told him to lay low for a while. He got his friends together, all on his own, and sent messages to every harbor to watch for me. One of those friends brought me here." He leaned his elbows on his knees, and gazed far away. "Saved my life." He straightened. "As far as my employer, he can go to the Fire for all I care. I think he knew Zia was false, and set me up to fail. I mean to find out why."

When we returned to the house, Pearson told me three letters had arrived. The first was a double-sealed letter with a silver-edged white envelope and the Diamond Family's symbol traced in silver on the flap. It read:

My dear Mrs. Spadros —

It is my pleasure to inform you that the matter we discussed earlier has been confirmed. Never fear: I did not give particulars to the gentlemen involved. Please advise your friend to go to the poorhouse outside the Spadros Pot at 10 pm on the last day of the month. Our mutual friend plans to send a carriage.

Most affectionately yours,

Gardena Diamond

I chuckled. So this was Gardena's idea of secrecy. No matter; the seals seemed untouched.

I tossed it in the fire and rang for Pearson.

He opened the door. "Yes, mum?"

"When did Mr. Spadros say he would return?"

Pearson checked a notebook. "For dinner, mum."

Perfect. "Then I'd like to go down to Madame Biltcliffe's and pick up my Spring gown. I'll need it for the Celebration."

"I can send someone to get it if you like."

"No need; I'd like to go on a ride. It's such lovely weather. I should be back in time for tea."

Indeed, the day had turned overcast and chill. But Pearson only said, "Yes, mum," and turned to leave.

"Pearson, did you ever learn when Mrs. Molly is 'at home'?"

"Yes, mum. Every day, it seems. Forgive me, the matter must have slipped my mind."

It was unusual for anything to slip Pearson's mind. "Thank you." I turned my attention to the third letter. Also from Gardena, it invited me to luncheon on the 1st of March. This must be when we were to meet with her blackmailer. As long as I was back in time to dress for the Celebration, I didn't think Tony would mind.

I still needed to see Molly in order to learn why Tony never knew of my lessons. But did I really want to go to Spadros Castle?

In the five years since it was built, we had never been invited there. Part of me wanted to visit simply out of curiosity, but the thought of facing Roy Spadros in his home gave me pause.

Perhaps there was another way. I took out paper and pen.

My dear Mrs. Spadros —

I hope you are well.

I did indeed hope she was well. Her husband Roy had a habit of hurting her when angry.

I hope to have the pleasure of your company for tea at the Spadros Women's Club the Twenty-Seventh of February.

Yours very truly,

Jacqueline

I gave the letter to Pearson on my way out.

Molly was "at home" every day? Did she never go calling? I remembered my lonely days "at home," waiting for callers, and began to regret never visiting her.

Perhaps this social call business had merit after all.

When I entered Madame's shop, neither Madame nor any other customers were there. Tenni stood behind the counter. "May I help you, mum?"

"Yes, I believe you are exactly the one who might help. I want to speak with a messenger boy."

Tenni blinked. "But ... why come here?"

"I have a message which can't be written."

"Oh." After pausing for several seconds, she said, "I know just the boy you want."

She went out front and waved a messenger boy over, then bent to speak with him. She came inside. "He's going to get him."

"Very well. I wanted to pick up my Spring gown, too."

Tenni smiled. "I'll box it up for you."

Honor stood out front, squinting in my direction.

I turned to Tenni. "Is Madame not here today?"

"She's preparing her fees, mum. For January. Your men will be here in a few days to collect their packet."

I forgot the realities of life for businesses here in Bridges. Late payment of Family fees had unfortunate consequences. "Has Madame done any sketches of my Summer dress?"

"Oh, yes," Tenni said. "Come this way."

She led me to a table near the front windows filled with sketch books and opened a thick one with my name on the front. She flipped to a page.

"Very nice," I said. I glanced up; Honor watched me. I waved at him; his face reddened and he turned away. "I think I'll page through this for a while until the boy arrives."

"Yes, mum."

A few customers came and went. After an hour, the boy returned with three others. The smallest was about nine, with white-blond hair and blue eyes, wearing a bright red jacket.

"Tenni, bring the boys to the counter."

"Yes, mum."

I brought the sketch book to the counter as well, about a yard away from the boys. The various mannequins, racks, and displays hid me from Honor's view. "Hello," I said once the door closed behind them, "are you a boy who can remember things?"

The little boy nodded. "I'm a Memory Boy, mum. That's why I wear the red jacket. I remember everything."

What an adorable child. "What's your name, sweetie?"

"Werner Lead."

I glanced at the large windows: Honor was nowhere in sight. "Well, Werner ... I want you to say this: Tô zami çé isit. Kékènn olé chué twa. Mo konné komen édé twa kité lavil. Va koté lamézon moun pov a diz èr. T'alé trouvé in boggé lá pou twa. Mo linm twa é mo sa lá ak twa kan posib."

This was Kourí-Viní, the language we spoke at home, just me and Ma. I didn't know anyone else who spoke it. "Do you think you can remember that?"

The boy repeated it perfectly.

I beckoned him over and whispered, "To Fanny Kaplan at the Cathedral, Spadros Pot. Okay?"

He looked up at me with his big innocent eyes. "I need extra to go there."

I smiled and handed him a dollar. "Okay. Will this do?"

He grinned at me.

"The men are big and scary there, but they won't hurt you." I gestured to Tenni. "Return here with the answer."

"Yes, mum," Werner said. "Thank you, mum."

I said to the older boys, "You take good care of him."

They nodded. "Yes, mum, we will," and hurried out.

I put a sixpence on the sketch book then slid it across the counter to Tenni. "Thank you." I picked up my dress box.

"I'll send word when they return, mum."

When I went out to the carriage, Honor peered at me with a puzzled expression but said nothing.

Later, I watched Amelia fuss over my new dress. Would Werner get to my Ma and back safely? The adults wouldn't harm him in the Pot. But he had to get to the Pot, and children on both sides of that wrought-iron fence ignored convention.

The two older boys will look after him, I thought.

At dinner, I felt anxious, wanting to hear of the boy's safe return, of Ma's answer, something.

Tony said, "Is anything wrong? You've hardly eaten."

I laughed in spite of myself. What wasn't going wrong in my life? "No, I'm fine."

"I hear you went to pick up your Spring dress today."

I'm sure you did. "Yes, and I saw some sketches of my Summer dress. Madame was occupied, so I'll probably go back in a day or so to choose between them." The mashed potatoes were delicious. "She really has done a wonderful job."

Tony gave me an amused smile. "I remember when you first came here. They had to throw your clothes away, they were so torn and filthy —"

Morton glanced up from his meal, a question in his eyes, and I felt mortified. *After they stripped them from me without so much as an if-you-please ... they were all I had.*

" — and now ... I'm glad you get to wear pretty things."

That sentiment, coming from Tony, surprised me, cooled my anger. When I considered the matter, it seemed amusing. Even as a child during the lean times, when I would have killed for bread, fine clothes meant nothing to me. Warm clothes, now ... a different story. But once I spent my nights fed and in warmth, fancy dresses did garner a certain appeal. "Thank you; I appreciate them."

Tony gazed at me from the other end of our long dinner table for several seconds. "You deserve beautiful things. Those rags were what you had, I know, but they weren't worthy of you."

My cheeks burned. Why was he saying these things in front of Blaze Rainbow? "Thank you."

Tony drained his wine glass, set it down. A maid hurried to refill it. "I wish you saw yourself the way I see you."

This interested me. "And how is that?"

"To me, you're the most beautiful woman in the world."

I chuckled. Was Tony drunk? "I'm sure Master Rainbow is embarrassed by such talk."

Morton laughed softly. "Men in love are all alike. You're a very fortunate woman."

Interesting. "Have you ever been in love, Master Rainbow?"

He picked up his wine glass. "Can't say that I have. From what I've observed, it usually doesn't turn out well."

I laughed.

"Well," Tony said, "I plan to be the exception." He rose, and came round to my side. "Now if you'll excuse us —"

Morton grinned. "By all means."

The doorbell rang.

"Now who could that be at this hour?" Tony seemed more than a little annoyed.

"I'll get it, sir," Pearson called out, and the door opened.

Tony said, "I'll see what this is about," and went off around the corner. He came back a few minutes later, a perplexed look on his face. "Mrs. Spadros, there's a child here to see you."

I rose and hurried past him to the front door.

Little Werner Lead and the two older boys stood on the front porch. Werner brightened when he saw me. "She said okay."

"What?"

"The message. She said okay. I asked if that was all, and she said yes."

My mother hadn't seen me, hadn't even tried to get a message to me in six years. When I got a message to her that her life was in danger, all she said was, "okay"?

I woke at the pain in my scalp. I grabbed the hand pulling my hair as I fell hard to the floor.

Ma yelled, "After all I told you, why did you go after him? You could have had another year, maybe two. We could have gotten you out of here. You stupid girl! You've ruined everything!" She yanked me to my feet, dragging me by my arm to the carriage, shoving me inside.

I didn't know any of the women in there. "Ma!" I felt terrified. What was happening?

Ma shook her head as if disgusted at me and went inside without saying goodbye.

Didn't she even care enough about me to send a message? "What made you come **here**?"

Werner smiled. "The shop was closed. I saw you in the paper on New Year's. I know everyone's address in the city." One of the boys behind him laughed, as if they hadn't known that but weren't surprised by it. He turned to Tony. "Hello, Mr. Spadros."

Tony stammered, "H — hello." Then he gained his composure. "I've never met a Memory Boy before."

Werner held out his little hand. "Werner Lead. A pleasure to meet you." He turned to me. "I better get home." He started down the steps.

"How can we get in touch if we need your services again?" Tony said.

Werner gestured towards the messenger booth down the street. "They all know me," he said, and the three of them disappeared in the gloom.

"How remarkable!" Morton said, from behind us.

"We must recruit that child," Tony said. He turned to me. "Where did you find him?"

"The girl at Madame's shop knew him," I said.

Tony nodded. "Very good." He went back inside and to his study, presumably to make plans for what he might do while using the boy's services.

Morton and I returned to the table.

"Some bourbon, please, Mary." I felt relieved that the boy got to Ma and back safely with the message, but I wished I had the opportunity to ask Werner more about her.

Mary turned to Morton. "Would you like anything else, sir?"

"No, thank you."

She turned and left.

"Looks like you dodged a bullet there," Morton said.

"What do you mean?"

Morton leaned his elbows on the table. "It doesn't take an Inventor to see you don't love the man."

I thought of Mary, and Tony, and the vent below us. "That's rather impertinent, Master Rainbow. Not to mention untrue."

He shrugged. "I've never been known to mince words. And as you'll next tell me, it's none of my business."

"So why say it?" I feigned a laugh, feeling uneasy. "Next you'll be telling me you can take me away from all this."

Morton snorted. "I got cured of that nonsense long ago." Mary brought in my bourbon, then left. "No, you'll do what you need to when you're good and ready." He leaned back. "I just hope too many people don't get hurt in the meantime."

His words angered me. "You won't enjoy working for Roy."

"What do you mean?"

I spoke softly. "One day soon, you'll be given an offer you can't refuse. A loved one's location. A secret you'd rather not be revealed," I studied Morton, but he never moved, "and I wager you'll become Roy's creature, just like most other members of this household. And if you refuse ...." Or more likely, from what I'd seen so far, run. "Coming here will probably be what kills you."

Morton said nothing.

I really didn't want to talk with him anymore, so I went to Tony's study. He lay asleep on his sofa, an empty wine glass on the floor beside him. So I rang for Tony's manservant, and we got him into his bed. But I pondered Morton's words later that night. It bothered me that I was so transparent.

Perhaps this was why Sawbuck suspected me.

The Records

The next morning, I decided to have our staff outing at the Spadros Country House. With Jane's help, I began coordinating preparations with the housekeeper there. Tony was gone much of the time, and I considered using the target range on my own, but there never seemed to be a good time for it. Like when Tony was engaged with the accountant, Jane had many questions for me, and tasks which only I could do.

I wasn't able to get to Jake Bower's office until a few days later. This time I wore Madame Biltcliffe's mourning garb. Mr. Bower stared at me for several heartbeats, then hurried me inside, alarm on his face. "That veil's much too thin. I've never seen your face plainly, yet I recognized you from your portraits. If you plan to continue this, you'll need a better disguise."

Feigning amusement, I pulled the veil away from my face. He regarded me, then let out a laugh.

"What is it?"

"I recalled our last meeting. At the time, even with the bruises, I thought you might be a Hart. Now—"

I leaned forward. "Why do you think so?"

He sat back, hand to his chin, and his eyes narrowed. Then he shook his head. "I don't know, but it was my first thought. The shape of your eyes, the color of your hair. The way you move. How you phrase things." He paused. "Who are your parents?"

"Fanny Kaplan of the Spadros Pot gave me birth. Peedro Sluff claims to be my father, but —"

He gaped at me. "**You're** Peedro Sluff's daughter?"

I gave a bitter laugh. "As I said, he claims this." Peedro showed no love for me. For all I knew, he claimed I was his daughter to buy his way out of the Pot. But something in Mr. Bower's tone of voice made me curious. "Why? Who's he to you?"

Mr. Bower took a deep breath. "Peedro Sluff was once the finest marksman in Bridges." He glanced away. "It's a long, unpleasant story."

I leaned back. "I'm in no hurry. And he has never been one to suffer questions."

Mr. Bower snorted. "No, he never was, even then."

"So you knew him well."

"Yes," he said, "once, I did."

I heard this story many times before as I played outside the tan linen curtains in my mother's brothel. A police officer tasked to infiltrate a group of Party Time users, who then became addicted. Yet I sat in astonishment at the thought of my father being talented at anything.

The brown-haired man dashed towards us several blocks away, shouting urgently.

Peedro Sluff froze uncertainly as Daniel raced towards them. Then Peedro whipped out a revolver from behind his belt and fired, the motion smoother than I could ever have imagined.

My father could only have been acting as an assassin. Even deeply intoxicated, that night he shot steady and true. But who was his original target? Was it Roy, or someone else?

Daniel was no threat. If Roy had been Peedro's target, then my father betrayed someone. Someone powerful enough to feel he might survive the consequences of killing Roy, yet too frightened to do the deed himself. By shooting Daniel instead, Peedro angered both the Diamonds and whoever hired him to kill Roy.

"Sluff became more wretched with every month, until one day he disappeared. I thought him dead." Mr. Bower seemed more disturbed than glad to learn Peedro still lived.

Something in his tone warned me not to ask further questions on that topic. "Your letter said you had news?"

"I do." He glanced away, took a deep breath and let it out. "The workers at the plant told me they saw a man with a gun, and fled in terror. Jack Diamond came to help them."

I leaned forward. "Are you sure?"

"I spoke with several of them," he said. "Of course, that helps little. I had to pay them a great deal before they would even talk to me."

Something wasn't right here. "See what else you can learn."

He gave me a shrewd look. "Might you be interested in other information? I know you were against learning about the rest of the Diamonds, but I did stumble across an interesting item —"

"What is it in regards to?"

"Your family, if I may be so bold."

My family? Ma? What could he possibly be talking about? "Would you care to be more specific?"

"Not without additional payment, since you forbade me to undertake this investigation."

"Can you at least give me the type of information you're speaking of?"

"Financial records, for one."

"Financial records. For one." The way he said it made me think he had much more. "Involving both the Spadros Family and the Diamonds. But not Master Jack?"

He nodded. "Not Master Jack."

I leaned back, opening Madame Biltcliffe's fan. "What price would you put on such dry, tedious fare as financial records?"

Mr. Bower relaxed. "Ah, but the nature of financial records is anything but tedious. Who paid who, and for what, and why — and how often. These are all fascinating subjects, or could be, to the right mind." He paused. "For example, I could spin a scenario with these records which you would find most interesting."

I snorted. "Indeed. The right mind might put an unsavory spin on a great many deeds."

He gave me a sad gaze. "You don't trust me."

I shrugged. "Should I?" While I appreciated the information

about my father, I had learned through bitter experience to trust no one associated with him.

Mr. Bower said nothing.

This was ridiculous. "You call me here at great risk to my person, yet bring me little information, and that unusable. Then you try to gain further monies from me by making innuendo. I'm sorry if I don't find this conversation diverting."

He leaned forward. "I'm trying to help you. I like you. You seem sincere. I fear you're with associates who are anything but." He paused. "You won't like what I've found."

Interesting, and not in a good way. "I hope you understand my dilemma. I truly can't pay you anything further. While I have a wealthy Family, I'm not privy to their coffers —"

"But you might parlay this information into a great deal of money for yourself."

A great deal of money? This sparked interest for maybe a second, but something warned me against it. "— and I find I fear what you might have to say."

He nodded slowly, his eyes evaluating me. "Then we'll speak no more of it."

I didn't like this. "How do I know you won't sell this information to someone else?"

He gave me a wry grin. "Who would care about such dry, tedious matters as financial records?"

Who indeed. I closed the fan, tapping it on my chin. "All I need do is notify my father-in-law. Roy Spadros would be most unhappy if information were spread about his Family."

Mr. Bower turned ashen. "I meant no offense, madam." He stared at me in horror for a moment. Then his eyes narrowed, color returned to his face, and he spoke with determination. "I must protect my interests and charge fair price."

"I would need to see this information to know what a fair price was."

"But then once seen, I no longer have sole possession of it. You might even refuse to pay, yet how could I retrieve it? You must understand my dilemma."

"That dilemma is yours, sir, not mine. I will pay nothing for unseen information." I rose, but fear gnawed at my midsection. "I trust if you learn anything further about Master Diamond that you will inform me at once."

He bowed. "I am at your service, madam."

Repositioning my veil, I went out into the Plaza and wandered, not considering where.

Jake Bower had information about the Spadros Family he shouldn't have. Yet my words to him were a bluff, and he knew it. For me to inform anyone, I would have to reveal how I got the information, when I got it, and that I had lied to my husband to even meet with Mr. Bower. Alone. Unescorted, and all that.

I didn't understand Tony's obsession with my reputation, or with my safety. It seemed excessive, stifling. I could see why he might want me to be safe. But everyone knew I was a Pot rag — how could they possibly think more poorly of me than that?

I sat on a bench. I had to think.

My reaction to Mr. Bower's news about Jack Diamond bothered me. I had learned to trust my instincts and reactions on cases; they seldom proved wrong.

But what reason did Mr. Bower have to lie? He put himself into terrible danger even talking to workers at Jack's factory. One word from a worker and Jack Diamond might turn his attention to Mr. Bower himself. I began to regret my harsh words to the man. Perhaps he was just trying to help.

What about Mr. Bower's secret information? His words made no sense to me. What kind of financial information could Bower possibly have?

A mother and three small children passed by, and glancing up at them, I noted I sat in front of Pike and Associates. Going inside, I asked for Thrace Pike, and was sent up at once. "What do you know of your grandfather's associate Mr. Jake Bower?"

Thrace Pike still wore his same suit; I felt amazed that it still held together. He shrugged. "I've never met the man. All I know is what I've heard."

"Which is?"

"He's a good investigator, cunning, and gets information no

one else seems able to. He worked with the police at one time, but they had some sort of falling-out and he now despises them."

I nodded. I didn't know what happened with Mr. Bower's wife, but it seemed to cause him pain.

I felt Mr. Pike watching me; he blushed and glanced away. "Why are you here, Mrs. Spadros?"

"Mr. Bower has said things to indicate he has information which could cause harm. It frightens me. If he were to tell anyone I went to him, a blow to my face would be the least of my troubles." I gazed into his eyes. "I didn't know where else to turn."

Mr. Pike straightened. "You were right to come to me." He paused. "Has he threatened you?"

"No. He said he wished to help me, that he had financial information which could bring me a great deal of money, but —"

At the word money, Mr. Pike blanched.

"What is it?"

He shook his head. "My thoughts are horrendous; I dare not speak of it. If I were wrong —" He appeared to undergo some great internal struggle. Finally, he said, "No. I will not make such accusation of any man. Not even — no. Not without proof." Whatever his thoughts were, they distressed him greatly.

What could he possibly be thinking of? "What should I do?"

He paused for several seconds, then he came to a decision. "Leave the matter to me. I will find these records. No one will harm you, I shall make sure of that."

The Ambush

At the Spadros Women's Club, white stone steps with black wrought iron banisters led up to a black door with silver knobs. A man in black and silver Spadros livery opened the door for me.

Inside, the Women's Club was paneled in piano black and trimmed in silver, with silver-gray carpeting. At the black podium, a man in Spadros livery stood, glancing up when I approached. "Welcome, Mrs. Spadros, your family awaits."

My family? The invitation was for Molly.

Perhaps she brought Tony's little sister Katherine with her. While I liked Katie, what I wanted to discuss wasn't really suitable for a thirteen-year-old girl to hear. Perhaps I could find a way to distract her.

Or bore her. Even better. That'd be sure to make her want to leave the table, if only to go outside and play.

I smiled to myself as I followed the man to one of the private areas, curtained in diaphanous white.

Molly, Katherine, and Roy Spadros sat around the table, rising when I entered.

Fear, outrage, and confusion struck me, all at once: How did Roy get in here? The Club was only for women!

Then I realized: Who would dare to tell Roy Spadros he couldn't come in?

As ever, Tony's father Roy stared out at me through dead eyes of blue ice. The light shone on the snow-white strands in his black hair. "Good to see you, Jacq."

Molly smiled warmly and held out her hand, which I touched briefly. Why didn't she warn me he would be here?

Katherine said, "Jacqui!" She hugged me around my waist, her face in the top of my corset. "I'm so happy to see you!" Katherine Spadros had auburn hair and bright blue eyes. Her hair was pulled away from her face, a fresh rose caught up in it.

The attendant held my chair, and I sat, quite mindful that my back was to the curtain. "What an unexpected surprise."

Maids entered, pouring tea, bringing sandwiches. The private areas were as large as my private dressing room at Madame Biltcliffe's shop, with plenty of room for the servants to move about. But today, their movements were jerky, hesitant.

Once the maids were done, Roy waved them off and peered at me. "What do you want to know?"

He did tend to get to the point, but even so his abruptness startled me. "I beg your pardon?"

"You've never asked my wife to tea before. That you would do so now, after your argument with my son about 'teaching you to shoot' —"

Alarm spiked through me. One of our servants, listening at the door, reported our private conversation to Roy?

Roy let out a cold, mocking laugh. "It suggests to me you might have something you want to know."

Katherine had filled her plate with cucumber sandwiches, and was happily removing the cucumber from each of them.

"I suppose it does bring up a few questions."

Molly smiled. "We mean you no harm, my dear."

So she was in on this ambush? Roy didn't force her to keep his visit here a secret? But they meant me no harm. "Why can't Tony know about my lessons? He's so concerned for my safety."

Molly sighed. "He's always been anxious, the poor dear. And I suppose for good reason." She glanced at Roy, who didn't meet her eye. "It just seemed for the best."

They coddled Tony. They didn't believe in him. They didn't believe he could handle the truth.

When he learned of it he would be furious. It would make

him feel so disrespected. And it would hurt, especially coming from his mother. And by extension, from me. I shook my head. "This ... you can't keep this secret forever."

Roy smirked. "Certainly we can. Who would dare tell him? You?" He paused. "Now that you know we wish you not to? Why in the world would you do that? With the Cathedral so close at hand. It's just a short drive away." A sly grin crossed his face. "I bet you'd like to see your mother, wouldn't you?"

I stared at him in horror. "No."

Molly frowned. "Roy, dear —"

Roy ignored her. "Surely after all these years, you want to see her? Just for a few days, perhaps? I could invite her over for some entertainment — I'd even let you watch."

Katie had made a pile of the cucumbers. She held a slice of cucumber in one hand and the salt shaker in the other. She ate the slices one at a time, salting each slice before she ate it.

She had no idea what her father meant. I forced myself to smile, to keep my voice light. "That won't be necessary."

Roy waved to someone behind me, and a maid came in. He gestured to her to come close, and she stood beside him as if he made her skin crawl. Katie watched her.

"My dear," Roy spoke as if we were discussing the weather, "Let's get one thing very clear. This Family is mine. This quadrant and every person in it is mine. The dress you're wearing. Even that desk you love so much. All mine, to do with as I wish." He reached up to the maid, who stood trembling, head down, face pale, and patted her cheek. "Right?"

"Yes, sir," she mumbled, eyes filled with terror.

He smiled, a real smile this time. "Very nice." He dropped his hand to his side. "You may go now."

"Yes, sir," the girl said, and rushed out.

Katie's face was pale, "Mama, may I go out to the garden?"

"Yes, dear," Molly said. "Don't pick any of the flowers."

"Jacqui," Katie said warily, not looking at her father, "do you want to go with me?"

Roy said, "We're not done talking yet."

Katie looked between us; I nodded at her, giving her a small smile. "Okay, Daddy." She hurried out.

Once she was gone, Roy said, "And you are not to interfere with the boy."

For a second, I felt confused. What boy?

Molly's cheeks flushed, and she glanced away.

Suddenly, it all made sense. What happened to Amelia, what no one wanted to tell me: Pip Dewey was Roy's son. "You unspeakable bastard." He knew Amelia abused Pip yet he wanted it to continue. It wasn't enough to violate and terrorize Amelia. He tried to torture his own child! "You push the boy too far. If he takes his own life, he'll be no fun to you."

Roy stared at me, unmoving, practicality trumping whim. "Damn you," he muttered. "Fine." He sounded annoyed, but seemed secretly pleased with me.

Oh, gods. Poor Amelia.

Roy let out a short ironic laugh. "I suppose we're done with lessons. Unless there's something else you'd like to know."

I might as well ask. "I'd like to learn to hit moving targets."

The surprise which flashed through his eyes made me almost think Roy Spadros was human. "Hmm. The Gentleman's Club has moving targets, but I can't bring you there. So you must move. I'll instruct the men to allow you to use your target range."

"I suppose I should feel grateful for that."

He studied me for a long moment, and I felt afraid of what my request might have told him.

Roy must have threatened Amelia into carrying the child. This was what Peter meant when he said they thought they might be safer at Spadros Manor. They must feel trapped.

I might not get another chance to ask, Roy in a good mood and all. And another question might distract him. "How did you learn of the ambush on my husband and his men?"

Roy hesitated.

"Please, sir, I must know. My husband believes there are more spies in our household." *Besides yours.* Did Tony know his men's first loyalty was to Roy?

He sat still for a moment. "After we visited, I received a letter. An anonymous letter, mind you, so I questioned the boy —"

I gasped.

Roy let out a short laugh. "I have better things to do than play with messengers. I merely asked whence came the letter. A black-haired young woman with pale skin is all the child knew."

A black-haired woman? Molly had black hair, but a boy would hardly call her young.

He shrugged. "When I sent men to the address the boy said he received the letter from, they found the building abandoned."

I nodded. "A taunt from our enemy." I rubbed my forehead. "How many do these scoundrels command?"

He snorted.

"Do you have the letter? I want to compare it to others we have received."

Roy gave a short laugh. "Do you now? Perhaps I should just take the ones you have."

I shrugged. I would burn them before I let him have them. "I can be of help to you. You don't have to do the investigation on your own."

He peered at me. "Very well. You may pick them up at Spadros Castle. Don't bother sending anyone; if you want them, you'll have to come get them yourself."

I sighed. "Agreed." So he'd force me to come to him after all. Roy would do anything to cause others distress. To him it was like food. And I had a thought: *Perhaps my greatest weapon is for him to believe I'm unafraid, no matter what his next ambush might be.*

The Stalemate

When I got home, Tony met me at the door, face pale. I glanced at Pearson, who seemed unperturbed. Tony took my hand. "Come with me." He drew me out of sight by the stair. Then he turned to me, voice shaking. "Did he hurt you?"

"Tony, I was at the Spadros Women's Club, taking tea with your mother."

The color returned to his face. "I got word that my father was also there. My father went into the Women's Club itself!" Tony sounded scandalized, and ashamed of his father's behavior.

So Tony had his spies as well. "I invited your mother to tea. The rest was ... most unexpected. But all's well. I'm unharmed, although somewhat wiser."

Tony pulled me to his chest in a tight hug. "Thank the Dealer." He kissed the top of my head. "My father delights in finding ways to hurt me."

I hugged Tony back, moved by his misfortune of having Roy for a father. My father Peedro Sluff might be foul and lewd, greedy and slothful, but he had never intentionally hurt me.

And suddenly, I had a new name for the list of people who had motive to hurt me: Roy Spadros. While I always thought he reveled in causing me harm, the idea that he would deliberately harm me in order to hurt Tony was new.

Tony let go of me and took my hand. "I have news." We went into his study, where Sawbuck already sat. Tony sat at his desk, opening a ledger stuffed with notes. I sat in a chair next to Sawbuck, wondering what this was all about.

"Your suspicion that these scoundrels are using our own money against us was correct," Tony said. He picked up a list. "They've bought — black cloth — damn them! The cloth I wanted for the casino!" A spasm of annoyance crossed his face. "Stamp ink, red. Well, that's no surprise, they **are** making those cards, after all. Ammonium nitrate — diatomaceous earth — paraffin — clock parts?" Tony shook his head. "I can't make sense of it."

I said, "May I use your library to investigate these items? Perhaps I might find a common thread."

Sawbuck nodded. "That's a good idea."

"Yes, it is," Tony said. "But you never had to ask — you're welcome to go there anytime you wish."

I chided myself for not asking earlier. Tony had a great many books which might be helpful to me. "When the accountant tells us more ...?"

"I'll pass it along to you at once," Tony said. Then he paused for several seconds. "Why the cloth? I planned it for the draperies —" He returned to musing, hand to his chin.

After a minute of this, Sawbuck stirred. "Do you have any orders, sir?"

Tony shook his head, waving Sawbuck away. "No, not yet. Once we deduce what they're up to, I'll know what to do."

"Yes, sir." Sawbuck left, closing the door behind him.

"Tony?"

He closed the ledger and placed it on the desk, leaning his elbows atop it. "Yes, my love?"

"How many of your men were once your father's?"

Tony didn't react. "All but Ten. He dislikes my father and refuses to work for him." He gave a slight smile. "One reason I trust him." He paused. "So you've perceived our predicament."

He sounded impressed, but it didn't take too fine a logic to reason out that one.

"But Ten's goal is to find loyal men." The thought didn't seem to bring Tony any happiness. "I can't do anything overt to my father — at least, not in front of the men — nor can he do anything overt to us. A stalemate, but better than the alternative." He paused, his face pensive. "My life seems filled with such tactics these days." He yawned, rubbing his face with his hands.

"Tony, I know something's wrong ..."

He sounded weary. "Jacqui —"

"I ask you, you deny it. I ask Gardena, she says ask you. Ever since she was here, you don't sleep, you're barely eating ... I care about you. I'm worried for your welfare. You let me help you in other matters; I want to understand why I can't help with this."

Tony put his face in his hands for a long moment. "Jacqui —" He raised his head. "Please stop. These questions aren't helping."

"But —"

"Leave Gardena alone. She's — she's in tremendous danger." He hesitated. "In the most danger of anyone involved. I — I can't — I wish I knew how to tell you without making things worse. The best way to help is to trust me."

I nodded, not at all understanding. Could it have to do with her grandfather's death? Why would something that happened six years ago put her in such terrible danger now? "Then I'll remain silent. But you must promise to eat and sleep. I don't want you to fall ill."

He smiled at that. "I'll try."

Tony sat silently for a long time. Then he said, "I'll be gone tomorrow until late."

"More work at the casino?"

He nodded, looking at his desk. "You may be asleep before I get home." He took my hands. "I love you, Jacqui. I'll do whatever it takes to make you safe and happy."

I couldn't make the connection between working late at the casino and my safety. Or happiness. What did he mean?

**

I spent the rest of the day reading in Tony's library. I wasn't good at reading, having come to it late in life, but I did enjoy it.

I took the list of items from Tony's investigation and ran down it.

Black cloth ... that could be used for any number of things.

Red stamp ink seemed obvious. I imagined that when the

accountant finished he would find large purchases of business cards as well.

I found ammonium nitrate in a book of Tony's called "Chemical Compounds." Most of the chapter contained material I didn't understand. But one section interested me:

> Uses: primarily used as a fertilizer, although it can be explosive if handled incorrectly. Must be sealed well or will absorb water and coalesce into a solid mass.

There was more of interest:

> Diatomaceous earth: fossilized remains of the diatom, a hard-shelled algae. Used as a filtration aid, a mechanical insecticide, an abrasive in metal polishes, an absorbent, a stabilizing component of dynamite, and a thermal insulator.

> Paraffin: a type of wax used to make candles. Also used as a sealant.

I rubbed my forehead. Fertilizer, insecticide, candles? Did these false Red Dogs mean to run a farm? No, that couldn't be it. What was this about dynamite?

I searched the book but could find nothing on the subject. I knew dynamite was used to destroy the bridges during the Alcatraz Coup. Did they want to destroy more of them?

I put the book away and searched Tony's library for any book which might shed light on how one made dynamite. The closest I found were the volumes, *The History of Bridges,* which spoke of the Coup. But they were silent on how the substance was made.

I set the book on my chair and went outside. The gardeners were busy planting for the spring, and I went to one of them. "Excuse me."

The man was perhaps sixty, with part of a folded newspaper stuck in his back pocket. "Yes, mum, how may I help you?"

"Ammonium nitrate. How is it used?"

"Ah, mum, we don't use anything like that here. The big farms in Clubb quadrant use that stuff. Don't need it in a small garden like this."

Our gardens were ten times the size of Ma's back home. "Why not? Is it dangerous?"

He shrugged. "Anything's dangerous if you don't know how to use it. But like I said, don't need it. Spadros soil is good enough without it."

"Thank you." I turned aside, then said, "If you were wanting to blow something up, would you use that?"

"Mum?"

"Ammonium nitrate."

He paused. "Well, you could, but why would you go to the trouble? You could buy explosives for a lot less bother." He took the paper from his back pocket and unfolded it. "Look there."

He pointed to an ad:

Extra Dynamite

Strong enough for mining

Safer than nitroglycerin

Contains 65% ammonium nitrate

Interesting. If the Spadros Family began buying up dynamite, someone would surely notice. But this? A sly move indeed. "Do you know how this is made?"

"No, mum, but my father used to work in the mines. He turned his cards in last year and we still got all his stuff. I'll see if he had anything about it."

"Thank you so much. This would be most helpful."

"My pleasure, mum."

I went to Tony. "I think they're making explosives."

His eyes widened. "To destroy what?"

"I have no idea."

***

Unable to move, I watched in horror as a dark-skinned man in white walked through the factory. He looked straight at me —

189

I woke with a start. Tony slept peacefully.

Something wasn't right.

I was so afraid that day at the factory, I might have believed anyone approaching in white to be Jack, but now ....

The man in white I saw seemed heavier, shorter. Was someone impersonating Jack Diamond there at the factory?

Why would someone do that?

Why would Jack allow someone to do that?

Ah, I thought. To provide an alibi.

My heart sank. A stalemate, indeed.

Jack must have told his workers to say this imposter was him.

Another way to discredit me. If I brought charges, yet Jack could prove beyond doubt that he was somewhere else at the time, I would never be given another chance to speak against him. He would get away with everything he had done.

The Liaison

The next day, after all my household duties were done, I went to my study. Since Tony would be away, I decided to do some of my social calls. That night, I would finally have the chance to see what Marja knew about the threat against Ma. So I wrote a letter:

> Vig,
>
> I need to meet a friend outside your bar. 7 tonight. — J

I sent that note with Pearson in a stack of my usual mail, and asked him to get the carriage for me.

I detested social calls. Hours of sitting in one stifling parlor after another, repeating the same banalities with women who hated me. I had my flask with me, though, and after each call, I celebrated its end with a good stiff swig. When I approached Honor at the last call on the list, he said, "Spadros Manor?"

"The Kerr house, if you please." Since I was out, it seemed a good opportunity to visit Joe to see if he even remembered our prior meeting.

Honor nodded. "Yes, mum."

I shook my flask, which had been full of bourbon, but it hardly sloshed. Only a bit remained. No matter: Josie would surely have something to drink there.

I would be proper as any upper, and I would set Joe straight. I couldn't allow Joe to believe we had any future together.

The maid ushered me to the Kerrs' parlor, directing me to a battered armchair which faced away from the door.

I pointed to the sofa, where I might see Joe and Josie enter. "I'd rather sit here."

"They were specific, mum. Miss Josie said it was a surprise."

I sighed. "Very well."

I wanted to see Joe for as long as I could. All my other visits today had been of the fifteen minute variety; if I lingered too long here it might arouse suspicion.

But if they had set a surprise for me ...

I heard the door open behind me, and close, then Josie pushed Joe around the sofa in his chair. Joe smiled his glorious smile when he saw me. "Hi, Jacqui."

The bandage on Joe's head was gone; a red patch at his hairline remained. He had a cast on his arm, and his thigh was now in a cast as well. Josie pushed his chair between my armchair and the sofa, so Joe faced me, yet sat to my left. We almost touched. Josie sat on the other sofa, to my right.

"I hope you both are well?"

"Very well," Josie said. "And you?"

Joe sat so close I could smell his scent, feel his warmth. It took all I had in me not to touch him. "Very well indeed."

Josie smiled. "I'm glad to hear it."

Joe said, "Josie, would you play for us?"

"I would love to." She rose, going to the piano, and once she sat behind it, the top of her golden curls was all I could see.

It was then I noted that the sofa was unusually far from the table, with plenty of room to wheel Joe near me. So this had been their plan all along.

Josie began to play a soft tune.

Joe said, "How are you, really?"

I smiled, feeling quite warm. "I'm well. How do you feel?"

"I feel well. The doctor says I'm making good progress. I should be out of this chair soon."

Relief washed over me. "I'm so grateful."

"Josie told me of your work. Are you in danger?"

It seemed I was always in danger, but to say so would only

worry him. "I only take simple cases; in this one, I'm more of a debt collector than anything else."

"Ah," Joe said, leaning back. "It seems so menial for you."

Josie played much better than I did. "It's a bit more complex than I made it seem, of course. But I don't want you to worry."

He gazed at me with those beautiful eyes. "Josie also told me of your fears. I'm not ashamed of anything I said when last we were alone."

Oh, dear. "You remember?"

"I meant every word." He leaned over and kissed me.

I don't know how long we kissed. I don't know what Josie played. But when our lips parted I felt breathless, dizzy. I whispered, "How can this possibly be?"

"We were meant for each other." His lips brushed mine, then our foreheads touched. "I only think of having you in my arms."

The thought of what might happen to Joe if someone walked in right now frightened me. "If anyone should learn of this —"

Joe brought his good hand to my cheek. "Josie loves you as much as I. She would never betray us. No one else shall ever know." He pulled me close, kissed my forehead; my hand lay on his chest. "This place can be our haven, if you wish it."

I wanted Joe more than anything in the world. But how could I betray Tony's trust and come here under false pretenses? How could I put Joe in this kind of danger?

Joe's fingers dropped to mine. "I'm sorry."

"You have nothing to be sorry for." I stroked his fingers with my thumb, wanting desperately to kiss them.

I had to be strong. I had to set Joe straight. "Tony's a good man. We've been together many years now. He loves me."

"Josie tells it different. You're unwilling. He violates you every night."

"It's not like that." The carpet had a hole in it near the table leg. "He thinks I go willingly." Joe's eyes, normally green, were amber in this light. "Roy Spadros threatened to kill me if I revealed I was forced to marry. Tony doesn't know."

"His father has you trapped."

I moved my hand to the arm of my chair. "It's more than that. I ... to do this ... it would be horrible. I love Tony as a brother. He relies on me. He ... he bares his heart to me. He's a good man, but not a strong one. If he learned of this, it ... it would destroy him."

"Why do you care?"

"I've known him since I was twelve. I care about him. He's a good man, doing the best he can in a terrible situation."

Joe shook his head. "He's a murderer many times over. He killed Ottilie, and Poignee, and Treysa — our friends. He shot them in the head and dumped them in the Pot. Or don't you remember? I don't understand. Why are you defending him?"

"I don't defend what he does. He's in the Family. He has to do things which you or I would shudder at. But he hates it. He wants to take me and leave here. He stood up to his father for me, which no one in this city ever dared do."

Joe didn't speak for some time. "So he defies his father. He takes you and leaves Bridges. And then what? Is he going to suddenly not become a murderer? Are you going to stay with a man, sleep with a man, who you feel for only as a brother? Live a lie for the rest of your life?" He paused. "Why?"

I hadn't thought that far.

"You used to think for yourself, Jacqui. Have these people turned you into one of their puppets?"

Had they? The thought shocked me.

I didn't care what Tony had done. He surely had never pulled the trigger on anyone, with the exception of Duck. I couldn't see him even ordering someone's death without the fear of his father and men driving him. But Joe was right; even if Tony and I left Bridges tonight, our marriage was doomed.

"I know we can never be together," Joe said, "but I thought — maybe, if you wanted, we could have some moments here." Joe's shoulders slumped. "I thought perhaps you still loved me."

My heart tore in two. Crying out, I took hold of his beloved face and kissed him again and again. "I do, I do ... oh, gods, how could I not? You're everything to me." I began to weep. "You're the only thing that's kept me alive through all this."

His face lit up. "You love me." He held my hand to his chest, eyes closed. "All this pain has been worth it."

It was as if he spoke my exact thoughts. I leaned over to touch his soft, soft hair, his beautiful face. I whispered, "I'll tell you a secret. Every night, I love you. You're in my arms, you're inside me. I kiss your lips; I pull you to me."

He peered into my eyes. "Truly?"

At that, I felt sad. "If only it were. But in my heart we've been together these past three years." I told him then what Ma told me to do, how I searched inside myself during that terrible wedding night, and how I found him there.

Joe kissed my forehead. "Then tonight, I'll seek you as well."

When I left Joe's I felt light as a bird. He loved me.

I could visit when I liked. And Joe could come visit me. It wasn't much, and we might never have anything else, but for now, it was enough.

On the way home, I reached for the brass speaking tube. "Stop by Dame Anastasia's, please."

"Yes, mum." The driver's voice sounded tinny.

Why didn't Anastasia tell me what she was doing? Didn't she trust me? Perhaps she thought I might disapprove of her liaison with Frank. Which was interesting. If he knew we were friends, calling me over to her house would have been the perfect way for him to capture me, without having to kidnap David at all.

What was Frank really doing? I needed to talk with Anastasia to see if he had given her any clues as to his plans. But Dame Anastasia wasn't home, so I left my calling card.

It was very strange; she had never not been "at home" when I stopped by before.

***

That night, I told Pearson I felt fatigued. I would be retiring early, so there was no need to make dinner for me.

After Amelia helped me undress, she left. I put on my disguise of widow's brown, with the shoes, hat, and thick veil I only used while on cases. Then I slipped out of the house, past my guards, and soon I was on my way to my friend Vig's bar.

Vig Vikenti always greeted me loudly. So I didn't go in the front door, rather around to his side entrance, raising my veil when I opened the door. A trumpet played jazz music far up front, muffled by walls and closed doors.

Vig's mother gave me a glance, nodding as she stirred her pot in the lamplight. The room smelled of frying meat. "Vig say you come here. Bad luck, woman wear brown." She herself wore brown, but I never tried to understand the logic of the old. "Go to Vig's room."

I patted her shoulder as I passed.

The hall past her was lit golden by a gas lamp at the far end. Halfway down the hall, the window blind on the left spilled slits of blue-white light onto the wall from the electric street lamp outside. Doors lined the right; Vig's room lay past them all.

When I got to the blind, the door across from it opened. A dark figure came around to face me, the slits of light shining on his face. I stared at the man in horror.

"Blitz Spadros. What the hell are you doing here?"

The Meeting

Blitz Spadros was Tony's cousin, our night footman, and sometimes (during the day) played piano in Vig's bar. "I could ask the same," he said. "I'm supposed to be protecting you. But I find you here. Why are you here, Mrs. Spadros?"

"That's none of your concern."

"I must be particularly inept at speaking tonight, because you're not understanding me. My **entire** concern is where you are, and more to the point, why you're here."

"Why do you care?"

"I thought it would be obvious. My loyalty is to the Spadros Family." He paused. "Who is your loyalty to, Mrs. Spadros?"

I tried to push past him, but he grabbed my arm. "You haven't answered me."

I turned to him; the lamp down the hall lit his face. "I'm sorry you don't trust me, Blitz. I'm not doing anything to hurt my husband, or to hurt the Family. I'm only meeting with a friend."

He let go of my arm. "Meet with your friend, then."

I knocked on Vig's door. The brown-haired woman Vig called "Gypsy gal" answered, gesturing for me to come inside. Blitz stood outside, arms folded; she shut the door in his face.

"I have dress for you," she said, bringing out one of hers.

"I don't know your name," I said. "Vig called you —"

"Vig call me all sort of name," she said, as if irritated at him. "But I'm Natalia." She began helping me out of my dress.

"A pleasure to meet you, Natalia. Where are you from?"

"I'm of the Romani. We travel. But we're here long before the Troubles."

I frowned, not understanding.

"Ah, you call it Catastrophe." She paused, pensive. "Yes, my people say it very bad." She paused. "Like that name he call me," contempt laced her voice, "Gypsy. It be like 'Pot rag' —"

I flinched. Yes, I had heard that one enough times.

"Very bad." She tied a scarf on my hair. "There. You look like me, enough to fool cops." A shot rang out in the street behind me. "Now go."

"Thank you."

Vig's other door opened to the street, and I peered out. A figure lay several feet to my right. Sawbuck stood over it.

What the hell was Sawbuck doing here?

I ran to them; the figure on the ground was Marja. I stared at Sawbuck in horror. "Did you kill her?"

He shook his head. "I found her like this."

I knelt beside her. "Marja, what happened? Who did this?"

Marja shuddered, a dark red pool spreading beneath her towards the curb. Her eyes filled with tears, then glazed over. "Ahhh ... Josie ...." She never breathed in.

I closed Marja's eyes as grief crushed my heart. "Even dying, you loved her." I looked at her face, vision blurring. *I'll keep Josie safe, Marja. I promise.* I took Marja's hand, kissed it. "May you be dealt better cards next time."

"We need to get out of here," Sawbuck said.

Who did this to her? Why? I searched Marja's pockets: nothing. But she held a crumpled paper; I stuffed it in my pocket.

A gunshot. Whistles, from far off. Police hats bobbed far past Sawbuck, running towards us from beyond the front of the bar.

"Run!" Sawbuck grabbed my arm, and we ran around to the other side of the building. A taxi-stand was across the street, and we went round the second corner to the door I went in at first.

A shock of surprise as Morton ran up panting, eyes wide. "I saw her. The woman I told you about. She just shot at me!"

We sat in the carriage on the way to Jack Diamond's Party Time factory. Morton stared at the floorboards as he told his story.

"Zia and Frank brought me to a third-floor office with a name-plate on the door," Morton said. "Frank Pagliacci, Assistant to the District Attorney, Clubb quadrant. When we went in for the meeting, a woman with black hair sat behind the reception desk. He called her Birdie."

I stared at him, remembering Roy's story of the anonymous letter sent by a black-haired woman.

"What woman?" Sawbuck sounded confused.

"Follow me." I ran to the door. I didn't know how they found me, but I had to get my dress back.

The men followed me inside. Vig's mother was nowhere to be seen, but a great commotion of police sounded to be in the front hall of the bar. Blitz leaned against the wall in the hallway, turning to face us as we entered. I opened the first door, surprising an unclothed couple, who after a glance, ignored me.

The next room was empty. "Go in there. I need to change clothes before they get here." The men went inside. I ran to Vig's room, scooped up my dress, and hurried my way into it. After I put on my hat and veil, I shoved Natalia's dress under Vig's bed.

I sat on Vig's bed. So Tony set Blitz, Sawbuck, and Morton to follow me tonight. Why would he think I'd go anywhere?

I returned to the room and double-knocked. Blitz opened the door. "Come on in."

Sawbuck pointed a gun at Morton, who sat in a chair by the wall, an alarmed look on his face. "It seems Master Rainbow hasn't been entirely truthful. He knows Frank Pagliacci."

I went into the room. "Don't be ridiculous, there's no need for pointing guns. Master Rainbow told me this earlier. He's yet another of Frank Pagliacci's victims."

Morton looked dismayed at my analysis, as if he hadn't considered it that way before.

Sawbuck didn't budge. "When were you going to tell us?"

"Come on, Master Hogan. Think. We have a bigger problem."

Sawbuck holstered his gun. "What?"

Blitz said, "Getting out of here, for one. It won't take long before the police start searching rooms."

I laughed in spite of myself. "Well, since the mayor's in the room next door, I hope they do. But that wasn't what I meant. I came to meet a friend who warned me my life was in danger," I told Blitz, "and Master Hogan here found her outside, shot dead."

Blitz was no longer smiling.

"Whoever shot her might still be out there," I said, in case they hadn't figured it out yet. Sure, it was Ma that Marja warned me about, but I didn't want to tell them about her.

Blitz said, "Why'd you come **here** to meet her? We could've had her brought to Spadros Manor."

I hadn't considered this, so I had to think fast. I remembered the taxi-stand across the street. "She was in Hart quadrant. Could you still have had her brought here?"

"Good gods," Sawbuck said. "I knew it was a mistake for Mr. Anthony to speak for Hart the night of the dinner." He twitched, then glanced at me. "Sorry, mum."

Somehow I felt unsurprised at his knowing this.

Blitz had been listening at the door. "I think they're gone; this might be our chance to escape." He opened the door a crack, then his hand jerked towards his revolver.

Natalia's face came into view. "Ah! There you are. The police are searching rooms. You," she gestured at Sawbuck, "take the lady. Come with me."

Sawbuck offered his arm to me and the others followed.

Natalia brought us back through the kitchen. But instead of leading us out of the side door, we turned left down another long hallway with windows to the right. Police filled the street, rushing to and fro. At the end of the corridor she pressed on a wall panel on the left, which clicked, opening onto a hidden door. I thought the door might lead to the lobby, instead it revealed a long flight of stairs headed down. "Go there, then right. At the end of the hall, go up. Knock three times. Tell them I sent you."

I handed her a dollar. "Thank you."

She winked. "You were never here."

We went down the stair; the lock clicked behind us.

The stair was narrow, yet well-lit, as was the corridor, which more than crossed the street. After going up the stair, Sawbuck knocked three times. The door opened; a man stood with a gun pointed at us. Sawbuck turned to me, face filled with alarm.

"Natalia sent us," I said. The man put away his gun.

I smiled at the sighs of relief around me.

The man gestured for us to follow. We went through an ordinary-looking pantry, ending up in the back alley.

Once to our carriage, Blitz held out his hand, as Honor usually did, but I stopped, speaking quietly so the driver might not hear. "You men did your duty, and I'm grateful. But I'm worried about my husband's distress should he learn of this meeting. Is it necessary to tell him?"

Blitz looked to Sawbuck; apparently Morton had no say in the matter. Sawbuck hesitated. "We'll say nothing for now. But if he finds you dressed in this fashion, or anyone comments on your absence, all bets are off."

I smiled. "Fair enough."

After helping me into the carriage, Blitz took his place in the back as our footman. Sawbuck and Morton sat silent.

Someone must have seen me leave the house: it was the only way they could've found me. I hoped it was one of these men.

Amelia claimed she never told Roy about my business or the times I went out at night. Tony claimed Sawbuck hated Roy; Morton (as far as I knew) never met him. That left Blitz Spadros. Who did he report to? "Should I expect a meeting with Mr. Roy?"

Sawbuck glanced at Morton. "A footman who betrayed his mistress would soon be out of a job. They report to me."

They reported to Sawbuck. And he didn't trust me. "I only want what's best for my husband."

"Then we're in perfect agreement," Sawbuck said.

At my insistence, Sawbuck stopped the carriage a block away so I might get in the house without notice. As I hoped, Tony wasn't home yet, only much later slipping into bed beside me.

I lay pretending to sleep as Tony tossed and turned, paced and mumbled, yet I could only think of one thing: Marja was dead. And I couldn't help but feel I had something to do with it.

The Reality

Tony got up at his usual time, just as the sky began to pale. Once he went out to do whatever he did every morning, I lit a candle and went to my closets to search the pocket of the dress I wore the night before. The piece of paper Marja had in her hand lay crumpled there. Something was written upon it in pencil, but between the crumpling, the blood stains, and the dirt, I couldn't make out what it said.

Deflated, I put on my robe and locked the note in my dresser. Perhaps I could find a way to decipher it later.

Joe and Josie would be devastated at Marja's death. Their mother died bearing them, and Marja had been one of the few people who watched over them. I remembered Marja brushing Josie's hair in front of the fire, bringing her food, rocking her.

Who would kill Marja? She was just a woman from the Pot. Certainly no one worth going to the trouble of killing. How did they know we were to meet last night? What did she have to tell me that someone found so dangerous that they would kill to silence it?

I crawled into bed. A copy of the *Golden Bridges* arrived while I was at the Kerr's, and I felt curious to see what these men thought of the miracle gems.

Indeed, they had an editorial on the subject:

Gem colored price bubble?

The "miracle gem" craze sweeping the city of Bridges is a great deal for the gem sellers, most notably a certain wag with the moxie to call herself Queen in a city ruled by the Diamonds. Whether these gems (or their "elixirs") actually do what they're claimed to do is unknown. Who knows this Dr. Overs Gocow, or his qualifications? But this is of little consequence to the mad sellers of gems, who will claim just about anything to part with their goods, for a price.

I would bring your attention to the "secret penny" craze of the 1870's. A few misprinted pennies ended up selling for thousands of dollars until people tired of the sport. Prices fell dramatically, those holding the pennies at the end after purchasing them for vast sums unable to sell them for more than a penny. Will this finish the same way, with buyers left holding worthless merchandise after squandering their fortunes? I suppose it's lucky the gems are pretty. We shall see.

Many people considered the *Golden Bridges* to be tawdry, but lately it seemed to have more sense than the *Bridges Daily.*

That made me think of Mr. Durak. I hoped he might recover from his melancholy and return to the productive life he once had.

When Amelia came in, she had a book with her. "The gardener said you requested this."

"Oh, yes! Thank you." I opened the book, *Formulation of Explosives,* and paged through it while drinking my morning tea. It spoke of how the dynamite sticks were dipped in paraffin to seal them, how to set charges, place fuses, and (most interesting) the construction of timers.

Air would have loved this book. My best friend, born in the Pot the same day as I, murdered in front of me when we were twelve. In a different place, Air would surely have become an Inventor.

At breakfast, I reminded Tony of Gardena's luncheon and told him we planned to visit the gardens at the Women's Club. "We might even stay for tea, depending on the weather. She's invited her sisters-in-law, and her brothers may take us boating if the day turns nice. Jonathan is keeping Jack occupied."

"That's a relief," Tony said. "I don't suppose too much could happen in the Women's Club. Unless you get soaked again."

We were not to meet her brothers at the Women's Club at all, but rather at the Plaza on Market Center. Many buildings there had easily accessed roofs one might observe from. Also, the Plaza was crowded, so we might come and go without attracting notice.

"Make sure you return right after tea," Tony said. "We should leave as early as possible for the Celebration."

I was not looking forward to this.

Tony placed his hands on my shoulders. "I know this isn't a blessed day for you, or even an enjoyable one. I understand; today we celebrate the destruction of your home and your people's descent into ruin, instigated by my ancestor." He spoke as if this hadn't occurred to him before, and paused, gazing to the side for a moment. "But this event tonight is something we're expected to attend. Can you at least appear to be happy?"

I laughed in spite of myself. "That I can do."

The biggest challenge I faced was leaving the Diamond Women's Center without my men noticing. I had instructed Gardena to bring a dark dress in my size with a plain hat and thick veil. I instructed Amelia to pick out a brightly colored dress with a feathered hat. "We're going to have such fun! First we'll have luncheon, then promenade, then perhaps go boating, then have tea ... it should be a lovely day."

Amelia smiled. "I'm glad, mum. I do like Miss Gardena, and her brother's such a gentleman."

"He is. He won't be there today, but I'll send your regards."

She shifted, glancing away. "Servants are never brought into conversation with fine folk." Her face grew stern. "I know Mrs.

Molly taught you this."

"She did." I thought of what Roy had done to her and my eyes stung. "How do you stand it here?"

"I'm most grateful to be here, mum."

After everything that happened. "Why?"

Amelia gave me an incredulous stare. "Mum, I grew up in the slums. My father died when I was small." She spoke as if this explained everything.

"I'm sorry, Amelia. How did it happen?"

"He worked in a Party Time factory; a canister fell and opened in front of him. He breathed the dust, him and five others, and it killed them." Her face turned pensive. "There were ten of us children, the youngest just a baby. After he died, we never had enough to eat, or proper clothes, and barely time to sleep. I worked as a street sweeper from the age of eight, sixpence for a ten hour day, and helped my mother with the washing at night. It was sheer Fortune that Mr. Roy's mother took notice of me." She paused for a while, gripping the chair in front of her, knuckles white, then took a deep breath. "My life has been hard, yes, but my mother is cared for and my girls have food and good clothing. Someday, they may become lady's maids to your children. Everything that has happened was worth it, for them."

I spoke gently. "And what of your son?"

Amelia said nothing.

"Amelia ... " I wasn't sure what to say. "What Mr. Roy did to you is not Pip's fault."

Amelia stood silent for some time. "Maybe it's for the best that he live with the men." She took a deep breath and let it out, then picked up my handbag and gave it to me with a fake smile. "I'm sure your carriage is ready."

The Message

As I got into the carriage, Pearson came up with a message. "The boy said it was urgent." He handed it to me. "Oh, and I learned about the warehouse."

I blinked, confused. "The warehouse?"

"The one you asked me about? Where your letter came from."

The building Marja sent her note from. "Oh, yes, I'm sorry."

Pearson spoke to me kindly. "It's of no consequence, mum. The building's owned by the Clubb Family."

By the Clubbs? "I didn't know they owned buildings here."

"Well, yes, mum. It's complex. They own the building, we own the land. But as it's one of their produce distribution houses, it's best for them to keep up the maintenance."

Why would Josie's uncle manage a building in Spadros quadrant owned by the Clubbs? "Thank you, Pearson."

He bowed. "Have a pleasant trip."

Once the carriage was underway, I read the message:

My dear Mrs. Spadros:

I must leave in haste. You'll hear many things about me once I'm gone; I suppose most of them are true. I was a foolish old woman who should never have trusted Frank Pagliacci. I helped him. I loved him. But he has no love for anyone but himself.

Although the charade with the Doctor was

Frank's idea, I gave you the case so you'd take the necklace. Dismantle it at once and sell the gems to one of my appraisers. Please don't hesitate; do it now.

Your fondest wish has always been to leave Bridges. If you sell the gems in the next few hours, you should have more than enough money to do so. That will make this whole debacle worth it.

I truly am fond of you, and I wish you well.

All my love,

Anastasia, Dame Louis

PS. Thank you for the clock. Such a heavy package for its size! I'm most intrigued. I will follow your instructions and wait to open it until we have passed through the Aperture.

I gave her no such gift. To ask me to destroy her necklace with such haste made no sense. And she neglected to use the code wordings we normally used when writing to each other.

This felt wrong, dangerously so.

Was this message indeed from Anastasia, or was this another forgery? Or was this message in some code? Was the package real? If so, what was really in the package? If the note was a forgery, what was the forger trying to tell me?

I took the brass calling tube. "Driver."

"Yes, mum."

"Clubb quadrant, zeppelin station, please."

"I'm sorry, mum, I can't do that."

"Why not?"

We continued on, and Honor came round outside the open window, standing on the running board. "Mr. Roy said not to enter Clubb quadrant until time for the Celebration."

"Do you know why?"

"No, mum, I don't." He disappeared back to his post.

Why would Roy forbid us to go into Clubb quadant?

I took up the tube again, meaning to go to the bank on the way to the Women's Club. "Driver?"

No answer.

But then the outside lock clicked into place. I was trapped.

***

While overcast, the day was warm, and rain seemed unlikely as we approached the Diamond Women's Club. The street was crowded; many women went up and down the Club's steps. The dining room and lobby were full. Gardena stood out of sight of the street, beckoning as I approached, and led me to a side room.

I closed the door behind us. "I must find a taxi-carriage."

Gardena blinked. "Whatever for?"

How could I tell her that my men (probably under orders from Roy) locked me in my carriage and forced me to come here? That I had a terrible feeling about all this? "I can't explain it now."

"Jacqui, no. You promised you'd come with me! You can't just leave me here! I did everything you asked me to."

You're at your best when you think, and reason, Tony said, *when you have the urge to act.*

I took a deep breath. Tony sent outriders with me for a reason. By now, everyone in Diamond knew Mrs. Spadros was in the Women's Club. Despite what I told Tony, Jonathan was still at his Country House, not in the city keeping Jack Diamond occupied. Jack could be loitering around the corner at this very moment waiting for an opportunity. What was I thinking? "You're right; I'm sorry."

Gardena smiled and patted my hand. "Whatever it is, all will be well. Let's get you changed and catch this scoundrel."

She made it sound as if going on a lark, but I wasn't so sure.

I changed into the navy blue dress she brought, covering my hair with a black scarf. The hat and veil were also navy blue, and hid my face well. I stuck my handbag in my pocket. "Ready."

Gardena also wore a hat with a veil. So disguised, we walked into the crowd of women on the street and past my men without them noticing us. It worked just as I planned.

Around the corner and down the street, a Diamond carriage awaited us. Gardena's footman opened the door. A man wearing brown sat inside.

Morton said, "Hello, ladies."

The Briefcase

How did Morton find us?

"Master Rainbow!" Gardena said. "Whatever are you doing here?"

I turned to her, astonished. "You know him?"

"Why yes. He works for the Harts." She climbed into the carriage, and sat across from him. "He's a friend of my father's."

"How remarkable!" The footman helped me inside, and I sat next to Gardena. I told Morton, "I didn't know you and Miss Diamond were acquainted."

"I didn't know you and Miss Diamond were acquainted either," Morton said. "Although I haven't been to call on the Diamonds for some time."

The footman shut the door.

Gardena said, "So I take it the two of you know each other."

I glanced at Morton. "We've been introduced."

Gardena appeared perplexed.

"I've been tasked with your protection, my dear," Morton said to no one in particular, "so here I am."

Gardena beamed at him.

It was clear Tony had asked him to follow me. "I hope your companions are well?"

"Indeed," he said, and the way he said it made me think they were alert to the fact that I might try to slip past them.

Morton's presence was a major impediment. He surely gave

Tony's men a contingency plan if he didn't return after a certain time. They would send one of our outriders to search for him, and not finding him, return and inform Tony.

This was not going to end well. Perhaps I could tell Tony that Gardena changed plans at the last minute — as long as Morton played along.

Gardena's expression became shrewd. "Evidently, Master Rainbow is a widely traveled man."

Morton grinned. "I do meet with many in my travels, although I haven't had the pleasure of visiting the Clubbs."

"I'll have to introduce you," Gardena said, then blushed.

"Miss Diamond is being courted by the Clubbs," I said. "The heir, to be precise."

Morton's eyes grew wide. "Indeed?"

Gardena began chattering in great detail about her meetings with Lance Clubb.

I gave up the idea of reaching Anastasia before she left. It was clear she planned to leave the city before her forgeries were discovered. But why stay in the city a moment longer than she had to? Why not leave earlier, hiring me instead to sell her belongings and send her the money?

Perhaps she never wanted me to know where she was going.

That hurt; she was one of the few friends I had in Bridges.

"You're so quiet," Gardena said. "I hope all is well?"

Anastasia helped Frank Pagliacci. "I recently learned that a friend may have betrayed me." I couldn't help but notice Gardena's flinch and Morton's evaluating gaze of us both.

I wondered what Gardena had done, why she sounded so contrite, so remorseful, at Queen's Day dinner. Why she had begged Tony to tell me something important, and if it was so vital, why he failed to do so. Why Tony thought she was in such terrible danger. Why Jake Bower thought I could gain a great deal of money from his information. What Thrace Pike thought was happening which upset him so.

I was missing something — as usual. Something important, something I should be able to deduce.

Gardena wasn't in love with Tony; she never acted as if she

loved him in all the years I had known her. She seemed more irritated with him than anything else. She had never treated me badly nor acted jealous of my relationship with him. And instead of moping or doing the other things a woman in love with someone she couldn't have might do, she was happily accepting suitors. "I don't know why she's done this. I can't even find her to talk with her."

Gardena put her hand on mine. "I'm sorry." She gazed out of the window, and we held hands the rest of the way there.

***

The carriage pulled up in an alleyway near the Plaza on Market Center. Morton, Gardena, and I went into the side door of an office building, then up several flights of stairs to the roof. Five men stood there, all tall, very dark, and handsome. Or the oldest would be, if he wasn't scowling. They wore black business suits and top hats, looking a bit too dapper for this sort of work.

He gestured at me. "Why did you bring that creature here?" His brothers shifted, glancing away, embarrassed.

"For shame, Cesare!" Gardena said. "This is Mrs. Spadros, my friend, who has risked her life to assist me."

Cesare smirked. "This is a Pot rag dressed in your finery, Gardena, nothing more." His gaze went past me, and he tipped his hat. "Afternoon, Master Rainbow. So my sister has ensnared you into this farce as well."

Morton seemed amused. "My pleasure, sir."

We were near the bank; from there I could catch a taxi-carriage. "Very well. If my services are no longer required, I'll —"

"No!" Gardena said, grabbing my arm. "You must stay. Please don't leave. Cesare, you will apologize to —"

"I'll do no such thing." He turned to me. "Have I said one inaccurate word?"

I chuckled. "Not one." I turned to Gardena, who appeared mortified. "I find men who speak their minds refreshing. I see you two are much alike."

"No." Gardena glared at her brother. "We are nothing alike."

I sighed, turning so I might face them all. "Are we here to argue, or to capture your blackmailer?"

Morton's eyes went wide.

I did neglect to tell him what he was getting into.

Gardena turned to me and said, "What shall we do next?"

Why did she think I would know?

I shrugged. I was a Watcher for many years as a teenager in the Pot, although we never shot anyone. We only watched for those we might steal from and signaled to the ones lying in wait below. "If I planned to capture someone, I would place someone on each of the roofs around where the meeting is to be, with a pistol at least. Although if you think you might really want to shoot him, a rifle would be better. Then at least two armed men close to you in case the man does something upsetting."

Her brothers looked at each other, impressed.

Cesare said, "She's not going anywhere near that spot."

Quadrant-men were so predictable. "Then this is a perfectly safe place to wait. Although I fail to see why the man should come forth when he sees she's not there."

"Oh," Gardena said. "My maid's down there, dressed as me."

I gaped at her, appalled. "You would put a maid into such danger? For shame, Gardena!"

She frowned at me in puzzlement. "She's only a maid, Jacqui. And my brothers will be there."

I let out a breath, exasperated. These people didn't see servants as anything but disposable. "Then why are we here?"

Gardena seemed put out. "Why, in case I recognize the man, I can identify him." She opened a letter. "It says he will be, I quote: 'dark of skin, wearing brown, carrying a brown briefcase.' I'm to give him the money in exchange for the briefcase of information."

Morton chuckled. As usual, he wore brown, a medium chocolate brown, but he carried no briefcase, and no one would ever say he was dark of skin.

I peered over the edge into the busy Plaza; at least 500 men wore brown. "Well, that narrows it down."

Men wearing brown had become the bane of my life. I had been followed by men in brown for the whole month of January. Every man in the city seemed to be wearing that color this season. Few carried briefcases though, as it was a Saturday, and offices were closed.

Gardena peeked over and laughed.

Morton said, "How may I help?"

"I could use a man on the roof over there," Cesare pointed across the street. "Can you whistle?"

Morton grimaced. "Not well." He took a small mirror from his pocket. "Perhaps this will suffice?"

"Perfectly." The two men shook hands; Morton tipped his hat to us and left.

Her brothers conferred with each other, then Cesare remained with us, peering at the crowd on the Plaza, while the rest went downstairs. Two of them took positions near a woman dressed in one of Gardena's gowns carrying a large satchel and the other two went to separate roofs.

"I had the pleasure of meeting your son," I said to Cesare. "He's a beautiful child."

He frowned at me. "What?" Then he glanced at Gardena and back at me. "Oh. Yes. Thank you."

An odd reaction for a man whose child was just praised. But he did seem rather distracted. Gardena's face showed nothing.

"Oh, by the way," Cesare said to Gardena, "Master Clubb wrote me this morning. Your package is on its way."

Gardena and I both said, "Oh?"

He chuckled. "Indeed. Should be loaded into the cargo hold as we speak."

Already? "What's this, Dena? I thought it would take longer."

Gardena pulled me aside. "He doesn't know it's a person. Lance knows a person is going, but not who. You said you wanted it secret."

On a first name basis with Master Clubb already, are we? "Well, I did, but I thought they would need training or something. I wanted to say good-bye to my mother before she left."

She smiled. "I'm sure she'll write once she gets there."

I knew they were being smuggled out, but I never imagined this. How long would Ma be in there? Would she be safe?

The clock struck half past two, and I wished for some shade. Wearing a navy blue dress to a rooftop gathering was a mistake.

"What time was this man supposed to arrive?"

"Shortly," Gardena said.

Cesare called out, "There he is!"

Two of Gardena's brothers held a dark-skinned man in brown who clutched a leather briefcase to his chest. The man's eyes were frightened, and his mouth moved rapidly.

"Let's go," Cesare said, so we hurried down the stairs.

The stocky young man wore a brown suit which was too large for him. From his face, so much like Ferti Hart's except a very dark brown, I saw that he had the same impediment. "The man said give it to her," he yelled, almost in tears. He appeared more upset by not being able to hand it to the maid than by the two men holding him.

I ran to them. "Let him give it to her."

The man handed the briefcase over to the maid, then blubbered, "Thank you pretty miss. He said give it to her and I would do good."

I peered at him. "You did do good. Tell me about the man."

"He was nice. He told me to give it to the lady. Only her."

Gardena's brothers stood around the open case, frowning. "What do you make of this?"

I turned to them. "What?"

Cesare held up an envelope. "It's addressed to you."

To me?

I told Morton, "Let him go. He's not your blackmailer."

Morton snorted, and one of Gardena's brothers laughed. For a moment, I hated them both.

"What's a blackmailer?" The man glanced from one of us to the other in bewilderment as a crowd of bystanders gathered.

"It's nothing," Morton said. "You did well. You can go."

I stalked over to Cesare, furious at whoever used that man in this way, and snatched the letter from him. Inside the envelope was a photo of my lock-box with the jewels, and a note: "BOOM."

The whole world became silent.

Explosives. Timers. Clock parts. Anastasia thought her package was a clock ... because it was ticking.

I stared at Morton. "He's going to bomb the zeppelin."

The Train

"Who's going to bomb the zeppelin?" said Gardena.

The color drained from Morton's face. "Frank Pagliacci."

Gardena and her brothers said in unison, "Who's that?"

A group of police approached, Probationary Constable Hanger with them. "What is this disturbance?"

Morton took a step aside. "It's just a misunderstanding."

They didn't look convinced.

I turned to Cesare, suddenly grateful for my veil. "Do you have a way to contact the Clubbs directly?"

"We can send a messenger, but it's almost shift change. The traffic will be horrendous. It'll take an hour at least for a boy to get there, even if his carriage is waiting on the other side of the river."

I had been here too long; it was almost three. "In that time, everyone on the zeppelin may be dead."

Gardena and her brothers looked appalled. "What do we do?"

I turned away, trying to think.

I had an idea.

"The train! When does it leave?"

"Right now," a man said, passing by. He gestured with his chin. A tall plume of smoke spouted on the far end of the island.

"Where's the carriage?" I shouted. "We must get to the train!"

"This way," Cesare said, so we followed him.

I glanced back. The police were questioning the bystanders,

all but PC Hanger. He called out, "Wait!"

I fled around the corner with the rest.

The driver, a dark-skinned man with white hair, was asleep. It took a moment to get him to understand what we wanted. "You want me to take you into Clubb quadrant uninvited?"

I grabbed his hand. "If we don't get word to the Clubbs, we might have a zeppelin full of dead people."

The driver stared at us in horror.

"The train slows to a crawl at the bridge, but we won't get there in time on this side," Morton said. "We have to catch it as it goes into Clubb proper."

PC Hanger and a few men came round the corner. "Wait!"

We climbed onto the carriage and started off, the police following far behind on foot. "Gardena, you and your brothers stop at the bridge," I said, "some on this side, the rest on the other side. Tell them someone plans to bomb the zeppelin. See if they can contact the Clubbs directly."

Gardena gave me a blank stare. "Directly? How?"

"The Clubbs have a device which can speak through wires. We stole it from them last year."

Her eyes went wide. "Ohhh."

I chuckled. "But don't tell Lance that."

Her brothers peered at me. Then they glanced at each other, faces thoughtful.

We got to the first guard post. "Hey," the guard said, as we went past those waiting in line, "You can't do that!"

Cesare and two more of Gardena's brothers got off and began speaking with the man, who shook his head. Cesare pointed at the other guard booth. "Go!"

The driver took off over the wide bridge, weaving around carriages trying to cross going both ways. Finally, we reached the other side, and Gardena's other brothers got off.

"Go with them," I told Gardena.

"But —"

"Tony will be upset enough with me for doing this. But if we were both hurt, it … it would kill him."

She stared at me a long moment, eyes reddening, then kissed

my cheek, dashing tears away as she climbed out of the carriage.

Gardena's brother, standing beside the guard, shook his head.

The constables far behind rode horseback through the packed bridge towards us. I shouted, "We have to hurry!"

Morton said, "Why do you care so much?"

"My mother's on that zeppelin."

He stared at me in shock, then stuck his head out of the window. "Go! We must catch that train!"

Taxi-carriage drivers shouted curses at us as we barreled along the long wide street, the horses' hooves ringing on the cobblestones. We turned left once we passed the Pot and raced towards the train tracks along the river. The guard lights flashed and a plume of smoke slowly approached. Our driver stopped, pulling his goggles up on his forehead as we climbed out.

Morton went to the driver. "Get your people. Tell them if they can contact the zeppelin to do so. We'll try to get there before it's too late."

"Bless you, sir," the driver said. "And you too, miss." He turned the carriage round as the train chugged into view.

We ran to the tracks, then towards the rear of the train. A passenger car passed, and a boxcar, then a railing appeared. Morton grabbed my hand as I leapt aboard, the sound of approaching hoof beats. Clinging to him, I glanced back. PC Hanger and several policemen shouted at us as we passed the waiting traffic. Three dismounted and chased us, trying to get on the train themselves. "We have trouble."

Morton laughed. "I should expect that when with you."

The constables pulled out pistols.

I moved out of their view. "We had best get inside."

Morton locked the door behind us. We were inside a cargo car full of boxes. We climbed over and around them, I a bit more slowly than he. "These skirts are most annoying at times like this."

Morton chuckled. "I daresay."

Shouts came from the other side of the door, and gunshots hitting the lock. We hurried to the next car.

This car was filled with baggage. I took a red and white patterned scarf tied to one of the bags and shoved it in my pocket.

Morton stared at me but said nothing. We moved to a passenger compartment, full of people reading papers, smoking, and chatting. Morton locked the door, then we pushed past a waiter handing out drinks. We continued on to the next car, the police rattling on the far lock as we closed the door behind us. The waiter went to unlock the door for the constables.

"They're going to catch us soon," Morton said.

We entered a baggage car. The window on the far side of this car showed more people sitting. A black coat with red lining hung on a hook in the far corner. I grabbed it, then grabbed Morton by his coat and pulled him out of view.

He repositioned his Derby hat. "What in hell are you about?"

I ignored him, taking off my hat and scarf and tossing them aside. I pulled my hair loose, tying the red and white scarf around my hair in a quick tignon, then turned the coat inside out so the red lining showed. The door clanked as it opened far behind us. I put on the coat, shoved him into the corner, pulled his hat over his eyes, and threw my arms around his neck. "Kiss me."

His voice was husky. "With pleasure."

Footsteps approached, then stopped. Probationary Constable Hanger said, "Excuse me, sir. My apologies." The footsteps of the police moved on to the next car as our lips parted.

Morton's face was flushed, his pupils dilated. He took a deep breath and let it out. "Whoa."

"Don't get any ideas," I said. "It'll take them some time to get to the front of the train, but then they'll be back, searching everywhere, questioning everyone. We aren't done here yet."

He took his hat off and smoothed his hair.

I pulled off the patterned scarf and the coat, tossing them over a box as we pulled into a station. I searched for Gardena's hat and scarf, then put up my hair in a bun.

"Riverfront Station," a man's voice echoed from the car in front of us. "Riverfront Station. Continuing along the Promenade and to the Rim. Next stop, Bath."

I peered outside. A train sat on the other side of the tracks. The placard hanging from the roof said: Zeppelin Station. "We're on the wrong train." I picked up Gardena's hat, put it on, pulled down my veil, put her scarf around my neck, and went for the door. I glanced in the passenger compartment; the police were there. "Let's go."

We ran across to the other train and got in just as the train started up. Across the platform, I caught PC Hanger's eye and waved at him. The look of astonishment and anger on the man's face was priceless.

"Won't they stop the train?" Morton said.

How did he not know that? "They can't. It's on a timer. They only stop if someone's injured. The conductor must do that." I leaned back. "We can only hope we get there on time."

Morton picked up an afternoon newspaper from the seat next to him. The headline read: GEM PRICES FALL 2%. He turned the page to the crossword puzzle and took out a gold fountain pen.

Completing a crossword puzzle at a time like this?

The whistle blew as the train gathered speed. I peered out over the wheat fields, recalling the last time I visited the zeppelin station. A vast half-cylinder of stained glass set into beams of wood and steel ... it was the most glorious sight.

Dirigibles of all kinds entered and left Bridges by way of the Aperture, each majestic, each beautiful. The people on the train would be horrified if they knew a madman planned to destroy one of those treasures along with everyone aboard it.

The timing of this meeting with Gardena's blackmailer was too convenient. But Gardena and her brothers had knowledge of neither the bomb nor of Frank Pagliacci. Was the blackmail just another distraction?

This thought gave me pause. Would Jack Diamond blackmail his own sister? Or did he unwittingly reveal some information to Frank — or whoever directed them?

How did any of them know Gardena would come to me for help, or ask me to accompany her?

Trey Louis said Anastasia and Frank worked together. Anastasia's letter said she helped him. Did Frank use Anastasia as they used Mr. Durak?

This bomb could be a way for Frank and Jack — or more likely, the man who directed them — to silence her as he did the stable-man. As he tried to silence Morton.

Whoever this man was, his decisions chilled me.

The station came into view to our right, sun glistening on its surface. Several airships rose from the station. The Aperture, high in the dome, opened as we watched.

The Aperture was a truly monstrous mechanism, large enough that several massive dirigibles could pass one another with plenty of room to spare.

The gigantic brass plates gleamed as they moved. *The Kerrs built that. Yet tonight, the quadrants will cheer their downfall.*

"Magnificent," Morton said. "I never tire of watching it."

The train's wheels squealed as it took the last turn into the station, which was full of people coming and going. Tourists here for the Celebration on their way to their hotels. Quadrant-folk intending to stay for the event tonight. Workers changing shift.

Morton said, "Where to?"

"Gate 19," I said.

Morton surveyed the approaching platform with dismay. "How are we going to get through that crowd?"

I remembered Tony's little sister Katherine, and let my hair fall loose. I took a decorative hair-comb from my handbag and pulled my hair away from my face, securing it with the comb. Then I tucked up the top of my skirts up under my corset, so my petticoats showed around my ankles. Morton watched me with amusement. "What are you now?"

"Get up," I said. I picked up Gardena's hat with one hand and took Morton's hand in the other, leading him off the train into the masses of people buzzing about the station. Yellow roses lined the entrance, and I picked one, tucking it into my comb. I grabbed his hand and pitched my voice high as a young girl, shouting loud enough for the whole station to hear. "Hurry, Daddy! Hurry! We're going to miss the zeppelin!"

Morton laughed as we ran.

The Zeppelin

We pushed past hordes of people up stairs and through golden stained-glass corridors to a great arching hall of stained glass. Morton hurried to a man in uniform and handed over his newspaper. "Which way to gate 19?"

"Over there," the man pointed to the far corner.

"You must stop that zeppelin," Morton said.

The man chuckled. "Be hard to do, sir," he pointed. Eighty yards away, the door to the outside was being shut. "If you hurry, they might let you on."

To our dismay, hundreds of people lay before us. But we ran through them, pushing people aside, straining to get to the zeppelin before it rose. Finally, we got to the counter. "You must stop the zeppelin," I panted.

The woman smiled. "I'm sorry. Once it's taken off," she pointed at the top of the enormous structure rising through the air, "we can't call them back." She glanced at Morton. "I can book you and your daughter another flight. Where were you bound?"

I turned away. Roy expressly forbade me to come here. If I revealed who I was, I was dead.

If Ma died, did it matter?

I took a deep breath and faced the woman. "I'm Mrs. Jacqueline Spadros. There's a bomb on that zeppelin."

The woman stared at me. "What?"

"There's a bomb on that zeppelin," Morton said.

She blanched, then grabbed a microphone. "Bomb alert. Bomb alert. Jettison all cargo. I repeat, jettison all cargo immediately." She kept repeating the words.

Morton and I stared at the zeppelin as it rose, yet the cargo bay doors below stayed shut. Why didn't they jettison —

They knew people were in the hold.

"Um," Morton said, glancing down at the woman, "I —"

The zeppelin engulfed in flame.

Terror stabbed me. *Ma!*

A huge sound, as if the world exploded.

"LOOK OUT!" Morton pushed me under the counter at the same instant the stained glass windows shattered above us.

Huge sheets of glass fell to smash on the wooden floor, shards flying like bullets whistling amidst the screams of the panicked crowd as we huddled under Morton's jacket.

Silence. A huge sheet of glass crashed to the ground far down the concourse.

Then all was sobbing and wailing.

Morton held my upper arms, peering at me. "Are you hurt?"

I shook my head, tears running down my face.

Morton helped me up. I stood next to him watching the pieces of zeppelin fall burning from the sky.

Ma ... I tried so hard to get you somewhere safe. I sent you to your death. I leaned against Morton, weeping as he held me.

Then: *Oh, Anastasia.*

As the last pieces fell, I remembered the foolish big-eared man, Trey, who thought I might marry him.

Police and zeppelin officials swarmed the area shouting for doctors. People bled all around us. The floor was covered with glass, blood, bodies, crying children, people wailing as they knelt over loved ones.

Morton grabbed my arm. "We must leave before the police start questioning people."

We tried every door, every hallway, but they were all blocked, guarded. Finally, I put my hair up, my hat on, and tried to bully a guard into letting us out, telling him my name.

"I'm sorry, mum, but we can't let anyone leave. This is a

police matter. I can call Mr. Spadros if you wish."

I turned away, terrified. What would Tony say? What would Roy do?

But what could I do? I turned back to the guard. "Yes. Tell him I was here to see Dame Anastasia off." I pointed where the zeppelin used to be. "She was on that ship."

"I'll have someone contact him right away."

Morton found some chairs which weren't damaged, and not too covered in glass, and brushed them off. There we sat while doctors and assistants, police and officials, families and the dead were moved about, until Tony came and they allowed him to fetch us.

The Aftermath

Tony raged at everyone: Morton, Gardena, her brothers, and above all, at me. I told him of the letter Pearson gave me as I was leaving, how I persuaded Gardena to let me see Anastasia off, how Morton followed us (as Tony asked him to). How Morton protected me when the blast happened.

None of it mattered. Tony didn't know where I was, I was hurt (a small piece of glass in my leg), and I had been in terrible danger. Worse yet, I had appeared in public with a bachelor gentleman (and without a female companion), and it had been noted in the papers. He drew his revolver to kill Honor and my driver, but I begged him not to. I told him I disguised myself, evading them on purpose in order to see Anastasia.

He didn't speak to me or come to my bed.

For several days, I didn't leave my room. I suppose Jane Pearson took care of the household; to this day, I don't know. Nothing seemed real. Ma was dead.

Jane planned the outing. Madame Biltcliffe sent her mourning garb to me without my asking. We went to the memorial. I stood as the names of the uppers were read. No one mentioned the hundreds of Pot rags in the hold.

Ma was dead.

Anastasia was dead.

Marja was dead.

Tony didn't speak to me. After the memorial, I went to him.

"I'm sorry for whatever I did to make you hate me."

He pulled me to him with a cry, squeezing me so tightly it hurt. "I don't hate you, no, no, oh gods no. I came so close to losing you. I don't know what to say or do. I can't sleep or eat, thinking of how you might have died."

I put my arms round him. "But I'm here. Why do you not speak to me?" His grip loosened and I took a breath. "Anastasia was my friend, one of the few I had here." It was then the tears finally came for her.

"Dame Anastasia defrauded many," Tony said. "The papers are full of it." He let go and turned away. "Yet she came to my home, sat at my table. I exposed the three Families here at that table to scorn and speculation."

I said numbly, "It's not your fault she did those things. We knew nothing of her crimes. No one blames you."

He rounded on me. "You think not? Look at my mail. My verified mail. Look at the papers!" He held one up, shook it at me.

The headline read:

Families Conspire To Defraud The City?

Scam Artist Welcomed At Spadros Manor

Three of four Families present at secret dinner

"We're all being implicated by association. Except, of course, the Harts. No one's made the connection with Master Rainbow being at your side in the station, which I suppose is fortunate for them." He paused. "Merchants across the city who bought her gems and are unable to sell them are ruined. Gentlemen have gone bankrupt." His face turned fierce. "Bankrupt! They want someone to blame, and she's dead. Who else do they have to turn to but her associates for vengeance?"

I leaned against a chair, feeling faint. "Are we in danger?"

"My father's men have rounded up anyone in the quadrant speaking against our Family. And Mr. Durak no longer is editor of the *Bridges Daily*."

What? "Mr. Durak was a good man! Why —?"

Tony shook his head. "He let Pike's editorial pass. He let the financial speculators on his paper whip the people into buying these things. Then he let this filth," he threw the paper down, "about us conspiring to ruin the city pass as well. He's no use to us. It's good he's dead."

I took a step back. It was as if I no longer knew him. "Tony! How can you speak in this way?"

His face turned sad. "I can't always be your Tony. These days, I must be Anthony, heir to the Spadros Family. And that man must be cruel if we're to survive."

***

The next day, Tony and I went to the bank to retrieve Anastasia's gems. Mr. Roman confirmed what I feared: the necklace she made decades ago and passed off as worth thousands was a forgery, with clear "miracle" gems inside. "Worthless," Mr. Roman said. "But cleverly done; only a jeweler might know. That must be why she never met with us. Even the settings are steel, colored to resemble the patina of old silver."

I had the smaller gems made into necklaces for each of our servant women. The rest I had cut and placed into pins for our servant men to wear on their collars. At our outing, I presented them to our servants after I promoted Jane Pearson to housekeeper. Many of the servants wept in gratitude at the gifts and swore their allegiance to us again. That made Tony smile.

When I presented little Pip with his pin, he hugged me. "Thank you."

"Is the bed better than the stair?"

"Yes, mum, much better. And the men are kind to me."

I hoped Pip never learned he was Roy's son. But to me he was family. "I'm so glad you're happy."

***

The lock-box also held an envelope with the deed to a small boarding apartment in the artists' area of Spadros quadrant, made out in my name. It was half of a duplex, about to be sold for back taxes, but I asked Tony if I might keep it.

It was on a strange street: long, narrow, and winding. All the buildings on one side of the street were duplexes, separated front to back. Some called the road my apartment faced 33 1/3 Street, others called it Artists' Alley. The apartment had a kitchen, a dining room, four lower rooms, and one large upper room with picture windows. A shirtless, mustachioed man with his suspenders around his waist watered a rooftop garden across the way.

I said, "I've thought one day to be a patroness, and own property. Perhaps with this, I can do both. We can rent the rooms downstairs to artists, and rent this room out by the hour as a studio for photographers and artists to take portraits. It would show our dedication to making this quadrant more refined."

"I like this idea," Tony said. "Choose a housekeeper and put an advertisement for rentals."

And so it was done. But nothing mattered. Ma was dead.

From that day, I went nowhere without Amelia, not even into my own garden, and extra men followed every move I made.

My cage tightened around me more with each day.

***

Molly came to visit, and when I saw her, I broke down and wept in her arms. Amelia curtsied and left us alone.

When I calmed, Molly said, "I'm sorry about your friend."

I nodded, feeling numb.

"Your Ma is perfectly safe," Molly whispered. "I made sure of it myself. She never left the Cathedral."

Ma was alive?

The room turned gray and Molly took my hands as I half sat, half fell into the chair behind me. "You poor dear." She put my feet up, then smoothed my hair.

I stared at Molly through the haze, mind racing.

Tony didn't know. I never said a word to him, hoping against hope Roy never learned I contacted Ma. But now even that hope was lost. "How did you find out?"

Molly gazed back at me with a slight smile.

Gardena didn't know my Ma, nor did Cesare, nor Lance, and even if they did … they would never have spoken about her, least of all to Molly Spadros.

Cesare didn't know it was a person. Lance didn't know who it was.

I gasped. There was one other person who knew Ma was going to be on that zeppelin.

Molly clamped her hand over my mouth, her voice stern. "Outside. Now."

Frightened, I followed her past the maids in the hallway out into the garden. We sat on a bench where no one else might hear.

I whispered, "Rachel Diamond. How … why?"

Why would she spend her life pretending to be incapacitated?

"Rachel is ill," Molly said, "but not as ill as people think."

Molly and Acevedo, Julius and Rachel. They had been friends, in spite of the old hatreds between their Families. Julius and Rachel were there for Molly after Acevedo's murder. She was there for Julius after Hector and Rachel's terrible accident.

For some time after the accident, Rachel seemed lost, but little by little, her mind returned. "She began trying to understand what happened. But people said things around her they never would have before, and she began to spy." Molly glanced away. "We've had difficult times over the years, but then … they came to me with a small problem, and we realized we had more in common than we thought."

Molly spoke more to herself, it seemed, but then she straightened and faced me. "Rachel took an awful risk getting a message to me. She's weak and slow-moving, and if anyone knew she was in her right mind she would be a tempting target. She was an Apprentice once, and knows the secrets of both the Apprentices and the Diamond Family. But she's incredibly brave. You have Rachel Diamond to thank for your Ma's life."

Why would Mrs. Diamond help me? I never said a dozen words to the woman.

I remembered Gardena's tears at our Queen's Day dinner. "Why doesn't she tell her daughter?"

Molly's face darkened. "Gardena is a spoiled, willful child, who may get us all killed before this is over."

Gardena's own mother doesn't trust her. "Does Julius know?"

Molly smiled fondly. "Of course he knows. He's not as terrible a man as most make him out to be."

I didn't think I would get another chance to ask, so I did. "Why does Mr. Diamond hate my husband so?"

"That's for Tony to tell … I'm sorry, I promised him I wouldn't speak of it, no matter how much you entreated."

"Something terrible's happening to him. He doesn't sleep, he hardly eats. I want to help him. Why does he keep this from me?" Why did he trust me so little?

Molly laid her hands on mine. "When it's safe for you to know, you'll understand."

I stared at our hands. Who would decide that? Tony? Nothing would ever be safe enough for him, I saw that now.

"My Ma. What's to become of her now? Is Mr. Roy going to kill us? I didn't go into the Pot, I swear." I didn't know if his threats reached to contacting her. "Joseph Kerr's housekeeper sent word that whoever attacked Tony wanted to kill her too."

Molly gave me a smile meant to be soothing. "Never fear. There's no way we would ever let her fall into his hands."

We. Who was we?

Then I realized: whoever they were, they needed Ma alive.

She was their only hold on me.

I stumbled back to the veranda and sat at the table, staring at my garden. Molly spoke, and Pearson spoke, then Tony spoke. But I heard none of it, even when Tony carried me up to my room as my little bird chirped in the darkness.

Dame Anastasia was dead by Frank Pagliacci's hand. Frank Pagliacci was loose, Jack Diamond was loose, and Gardena's blackmailer was as well. The more I thought about it, the more I came to believe that Joe was right: we were not like these people.

Poor sad Mr. Durak's death was the final straw.

I couldn't live like this anymore. I needed to get me and Ma out of Bridges before we both ended up dead.

~This ends Chapter Two of the Red Dog Conspiracy~

Appendix

The Four Families

(Those members named)

Spadros

Motto: We never changed our name

The Spadros family has been in Bridges since the raising of the dome, being among the original laborers brought in to work on the project.

Patriarch: Roy Spadros (wife: Molly, daughter: Katherine)
Heir: Anthony (Tony) Spadros (wife: Jacqueline)
Inventor: Maxim Call

Retainers:
John Pearson, butler (wife: Jane, daughter: Mary)
Jacob Michaels, manservant
Peter Dewey, stable-man (wife: Amelia, son: Pip)
Skip Honor, day footman
Blitz Spadros, night footman
Dr. Salmon, private surgeon
Rocket, a bomb-sniffer dog
Poignee, kitchen maid (deceased)
Ottilie, kitchen maid (deceased)
Treysa, kitchen maid (deceased)
Anne, kitchen maid
Monsieur, chef

Business:
Sawbuck (Ten Hogan), Tony's right hand man
Crab, Associate (deceased)
Duck, Associate (deceased)

Diamond

Motto: Diamonds protect their own

A large group of immigrant workers from the South African diamond mines settled in Bridges in the early 1500s AC. Proud of their unique identity, this disparate group of families began to call themselves "Diamonds" and exclusively intermarry.

Patriarch: Julius Diamond (wife: Rachel)
Heir: Cesare Diamond

Other Sons:
Jack Roland Diamond III (Black Jack, Mad Jack)
Jonathan Courtenay Diamond, his twin brother

Daughter:
Gardena Diamond

Retainer:
Daniel, manservant (deceased)

Others:
Octavia Diamond, a nanny
Roland, a small boy

Hart

Motto: Ready for anything

Descended from Appalachian and Chinese workers, Crispin Hartmann led one of the early street gangs of the early 1700's. This gang called themselves the Harts and were a major player in the looting and other unpleasant acts seen during the Coup.

Patriarch: Charles Hart (wife: Judith)
Heir (and Inventor): Etienne Hart (wife: Helen, daughter: Ferti)

Under protection:
Joseph Kerr
Josephine Kerr, his twin sister
Polansky Kerr IV, their grandfather
Marja, their housekeeper
Daisy, a maid

Clubb

Motto: A golden harvest

Clover Banditerna was a worker on a farm near the zeppelin until the Alcatraz Coup. Seeing an opportunity, he and his fellow workers called themselves the Clubbs Of Justice and seized the zeppelin station, along with the controls to the Aperture.

Realizing no one could go in or out of the city without going through them, the group charged exorbitant rates and became extremely rich.

After the Coup, Clover Banditerna changed his name, calling himself Johnny Clubb.

Patriarch: Alexander Clubb (wife: Regina)
Heir: Lancelot Clubb

Daughter:
Kitty Clubb

Other players

Spadros quadrant

Dame Anastasia Louis, aristocrat and gemologist
Trey Louis, her great-nephew
Eleanora Bryce, a widow
Nicholas (Nick, Air), her son (deceased)
Herbert Bryce, her son (deceased)
David Bryce, her son
Madame Marie Biltcliffe, a dress shop owner
Tenni, her shop maid
Vig Vikenti, a saloon owner
Natalia, a woman of the Romani in Vig's saloon
Peedro Sluff (Jacqui's father), a liquor store owner

Market Center

Bridges Daily, a newspaper
Acol Durak, the editor
Doyle Pike, a lawyer
Thrace Pike, a law clerk, Doyle's grandson
Anna Goren, an apothecary
Probationary Constable Paix Hanger, a policeman

Other

Fanny Kaplan (Ma), a brothel owner
Major Blackwood, an old Army man
The Red Dogs, a street gang
Stephen Rivers, a Red Dogs "chip" (deceased)
Clover, a Red Dogs "ace"
Morton, their trey leader/Blaze Rainbow, a gentleman
Zia, his sister
Golden Bridges, a tabloid
Frank Pagliacci, a scoundrel

Acknowledgments

Many people have helped me with this book, and I'd like to thank them. I appreciate the beta reader input given by Andy Loofbourrow and Tasha Reese. I'd also like to thank Dennis McDonald for his support, advice, and example in self-publishing; Dr. Christophe Landry for his help with translation, Erin Hartshorn for her meticulous proofreading; and Anita Carroll for her gorgeous cover art.

I also appreciate my street team, The Commission, for helping get this book series into your hands! And special thanks to my Patreon patrons, Dave Kobrenski and Cristina.

This series would not be what it is today without the hours spent by my son (and awesome developmental editor) Corwin Loofbourrow. Thank you.

About the Author

Patricia Loofbourrow is a writer, gardener, artist, musician, poet, wildcrafter, and married mother of three who loves power tools, dancing, genetics, and anything to do with outer space. She also has an MD. Heinlein would be proud.

She is the writer for the websites Edible Landscape Design (http://www.edible-landscape-design.com) and Everything Cobalt Blue (http://www.everything-cobalt-blue.com).

She is also a Master Certified Guide for the Master Key Experience (http://masterkey.pattyloof.com).

You can follow her at:
- Her website http://www.jacqofspades.com
- Twitter @Jacq_Of_Spades
- Tumblr http://red-dog-conspiracy.tumblr.com/
- The Red Dog Conspiracy Facebook page.

Note from the Author

Thanks so much for reading *The Queen of Diamonds*. If you liked the book, please contact me, or leave a review where you bought this!

The Ace of Clubs

Coming October 2017

The one secret which could destroy everything ...

After financial disaster and the zeppelin bombing, the city of Bridges is reeling. Three of the four Families are implicated, and an inquest is called to investigate.

After her failure to prove Jack Diamond's guilt in David Bryce's kidnapping and the deaths of her friends, private eye and mobster's moll Jacqueline Spadros has had enough. While she and her former lover Joseph Kerr try to learn who killed their family friend Marja, they also begin making plans to leave the city.

But the secrets Jacqui has kept over the years are coming back to cause her serious trouble. Will she be able to escape Bridges? Or will she be forced to face the terrible consequences of her lies and trickery once and for all?